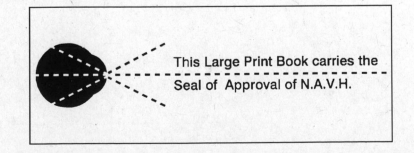

This Large Print Book carries the
Seal of Approval of N.A.V.H.

Rumor Has It

RUMOR HAS IT

CHERIS HODGES

THORNDIKE PRESS
A part of Gale, Cengage Learning

GALE
CENGAGE Learning·

Farmington Hills, Mich • San Francisco • New York • Waterville, Maine
Meriden, Conn • Mason, Ohio • Chicago

GALE
CENGAGE Learning®

ALL RIGHTS RESERVED
Thorndike Press® Large Print African-American.
The text of this Large Print edition is unabridged.
Other aspects of the book may vary from the original edition.
Set in 16 pt. Plantin.

LIBRARY OF CONGRESS CATALOGING-IN-PUBLICATION DATA

Hodges, Cheris F.
    Rumor has it / by Cheris Hodges. — Large print edition.
        pages cm. — (Thorndike Press large print African-American)
    ISBN 978-1-4104-8223-5 (hardcover) — ISBN 1-4104-8223-5 (hardcover)
    1. African Americans—Fiction. 2. Large type books. I. Title.
PS3608.O473R86 2015
813'.6—dc23   2015015209

Published in 2015 by arrangement with Dafina Books, an imprint of
Kensington Publishing Corp.

Printed in Mexico
1 2 3 4 5 6 7 19 18 17 16 15

ACKNOWLEDGMENTS

This book was truly a labor of love and just a good time. As always, I have to pause and thank the people who keep me writing. My parents, Doris and Freddie Hodges. My sister, Adrienne Hodges Dease, and my niece, who is an inspiration to me every day, Briana Dease.

To all of the book clubs, libraries, and bookstores that have been in my corner since I started on this journey, thank you! I have to thank the ladies of my street team: Louise Brown, Lynne Bradley, Jennifer Copeland, Erika Parker, LaSonde Jones, Deborah Fotner, and Donisha Rosebud. LaSheera Lee, Yolanda Gore, Sonia Corley, Erica Singleton, Ashley Fayton, thanks for the support, for challenging me, and for listening to me rant about Wonderland.

CHAPTER 1

Sitting at a table in the middle of Starbucks, Liza Palmer pushed her steaming caramel latte aside and focused her ebony stare on her friend, Robert Montgomery, as he explained why he was going to run for North Carolina Senate Seat Forty-Five. His brown eyes sparkled with passion as he talked about serving the people and that look ignited her like a firecracker. "Yes! I think you will be a great senator and I know some people who can help us build a buzz around you. This is just awesome, Robert. I can't wait to . . ."

"Slow down," Robert said. "You're talking as if I'm one of the brands you represent." She frowned at him and Robert threw his hands up. "Not saying what you do isn't serious, but I don't think marketing me like a cashmere sweater is going to work. People are going to have to connect with me and know that I'm going to Raleigh to represent their best interests."

Liza rolled her eyes and toyed with the lid of her cup. "Of course not, but a grassroots campaign got Barack Obama into the White House. You need a Twitter account, Facebook fan page, and website where people donate to your campaign." Liza pulled out her iPad and started taking notes. Robert laughed.

"You take that thing everywhere, don't you?"

She nodded. "Got to stay connected. You know who would be a great campaign manager for you: Dominic Hall. He has been behind some of the biggest campaigns in the city and the state. Remember that contentious fight for the chairmanship of the board of county commissioners? Dominic was behind the winner. And he systematically shut the other guy down."

"Funny you should say that," he said. "Nic and I met this morning and he agreed to work with me."

"Awesome! But you still need me."

Robert placed his hand on top of hers. "I know. One thing I know for sure is that you have my back for real. Together we're going to be unstoppable."

"That's right, Senator Montgomery. Now, about your social media life. Do you tweet?"

"As the law firm, but I don't have a personal account. I don't understand that whole Twitter thing."

"Good, I'll be happy to explain it to you. More people get their news from Twitter than the local TV stations. So, you kind of need to get on board," she said, then stroked her cheek. "Your personal life is going to be under a microscope — especially because you're single. Anything or anyone out there with an ax to grind?"

"Did you just say 'anything'?"

Liza rolled her eyes and flipped her shoulder-length auburn tresses back. "I've seen some of the women you've dated, Rob. 'Anything' was being kind."

"And you don't have much room to talk. Remember your thug life stage? You really can't hold my hood rat phase in college against me."

Liza giggled. "Where did you import those hood boogers from? I wasn't aware of a hood within walking distance to Chapel Hill."

"See, you can't be saying stuff like that." He looked around the semi-full coffee shop to make sure no one was paying them any attention.

"Well, if you're running as a single candidate, you need to be seen with a higher

9

class of woman."

"Are you suggesting a fake relationship?" he asked, raising his right eyebrow. A frown marred his handsome cocoa brown face.

"No, people would see through that like glass. I'm suggesting you meet some nice ladies at my dinner party on Saturday, which you didn't RSVP for."

"I'll be there."

"When are you filing?" Liza asked.

"Dominic and I are going to discuss that tomorrow. I need a war chest and Dominic said he has a list of donors willing to help."

"What platform are you running on?" Liza asked in between sips of her cold latte. "You really need to consider the problems in the district. There are three issues getting military family behind you and . . ."

"Business development is my main thing. I know the military's important, but Charlotte and the surrounding area need jobs."

"Yeah," she said, then drummed her French-tipped fingernails on the lid of her cup. "But people are wary of politicians who are for big business. You need to play up your roots."

Robert's handsome face darkened. "I don't want to be some sad-sack politician that people are drawn to because of their shortcomings."

"Whoa! You're starting to sound like a Republican."

"No, you're misunderstanding what I'm saying. I'll acknowledge everyone who helped me, but I'm not going to tell the state and the world that I was born to a crackhead who left me at a fire station."

Liza held her tongue; she knew how hurtful Robert's past was. But the public relations professional inside her knew people would cheer for a man who came from absolutely nothing to go on and breeze through college, then law school. Maybe he'd listen to Dominic about telling his story. "Anyway," she said, "I am so proud of you, Rob. I remember when we were in that political science class together and you did that mock campaign for president. I knew two things that day." She brought her cup to her lips and took a final sip of her latte.

"What?"

"That you'd be president one day and I wasn't going to get a degree in political science."

"President, huh?" Robert smiled and Liza knew his picture-ready smile would win hearts even if he didn't talk about his past. "You expect a lot from me, huh?"

"Actually, I do," she said, then pushed her cup away. "I believe in you, Rob. And I

11

don't say that lightly. You're the embodiment of the American dream and the people of North Carolina will be lucky to have you."

"Great, that means I have one vote."

"You'll have more than one vote. How many people are going to be in the primary, I wonder," she said, then looked down at her iPad as it chimed. "Oh, hate to run, but I have a meeting in twenty minutes with the Hornets' new player relations manager."

"There you go, moving and shaking things in the city," Robert said as he watched his friend collect her things.

"Next, we're going to move and shake this election." Liza gave him a quick kiss on the cheek, then dashed out the door.

CHAPTER 2

Jackson Franklin hated the term *hero*. He wasn't a hero. He was a soldier. He'd joined the Army to serve his country and to earn money for college. He went to war because the commander in chief had ordered it. He saved his platoon from a roadside bomb in Kabul because that had been what he was trained to do. But when he returned to Fort Bragg, North Carolina, he was branded a hero. However, the injuries he sustained in Afghanistan forced him out of active duty. And damn it, he missed it. Big-time. Working as a transition counselor for the Veteran's Association in Charlotte made him feel alive again. Feel as if he was still serving his country by helping broken men and women become whole again.

Sitting behind the oak desk in his small office, Jackson knew there was more work to be done and he knew he couldn't do that by just working with the veterans at the center. He looked out of the windows in front of him and watched the men and women in the lobby filling out forms. Some of them had been in and out of the office more than a dozen times. What were they going to do if these doors closed to them?

The center needed a huge influx of cash in order to keep helping veterans. He'd written to the district representative in the General Assembly. He'd reached out to some of the city council members but help never came. But more and more veterans kept walking through those doors.

"Sergeant Franklin, we've got a problem out here!" Natalie Johnson, the receptionist, exclaimed from the doorway of his office.

Jackson rushed into the hallway expecting the worst. But he was greeted with a bunch of balloons and chocolate cake, followed by a chorus of "Happy Birthday." Jackson smiled for two reasons: one, he'd actually forgotten his birthday, and two, the staff knew in order to get him out of his office they had to fake an emergency.

"You guys didn't have to do this," he said. Jackson was happy to see so many of the men and women he'd worked with over the last year standing there ready to celebrate with him. Their healing had begun. But in the back of his mind he was pissed because this time next year, the doors to this office could be closed.

"Come on," Natalie said, "let's go cut the cake."

Jackson wanted to send them down the hall without him; he had to figure out who to lobby to for money.

"Hey, Sergeant Franklin," Dena Washington, one of his clients, said. "Have you heard about the new district the General Assembly carved out?"

"I must've missed that," he said. "What's this new district supposed to do?"

Dena smiled. "Give us another voice in Raleigh. Maybe we'll finally get someone in there who gives a damn. You should think about running."

"I'm not a politician."

"That's why you're just what this district needs." Dena walked toward the conference room and Jackson stood there bewildered. What did he know about running for political office? Then again, he knew what the people he worked with needed. Was it too much of a long shot for him to throw his hat in the ring?

When Jackson walked into the conference room and saw all of the veterans, he knew just what he had to do if he wanted things to change. But what did he know about

15

politics? He couldn't be worse than the clowns already in Raleigh. Where was he going to start? Should he even run, or was he just dreaming out loud?

"Why are you scowling? It's your birthday?" Natalie said, then bumped him with her hip.

"We need to talk about a letter I received," he whispered.

"No bad news today."

"Today, tomorrow, the news isn't going to change." He folded his massive arms across his chest.

Natalie sighed. "Do you want to disappoint them?" She nodded toward the people enjoying cake and soft drinks.

"No," he said. "Let me get a slice of cake and smile."

"Good idea."

After the surprise party was over, Jackson and Natalie were in the conference room again, this time with the head of the counseling center and the other doctors who worked there. There was no laughing or balloons this time.

"We're closing," Daniel Keter said without preamble.

"Are you serious?" Jackson exclaimed. "Why are we closing when there is a strong need for the work we do here?" The letter he'd received said the center was in debt, but closing?

"The state won't accept federal money and they aren't funding us. I can't pay you guys, and no matter how much you love what you do, I know each and every one of you has to eat."

Natalie looked at Jackson and shook her head. "This is stupid. I feel like marching to Raleigh and . . ."

"Listen," Daniel said, holding his hand up to quiet the rumbling. "We have thirty days, and I need you all to line up referrals for our most serious cases."

"They're all serious," Jackson growled. "So, let me get this straight. Because the governor and the General Assembly have issues with the president, our soldiers are going to suffer?"

Daniel shrugged. "Jackson, there's nothing I can do. If I could, I'd recall the governor and send those greedy bastards in Raleigh to South Carolina. Or better yet, to the hellholes that our clients came from and see if they will stop this political bickering."

A chorus of "Damned straight" rippled through the conference room. "What are we going to do?" one of the doctors asked. "I mean, we need to stay open. Too many people are going to suffer if we close up in a

17

month."

"I don't disagree, but we need funding."

"How much?" Jackson asked, then frowned. It wasn't as if he had a few million dollars sitting in a bank account to give the center. Hell, he didn't even have a spare thousand.

"More than we have," Daniel said with a defeated tone in his voice. "We've been running in the red for a few months. To get out of the hole, we need a hundred grand. To stay open, we need twice that."

Jackson shook his head. "I'm going to run for that new senate seat because this is ridiculous!"

He was surprised by the applause that came from his coworkers. "You would be a great senator!" Natalie said.

"And I know the person who can run your campaign," Daniel said.

"I'll volunteer," Natalie said, followed by a bunch of other people promising to volunteer.

A smile spread across Jackson's face. If he had this level of support in this room, would he be able to win the senate seat?

"All right," Daniel said. "While this is great news, we have to get back on task and work out how we're going to provide seamless service until we find some mental health providers who will accept our clients."

Everyone returned to the work they needed to complete, and Jackson looked up a few doctors with a military background whom he could send his list of clients to. Being trained to work with mental issues was a lot different from actually understanding what the client was going through, in his opinion. When he'd worked with his own doctor, the fact that his doctor had also seen combat allowed him to open up more.

About two hours later, Daniel walked into Jackson's office with a wide grin on his lips. "Sarge," he said.

"What's up?"

"Are you serious about this senate seat? Because if you are, we're going to have a hell of a senator in you, and I know the best person to run your campaign."

Jackson leaned back in his chair. "You really think I can make a difference, because I want to be clear, this isn't about me. The budget cuts that the VA is facing make no sense. It's as if we sent these men and women to fight and then after the parade when they get home, we don't give a damn about them. When's the last time we heard any of our representatives say a word about the military?"

"You don't have to sell me."

Jackson squeezed the bridge of his nose. "Yeah, but what do I know about politics?"

Daniel clasped his hands together. "You don't have to know anything because Teresa Flores knows enough for all of us. Quite honestly, she's one of the reasons that we've been around as long as we have."

"How?"

"She knows the right people in Raleigh — hell, in Washington too. We've been up for closure three years in a row."

"If she's so good, why are we getting shut down now?"

"Too many god . . . too many rich people sitting in the General Assembly, and with the gerrymandering of these districts, we're going to be in trouble. That's why you have to run and you have to let Teresa help. She's tough but clean."

"That sounds good because I don't want to be a part of some mudslinging . . ."

"Listen," Daniel said, "it's not as if we have an incumbent to fight. No one has ever represented this district. The main thing we have to do is make sure that the new senator cares about what's important. And once in office that he can rally people to his side."

Jackson nodded. He knew it wasn't just the veterans and their families who were hurting. There was education, the economy, transportation concerns, and voting rights. There was a lot of work that needed to be done in North Carolina. Jackson had to make sure he was up for the task. He couldn't run off of emotions.

"When can I meet Teresa Flores?" he asked.

Daniel smiled. "I'll call her right now and see how soon we can set something up. This is going to be great, Jackson. Just great."

When he was alone in his office, Jackson logged on to the state board of elections' website to study what he needed to do to get his name on the ballot.

CHAPTER 3

Liza tilted her head to the side as she updated her client's Twitter feed and listened to the caterer for her party. "No," she said as she hit the tweet button. "I do not — I repeat — do not want a buffet. That's not the vibe I'm going for. I want servers to roam the room with trays of hors d'oeuvres. And I really want some of your famous canapés."

"Famous? You think so?" the caterer asked excitedly.

Liza rolled her eyes, glad that she wasn't Face-Timing with her caterer. "Oh, yes. And after this party, they are going to be Beyoncé famous. Then for the main course, everyone will be seated, so, if we can do some sort of festive plating . . ."

"What do you mean?"

Liza sighed. "This is a dinner party for some people who have the potential to change the politics in this state. The next

North Carolina senator may even be there. So, be creative. I know you can do this. And, I know this isn't protocol, but that chocolate cake from Hometown Delights is to die for. Please make sure we have one."

"You want me to get another person's food and serve it under my name?"

"No. That cake is for later. But it needs to be in the building," Liza said while she silently formulated a plan to get Chante and Robert alone sharing coffee and cake.

"All right, I'll make it happen."

"And that's why I love you. I have to go; call me back with the menu."

"Will do."

Liza hung up the phone and rose to her feet, stretching and smiling. She was actually done with her work for the day.

"I guess I should go pick out a dress for the party," she muttered as she dropped her iPad and iPhone into her oversized leather purse. But before she could walk out the door, her office phone rang.

"Liza Palmer," she said.

"Liza, it's Claude Richards. I need your help."

Dropping her purse on her desk, Liza knew this call from her troubled NBA client meant that dress shopping would have to wait. "What's up, Claude?"

"I'm in trouble," he said. "There's this woman who says she's having my baby."

"This is the third time this month."

"And it's the same girl," he said. "You have to make her go away."

"I work in public relations; I don't make people go away. Why don't you talk to this woman? Request a DNA test. But you need to stop treating women as if they are disposable sex toys."

"It's not my fault," he said. "These women are after my money."

"Then why are you letting this happen? Ever heard of saying no?" Liza sighed and silently contemplated giving up her professional athlete clients. "What do you want me to do?"

"Maybe I should just give her what she wants," he sighed.

"And what would that be?" Liza was now sitting at her desk with her feet propped on the edge. She was going to drop him as a client, for real. The financial hit wouldn't be that bad.

"An engagement ring."

"Richards! Didn't I tell you to stop coming to me with your relationship problems?! So, this pregnant girl is your girlfriend? What's the problem with committing to her?"

"What about my image and fan base?"

Liza closed her eyes and silently counted to ten. "This is Charlotte, North Carolina. People love a family man. Now, if you want to be a man-whore and build a fan base, get traded to L.A."

"What are you saying?"

"That playboy stuff doesn't work here. Do you love this woman?"

"She's all right. I mean . . ."

Liza blew into the phone. "Let me get this straight. She's all right but you slept with her without a condom. Did you use your scholarship to learn anything in college?"

"Wow, you're being really mean right now."

"Richards, grow up. Either you're going to accept responsibility for your child or you're going to be the stereotype of the NBA player who makes babies and runs. Which one do you want to be?"

"So, if I marry her and it doesn't work out . . ."

"Then we can go all Dwayne Wade, show you as a great father and go from there. But you can't allow her to start talking to MediaTakeOut, Bossip, and those blogs that will make you look like the biggest jackass in America."

"I guess you're right, but I think she

already went to the blogs."

Liza shook her head. "Give me her number and you need to call Eli Millou."

"Who is Eli Millou?"

"Your new best friend, the guy who's going to design the engagement ring that women are going to ooh and ahh over. And, I'm charging you double for this." Liza hung up on him, then sent him a text with Millou's number before tossing her phone across the room.

She couldn't stand an unfaithful and wishy-washy man. That's one of the reasons why she focused on her career. The other reason: Alvin Thorne. They'd come close to getting married, until she overheard a conversation with him and his lover two days before their wedding. In legendary Liza fashion, she'd called off the wedding and wrote a press release about the end of her relationship and posted it on her blog, which had about a hundred thousand followers at the time.

Alvin, who'd worked as an investment banker for a boutique firm, tried to make it up to Liza after he began losing clients. Of course, she turned him down, and then she became the most famous client of It's Just Lunch, a dating service that paired busy professionals together for lunch dates. While she hadn't made a love connection, she'd helped the company grow because of her blog posts about her dates and her willingness to talk about her love life — or more accurately, her lack of one.

While Liza's star rose, Alvin had been branded a cheater and disappeared from the social scene. It was a wonder that she represented someone like Claude Richards. But the money was good, she had to admit.

Was it worth it, though? Maybe that's why she was so excited to help Robert in his effort to do something meaningful. Being the next state senator was important, and Liza was going to do everything in her power to give Robert the image of being the perfect candidate. Picking up her desk phone, she called her best friend and sorority sister, Chante Britt.

"This is Chante."

"I hate that lawyer voice of yours," Liza said with a laugh.

"Girl, why are you calling me in the middle of the day?"

"What am I interrupting? Brief writing? A settlement offer because no one wants to face you in court?"

"You're gassing my ego. What do you want?"

"I don't want anything. I just want to

make sure that you're coming to my dinner party."

"Umm, about that . . ."

"Don't you dare cancel on me!"

"Liza, I have work and . . ."

"If you don't come to this dinner party, you're going regret it. And you might even pick up a potential client."

Chante sighed. "Really, L? You're trying to hook me up with some dude, aren't you?"

Liza laughed as she imagined her friend sitting at her big oak desk dressed in her lawyer gear while throwing a temper tantrum. "Chante, not just *some dude,* but the next state senator for district forty-five. You two will be perfect for each other. I don't know why I didn't hook you two up sooner. Oh, because you're always working."

"If you're talking about your friend Robert Montgomery, we've met before."

Liza rolled her eyes. "Yes, you've met him at several professional events, but you've never talked to him on a one-on-one level."

"And why would I want to do that?"

"Because you two would be perfect for each other. You're smart and understand this lawyer stuff. You won't be mad when he's late because of a court case. You can unwind with him and quote court cases that he understands. And Robert is pretty fine."

"Then why haven't you two ever been more than friends?"

Liza snorted. "You know I don't date."

"And you and Robert never hooked up?"

"Please! He's like a brother to me, and why would I try to hook you with someone I'd been with. Eww!"

"I'm just making sure you're not trying to make some sordid drama for a reality show or something."

"I hate reality shows and I really try to keep my clients off those things. But that's neither here nor there. Please be nice to Robert. He's going to be a big deal, and if you two hit it off, then I will be friends with one of the biggest power couples in the state."

Chante sighed again. "Liza, do you ever get tired of playing cupid? You deserve to be happy too, and allowing what happened with busted crotch to cloud your view of love is wrong."

"Nobody has time for that. I don't work for a huge law firm; I have to build my brand and do it in a way that doesn't put me on front street. After all, I'm not Marie Charles."

"Who's married and in Paris now. Yep, you are no Marie Charles."

29

"Whatever," Liza said with an eye roll that Chante couldn't see.

"I'm just saying," Chante said. "And I know you rolled your eyes at me."

Liza laughed. "Let's meet for coffee so I can go over the details of the dinner party and how you and Robert are going to have coffee and cake afterwards."

"You're always scheming something!" Chante said with a laugh. "The usual spot?"

"Yes, ma'am. See you in an hour?"

"Make it an hour and a half. I have to file a brief."

"I'll be waiting, with caramel salted brownies," Liza said. This time, she grabbed her purse and phone, then went out the door without giving anyone a chance to interrupt her again. Heading to Amelie's, the twenty-four-hour French bakery, where she and Chante often met and planned everything, many times in the middle of the night because of their schedules.

Liza loved the eclectic mix of people who flowed through the bakery at night. The artists and writers enthralled her because they seemed so free. She wanted to offer her services to some of the greats she saw come through those doors. Then there were those she wanted to tell to get a really good day job.

When she arrived at the bakery, Liza wanted nothing more than to sip a chocolate latte and nibble on the renowned sweets Amelie's was known for. But her cell phone rang again. When she saw that it wasn't Chante, all she could do was sigh.

"Liza Palmer."

"Liza, it's Robert."

"What's with the new number?" she asked.

"Nic's idea. Look, I want to talk to you about this campaign. I'm thinking that I need some assistance with getting the public on my side."

"I'm with you! What do you need?"

Robert went on about his need for a Twitter account, a blog, and the crafting of his story.

"I know I probably shouldn't have, but I have a file of all of that stuff."

"Liza, you are amazing. If you were anyone else, I'd think that file would be a little strange."

"I wish we were on a recorded line so that I could remind you of that later."

"I'm near your office. Why don't I stop by and we can get started?"

"I'm not at my office right now. I should be. . . . Why don't you meet me at Amelie's?"

Liza figured she could kill two birds with one stone: she and Robert could talk business and he could meet Chante before the dinner party. Smiling, she loved it when things fell into place. Walking into the bakery, Liza was glad to see there wasn't a long line for the delectable sweets.

She ordered three brownies and a large coffee, then took a seat near the door so that she could see her friends as they walked in. She pulled out her iPad and opened the file she had on Robert and his social media plan. *He should've just listened to me from the beginning,* she thought with a smile as she sipped her coffee.

"Must be some good reading," Chante said as she touched Liza's shoulder to get her attention.

Liza's head snapped up and she smiled. "Girl, you know me. Going over a social media plan."

Chante shook her head and then spotted the brownies. "Aww, you got them," she said as she crossed over to the table and picked up one of the treats.

"So," Liza said as she powered her iPad down. "What's new in the legal world?"

Chante rolled her eyes. "I'm sick of doing all of this work to prove to the partners that they need to go ahead and put my name on the door."

Liza nodded. "Myrick, Lawson, Walker, and Britt sounds good to me."

"Lawrence Walker's retiring and that's why I'm busting my butt to get this partnership."

"You're going to get it. You're too brilliant not to." As she spotted Robert walking through the door she added, "And, I'm going to introduce you to more brilliance."

Chante followed her friend's gaze. "That's Robert?" she whispered.

Liza nodded as he walked over to them. His smile lit up the room, and she noticed the twinkle in her sorority sister's eyes.

"Hello, ladies. I hope I'm not intruding," he said, then took a seat beside Chante.

"No, not at all," Chante said. "I'm guessing this third brownie is for you." Liza hid her laughter as Chante handed him the plate.

"So, have you two met?" Liza asked as she sipped her coffee.

"Not socially," Chante said, never taking her eyes off Robert.

He smiled and nibbled his brownie. "Oh, no, Miss Britt, I do remember seeing you briefly at a cocktail party, but before I could make a move toward you, you disappeared."

"I don't recall you making a move at all

that night," she said. Liza almost wanted to excuse herself from their conversation. But she was just too entertained by the dance between these two.

"If I didn't, I must have been drinking a little too much."

Liza drained her coffee cup and headed to the counter to get a refill. Glancing over her shoulder, she couldn't help but smile at the fact that the two hit it off so well. It was kind of weird, though, because Robert had been acting as if he didn't want anything to do with Chante or social media, and now he'd done a complete one-eighty. Maybe he had seen the error of his ways or maybe Chante was just that charming. Liza lingered at the counter a little longer watching the interaction between her friends. Though she couldn't hear what they were saying, she could tell that the conversation was going well by the way Chante smiled.

This is going to work out just fine, she thought as she headed back over to her friends.

"Excuse me," a smooth, deep voice said from behind her. Turning around, Liza was surprised to see Jackson Franklin standing there. Looking into his emerald eyes, she took a deep breath. Pictures didn't do him justice at all. This man was a living, breathing god — even if his tie was askew.

"Sorry," she said quietly.

"No problem, I just need some sugar and I'll be on my way."

Oh, I'd love to give you some sugar, she thought as her gaze fell on his full lips. She picked up the glass container and handed it to him.

"Thanks," he said, then smiled at her. Liza glanced down at his massive hands and forced herself not to think about him touching her. This man was the "enemy." He wanted a seat that clearly belonged to Robert.

"You're welcome. Excuse me," she said. Liza returned to the pastry counter just so she could get a look at that man as he walked out the door. "Get it together," she muttered, then ordered a cinnamon stick that she didn't really want. Looking down at the sweet treat, she shook her head thinking about how much it reminded her of Jackson's smooth skin tone.

Walking back to her friends, she chided herself for acting like a political groupie. Her job was to bring him down, not lust after him.

"Everything okay over here?" Liza smiled as she sat in the chair vacated earlier.

Robert returned her smile and nodded.

"Everything is fine. Chante and I were having a great conversation that I can't wait to continue at the dinner party this weekend." Liza expelled a sigh of relief — neither of them had seen her near meltdown with Jackson or noticed that he was in the French bakery.

Chante grinned. "I'm looking forward to this weekend as well."

Robert rose to his feet. "I know I was supposed to talk to you about some campaign stuff, but I have to get back to the office. Breakfast?"

"Usual spot?" Liza asked.

Robert nodded, then turned to Chante and took her hand in his. He kissed it, then told both women good-bye.

Once he was out of earshot, Chante expelled a sigh. "You were right," she said.

"What was that?" Liza quipped, then cupped her ear. "I know you didn't just say I was right."

"He's charming, good-looking, and single. Please tell me — again — why you two have only been friends all of these years?"

"Because Robert is just as driven as you are, and you know, I need attention."

Chante rolled her eyes. "No, you're playing Erykah Badu over here, bag lady."

"Anyway. You and Robert are perfect for

each other."

"I see the potential. And I like what I see," she said with a smile.

Jackson hung back at the coffee counter and watched the alluring woman talk with her friend. Something about her made him smile. Maybe it was the singsong quality to her voice or the fact that she had the most beautiful onyx eyes he'd ever seen.

Who was she? While he knew his time would've been better spent preparing for his meeting with Teresa Flores, he had to at least find out what her name was. When he saw that she was alone, Jackson crossed over to her and stood in front of her.

"Hi," he said. "Do you mind if I sit?"

She looked up at him with a shocked expression on her face. "Well, I'm a little busy." She nodded toward the iPad in her lap.

Unmoved, he extended his hand to her. "I'm Jackson Franklin, and you are?"

Clearing her throat, she took his hand and shook it firmly. God, she had the softest skin. "Liza Palmer, and I know who you are."

"Is that so?"

She nodded and smirked. "You're one of the people running for the state senate seat."

He smiled. "I hope that means I have your vote."

Liza slipped her iPad into her purse. "Not a chance," she said, then walked out the door, leaving Jackson standing there with his mouth wide open.

CHAPTER 4

Jackson had diffused bombs in Baghdad. He'd taken fire in Iraq and Afghanistan. But none of that prepared him for the force of nature that was Teresa Flores. From the moment he'd walked into her office, she had laid out his campaign, created his backstory and talking points as to why he was running for the senate seat. Even after drinking two cups of coffee, he was still having a hard time keeping up.

"Any questions?" she asked.

Oh, he had plenty, but he didn't know where to start. "Who had any idea that it took this much to run for office?" Jackson said.

"If you think this is a lot, then perhaps this isn't for you," Teresa said as she sat behind her desk and pushed her raven locks behind her ears. "Mr. Franklin, your life is about to become fodder for news stories, comedians, tweeters, and bloggers. You have to ask yourself right now, do I want to do this and why am I doing it?"

Jackson sighed. "I'm doing this because I've seen what happens when the government caters to special interests and puts the people who keep this country free on the back burner. I have to do this because I haven't heard anyone running for any office say anything about what the people need. I could sit back and watch other people try to fix the issues that are plaguing the military community, but I've done that and I haven't seen anything happen to make things better."

Teresa applauded. "You can't buy that kind of passion," she said with a smile. "Jackson, I think you're the real deal and will be a real asset to the people of this district. All I need from you is to be honest and to keep doing what you do. Don't worry about poll numbers; that's my job. We're going to make you the next North Carolina senator." She extended her hand to Jackson. "Now, you need a makeover."

"What?"

She nodded. "You have to look like a politician. A few suits and a haircut will give you just what you need to look like what people think a senator should look like."

Jackson rubbed his forehead. "What is

this, a dog and pony show?"

Teresa shrugged. "Yes."

"This is really not what I signed on for."

"Well, politics is about image as much as it is about substance. You don't think your opponents aren't doing the same thing we're doing right now with their staff?"

"I don't want to be that kind of man. If people can't accept me for who I am and what I have to offer, what is the point of all of this?"

"Do you want to win?"

"Of course I do, but not at the expense of my integrity."

"And, Jackson, I'd *never* put your integrity into question. You're one of the first men who has ever walked into this office and impressed me."

Jackson furrowed his brows. "How so?"

"You're honest, you have real concerns about this undertaking, and your passion about winning this seat is real. I've been doing this for thirty years and you're the second guy I ever seriously believed in."

"Who was the first guy?"

She shook her head and chuckled. "I'm going to plead the fifth on that one. All I know is, I will hire your videographer."

Jackson laughed hardily as he caught her reference. Then she handed him a business card. He read the lifted gold text, *Charles P. Dwight, Haberdasher.*

"Really?" he asked.

"Yes. We have to get you camera ready when you go file. Charles will fit you in a suit that will have you looking a leader and a military man at the same time. Voters will flock to you. We're not going to have you looking like a man who gets seven hundred–dollar haircuts or a career politician — we're just going to polish you up a bit."

"When should I go see this Charles guy?"

Teresa looked at her watch. "He's waiting on you now."

Jackson rose to his feet, in awe of his campaign manager. "Then, I'm on my way."

"And after you meet with Charles, I have a couple of donors that you're having lunch with at Chima. Make sure you wear your new suit. Jackson, I believe in you, and if you sell these guys on your passion, I think we have a serious shot of winning this election."

He smiled and tipped his hand to her as if he were wearing a hat. "Thanks for your faith in me."

"Don't make me regret it."

Jackson left the office and headed to Charles Dwight's shop in Uptown Charlotte. It wasn't lost on him that the clothier's business was across the street from the restaurant where Teresa had set up the meeting with the donors. "I hope this isn't the beginning of a mistake," he mumbled as he walked into the shop.

"Jackson Franklin?" a thin, tall man dressed in a pair of black slacks and a green and gold plaid shirt asked.

"Yes. Charles Dwight?"

"Guilty as charged. Now, Teresa neglected to tell me that I was going to be working with a model."

Jackson furrowed his brows. "I wouldn't go that far."

Charles fanned his hand. "Please, the last wannabe politician who walked in here needed a potato sack. You're going to be easy to clean up."

About two hours later, Jackson was dressed in a perfectly tailored navy blue suit, crisp white shirt with a North Carolina flag tie, and a pair of brown wing-tip shoes. He thought the tie was a little over the top, but glancing at himself in the mirror, he had to admit it worked.

Crossing the street, he headed to the Brazilian steakhouse and noticed that it was practically empty, except for a table in the center of the restaurant. The host didn't say a word; he just led Jackson to the table.

"Mr. Franklin," one of the men said as he rose to his feet.

"Yes, and you have me at a disadvantage," Jackson replied as he shook his hand.

"Excuse me?"

"I don't know your name."

The man chuckled and pointed his index finger at Jackson. "I like that. Stephen Winston, president of Charlotte Metro Credit Union." He introduced Jackson to the other men at the table. "This is Taiwon Myrick and . . ."

"General David McClain," Jackson said, then saluted the older man.

"Sergeant Franklin, I have to admit I was intrigued when I heard that you were running for office. Not many of us do this. But when I heard why you were doing it, I knew I had to meet you and see if I could support you."

"General, I'm honored to meet you. And we can't sit by and become the good men who do nothing while our brothers and sisters suffer."

Taiwon cleared his throat. "Excuse me, but don't we have other issues that we need to focus on?"

"Yes," Jackson said, turning to face Myrick. "The General Assembly has crippled education and social programs, and tax reform is a joke. It seems as if the government is out to keep the poor in their place while the rich keep getting a bigger piece of the pie."

"Sounds like you're running on a socialist platform," Taiwon retorted.

"Not at all," Jackson said, folding his arms across his chest. "But it's time to stop rolling over the poor in this state and this country as if they don't matter. Politicians are supposed to represent everyone, not just the special interests and people with deep pockets."

"You know, you can't win an election without money," Taiwon said.

"And some donors expect favors," Stephen said.

"That's what this meeting is about?" Jackson asked, looking around at the men at the table. "You want to bankroll my campaign and then keep me in your pocket?"

The men looked at each other and smiled. "I like this guy," the general said.

"It's easy to stand up when you don't have power," Taiwon mumbled.

Jackson gritted his teeth. "Listen," he began. "I'm not going to beg for anything. Either you want to support me or you don't."

David McClain applauded. "You've got

my support. That takes balls."

"So, no one stands up for what's right anymore?" Jackson asked.

"Nope," David said. "That's why I want you to represent district forty-five." The old general sat down and wrote a check for Jackson's campaign with more zeroes than Jackson expected.

The lunch meeting turned out to be a success. Jackson's honesty and straightforward way impressed the donors, and he left with more than a million dollars in donations — with no strings attached. Though he was a little wary of Myrick. When he got into his car, Teresa called him.

"I just heard great things about you," she said when he answered.

"I was just being me."

"That's all I want you to do, Jackson. Now, we need to get the paperwork together for your campaign account. But I don't want to overwhelm you today. Go home, get some rest, and we will hit the ground running tomorrow," she said.

"I'm going into the office. I need to check on my clients and make sure the referrals are going through. . . ."

"Yeah," Teresa said. "You're going to be a great senator."

After hanging up with Teresa, Jackson felt

as if his real life was coming back into focus. He was doing this because he wanted to make sure the military men and women he wanted to save were getting the help they needed.

As soon as he arrived at the office, Daniel cornered him and asked him about his meeting with Teresa.

"She is something," Jackson said with a smile. "Before I got there, she already had donors with checkbooks lined up to donate to my, what did she call it, war chest."

"I told you. I'm wondering who else is running in this race if Teresa's already lining your war chest."

Jackson shrugged. "I guess I should know these things," he said. "This is a lot harder than I thought it would be. Greasing palms, meeting people who could make a difference if they gave a damn . . ."

"Calm down, Jackson," Daniel said. "Politics is nothing but a dog and pony show. It's a game."

"With real people's lives hanging in the balance? This is bullshit."

"You do realize that it gets harder."

He nodded and closed his eyes. "This is why Raleigh is so screwed up. Men and women sell their souls for power."

"That's the difference between you and

them — you're not in it for the power." Jackson agreed but he was happy to change the subject.

"Where are we on the doctor referrals?"

"We have doctors for the clients, but the problem is, we have a few people who don't want to deal with doctors who don't know what they've been through."

Jackson sighed. "I was afraid of that. How much time do we have?"

"Not much. That's why you have to do this," Daniel said. "We need someone representing us who understands that our returning troops need this kind of help."

"Not only troops but all of our families who need help. I was reading some of the bills that the General Assembly is debating and I don't see how any of this helps the majority of citizens in North Carolina."

"Preaching to the choir. I understand how important you've been to our clients. You've been where they've been. I can't reach them the way you do."

"And they think another doctor won't be able to do that either," he said with a sigh. "But the government they fought to protect won't keep centers like this one open."

"You take that passion to the General Assembly and things might get done."

"That's the . . ." His cell phone rang,

flashing Teresa's name and number. "I have to take this." Daniel nodded and backed out of Jackson's office.

"Yes, Teresa."

"You impressed the right people at lunch today," she said.

"You already told me that."

"We have a breakfast meeting with the general and Senator Thomas Watson," Teresa said.

"What time?" he asked as he flipped through his calendar.

"Six."

"That's early."

"Well, let's not be naïve here, these donors are hedging their bets and meeting with candidates all day. You do realize that there are at least thirteen people who are rumored to be interested in this seat. I've looked at them and your real competition in the primaries is going to be Charlotte lawyer Richard, er, Robert Montgomery. He's been looking for a reason to throw his hat in the political ring for a long time and he's the typical Charlotte politician."

Jackson snorted. "That's the problem, isn't it? We keep sending typical politicians to Raleigh."

"That's true. But you need to meet the competition and see where you're the same

49

and how you're different." He could hear Teresa typing on her computer. "Sending you an e-mail about Montgomery right now. Oh, and he's probably going to attend the breakfast as well. Knowing him, with his entourage."

"Are we taking a page from his playbook?" Jackson asked, his head already throbbing.

"No. We don't do pompous. We're not assuming that we're going to win, although you will."

Jackson chuckled as his computer and smartphone alerted him that he had an e-mail.

"Review the e-mail and let's meet for a quick dinner at my office. I'm vegan, by the way, so if you can't go without meat, bring your own meal."

"Got it," Jackson said. Then Teresa hung up. He noticed that she never said goodbye. He'd have to ask her about that over dinner.

Liza yawned as she read over her guest list for Saturday's party. Just as she was about to call it a day, her phone rang — playing "Hail to the Chief," Robert's ringtone. "What's up, senator?" she answered.

"Getting ahead of yourself, sis." She could hear the chuckle in his voice. "Chante is a lovely woman. I need her phone number."

"Ah," Liza said, then rattled off her friend's number. "Why haven't you two exchanged these pleasantries before? After all, you run in the same legal circles."

"Well, when I saw her at a couple of NC Bar Association mixers, I just assumed that she had a man. Women like that — you included — shouldn't be single."

Here we go, she thought with a roll of her eyes.

"Anyway," Robert said. "I need another favor too."

"What's that?" she asked.

"There's a breakfast meeting in the morning with me and some heavy hitters. I want you to go with me."

"Ooh, why aren't you taking Nic?"

"He'll be there as well. Nic said we need to show these guys that we have an organized campaign team, and you know you're a major part of this team."

Liza beamed. "I'm glad you consider me a part of the team."

"Come on, Liza, you've always had my back. Hell, you've believed in me more than I believed in myself at times."

"Well, you're an easy man to cheer for," Liza said. "Who's this meeting with?"

"Some donors and possibly my competition. Ever hear of a guy named Jackson Franklin?"

"Briefly. I've seen a few local features on him. I haven't had a chance to really look into his background." Liza immediately typed his name into the search engine. Links populated showing photos and stories about war hero Jackson Franklin. People loved a war hero turned politician. This was going to be trouble as well as the fact that he was fine as frog's hair and had made her heart skip several beats when he shook her hand at the bakery.

"From what I just Googled, this guy is going to be a tough adversary."

"Why is that?"

"War hero, pretty attractive, and a down-to-earth guy, from what I'm reading online."

"What the hell does he know about politics?" She could tell that Robert was annoyed. That's why she didn't tell him that war heroes made good candidates and all he had to do was look at John McCain.

"It isn't about what he knows," she said. "It's about what the public will perceive he knows."

"How do we combat that?"

"You're not going to like the answer."

Robert groaned. "Liza, don't start this background bullshit again. I'm not going to advertise that my mother was a crackhead who left me on my own."

"Voters will identify with you and it will level the playing field," she said with a frustrated sigh.

"I'm not doing that, Liza, playing field be damned."

"Then what's your plan?" she asked.

"That's why I need you. And I need you to come up with something good."

Rolling her eyes, all Liza wanted to do was reach through the phone and slap sense into her friend. "I guess we can just go back as far as college. You made some great impressions on professors at UNC and we can get some of them to do some 'I knew he'd make it' endorsements."

"I don't know what I'd do without you, Liza."

"You'd suffer and never meet a quality woman to save your life."

"Whatever. Be on time, please," he said.

"I'm never late. Where is this meeting taking place?"

"Shooting you an e-mail with the details. Thank you, Liza."

After hanging up with Robert, Liza continued her research on Jackson Franklin. His pictures did him no justice at all. She remembered how he'd looked at Amelie's: tall, muscular, and a disarming smile. That made her nervous and excited at the same time. Women voters would flock to him, and men would probably put more trust in the war hero than the lawyer. *We can make this work. Jackson Franklin won't stand a chance,* she thought. But she couldn't stop looking at his picture.

CHAPTER 5

Jackson sat in front of his computer reading the information that Teresa sent over to him about Robert Montgomery. A criminal lawyer with a UNC–Chapel Hill education, a member in good standing with the North Carolina Bar Association, a mentor with the Charlotte area Big Brothers Big Sisters organization, and it went on and on. Jackson was almost ready to just jump on Montgomery's bandwagon. He seemed like a viable candidate. Maybe Jackson could funnel his ideas to Robert and instead of spending money to fight it out on Election Day they could use their money to work on some of the projects to help the wounded warriors and low-income families. Maybe he wouldn't have to leave the front lines to make sure things got done. Maybe he and Robert could be allies.

Closing out the files, Jackson decided that since he was going to meet this Montgomery guy in the morning, if he lived up to his press clippings, then he'd tell him they could work together on bringing change to the General Assembly. He knew for a fact that Teresa would be pissed and his career in politics would be over. He probably wouldn't even be able to get elected dogcatcher after doing this, but he wasn't throwing his hat in the ring for himself. He was doing it to help people. If he and Robert shared the same views, then only one of them needed to be in Raleigh.

Jackson smiled as he shut his computer down. Deciding to head for the gym, he was going to work on a plan to save the center where he worked, instead of a political strategy.

Jackson's cell phone rang as he changed into a pair of compression pants. "Damn," he muttered. "This is Jackson."

"I don't like to be stood up by my candidates. It is now seven P.M.; you were supposed to be here thirty minutes ago." Teresa sighed. "You're unsure about yourself, aren't you?"

"Maybe Montgomery is better for this than I am. From the looks of what you sent me, he's been spending his whole life getting ready for politics."

"Where are you? A gym or a bar?"

"On my way to the gym. Why do you ask?"

"Wanted to make sure you were actually thinking clearly. Here's the deal: Robert Montgomery has been getting ready for power. I don't think he's better. So, get over here and let's put a plan together."

Jackson sighed and told her he'd be right over. When he arrived at Teresa's office, he expected her to give him a stern talking to and threaten to quit. Instead, she handed him a thick file.

"We need to study this and make sure we can beat him." She offered him a seat across from her desk, which was covered with papers, newspaper clippings, and a plate of hummus and pita chips.

"You don't think he could be good for the district?" Jackson asked as he flipped through the file.

"Read page eight and your question will be answered."

Jackson read the copy of the *Daily Tar Heel* from fifteen years ago. Montgomery had been implicated in a sexual assault. He and three other guys in his fraternity had been accused of raping a girl at a party. Robert, who had been attending UNC on a scholarship, said he never would've done anything like that. At the bottom of the page, there was a note written about a settlement that was offered to the girl, who then dropped out of school.

"We all did things in college that —"

"This," she said, "speaks to his character. We can't have this kind of man representing us. Someone who throws money at problems? Someone who doesn't respect women? This kind of stuff doesn't go away."

Jackson gritted his teeth. She was right. But the one thing he was against was playing dirty. "What are we going to do with this information?"

"Nothing, but we have to know who we're running against. Don't think that they aren't across town looking into your past and putting together a file just like this. The difference is, anything that stains your past, they are probably going to use it."

Jackson chuckled. "Not saying that I'm perfect, but I don't have a criminal background, my service record is clean, and my ex left me."

Teresa smiled. "You think I didn't know that? Hillary McMillian, your ex-fiancée, had nothing but great things to say about you. She might call you — if your number is the same."

Jackson snorted, thinking that if Hillary called him, she'd be in for a surprise, since he changed his number the day he returned from Iraq and found her in bed with some random dude. He'd heard about loved ones at home cheating on servicemen, but he'd known Hillary was different. She had always been available when he called or Skyped her, and she sent letters. Every week he'd received a love letter from his woman detailing what they'd do as soon as he got home.

When he'd arrived home, trying to surprise his woman — the love of his life — the surprise had been on him. Hillary had been in bed with another man, screaming out his name while she rode him with zeal and zest. Passion that he'd thought had been reserved for him. Devastated and heartbroken, Jackson had to leave before he snapped. He went to the VA hospital seeking help. He felt as if the war had robbed him of everything. That's where he'd met Daniel. Before his second tour and the injury. The injury that removed him from active duty and branded him a hero. In some of his darkest days, Jackson had wished he'd died that day. It was because of Daniel that he'd been able to work through his posttraumatic stress and not swallow a gun.

"Jackson," Teresa asked. "Are you listening?"

"I was thinking," he said. "I've had some

dark times and some people might look at that as a weakness."

"Getting help and turning around to help others is what makes you strong," she said. "Is that why you thought you should throw in with Montgomery? Anyone that he's ever helped, it was because of money. He's what's wrong with Raleigh. That's not the man we need to hand this district over to."

An hour later, Jackson and Teresa had hammered out the talking points of his campaign. The one thing Teresa told him to do at the breakfast was to be himself. "Don't be slick and polished like I'm sure Robert will be."

Jackson snorted. "I wouldn't know how to do that if I tried." As he drove home, he couldn't shake Hillary from his thoughts. He hadn't thought about her in years. Of course she'd probably be interested now that he was doing something that would put him in the spotlight.

The next morning, as Jackson waited at the restaurant where the meeting was to take place, he wasn't surprised to see Robert arriving with three people in tow. It was the woman who caught his eye. He'd seen her somewhere before. Yes, at Amelie's. Liza Palmer. Glancing at her curvaceous figure stirred something inside him. *Damn, he's lucky if that's his wife,* he thought as he watched the shapely sister cross over to the table where Jackson was already seated. *I guess this explains why I couldn't win her vote with a handshake.* She sparkled in a polished, supermodel way, and a part of him wondered what she'd look like stripped bare. Hair down, face scrubbed free of makeup, and barefoot. *Stop lusting after this man's wife,* Jackson admonished as he rose to his feet. "Good morning," he said. "I'm Jackson Franklin." He extended his hand to Robert, who turned his nose up at him.

"I know who you are," Robert said. Liza stepped between them and took Jackson's hand.

"Liza Palmer," she said, flashing Jackson a smile that sent chills down his spine.

"Nice to meet you, again."

"I have to say," she began, "thank you for your service, but why do you think you're ready to serve in office?"

Bold question. "I think fighting in Iraq has prepared me for everything. What makes your husband ready?"

Liza's laughter filled the air. "My husband? I guess you think that a woman's place is behind a man?"

"Liza," Nic said, shaking his head. "This isn't the time." Robert shot her a look that quieted her right away.

"We're just here to meet with donors and maybe even sway Mr. Jackson to our side," Nic said with a plastic smile.

"Sergeant Franklin," Jackson corrected. *You pompous jackass.*

"Sorry about that," Nic said hollowly. Their chatter stopped when U.S. Senator Thomas Watson walked in.

The representative from the ninth district had been a member of Congress for fifteen years and earned every ounce of respect that flowed in the room. "Good morning," he boomed. "I was just expecting two people, but I guess it's a good thing I overordered." He worked the room, shaking hands with everyone. Jackson wondered if he'd ever be that smooth.

"Sergeant Franklin, it is an honor to have you here," the senator said. When he took his seat, everyone else followed suit.

"Senator," Nic said, "we are thankful to have your support. But I have to ask . . ."

"I love the state of North Carolina and I hate what the General Assembly has been doing. This new district is nothing but ger-rymandering. The last thing I want to see is two powerful black men tearing each other down to win a seat that — at the end of the day — won't mean much."

"What do you mean by that?" Jackson asked.

Robert nodded. "This seat is going to be important to a lot of people in North Carolina."

"That's total bullshit," the senator said with a laugh. "Either of you noticed what is being changed, here? The lines have been redrawn; the African American politicians are being pushed out. This new district is just a slap in the face to the work that has been done in this state."

"Senator, I don't think it matters about the redistricting rules. If the right man is in place to reach across party lines to build coalitions, then we can still help the citizens of North Carolina," Robert said with a smile. "I don't plan to run a dirty campaign. If Mr. Franklin agrees to make the same promise, then I don't see a problem. There are eleven other candidates running for this seat. Why are you telling us to drop out?"

As much as Jackson wanted to tell Robert where he could stick his campaign promises, he had to admit that he posed a great question.

"Two reasons: I don't think either of you is ready." The senator turned to Jackson. "And the hands-on work you're doing with wounded warriors is better than anything you would be able to do in Raleigh." He nodded toward Robert. "Your law firm has worked with the Innocence Project and gotten three people off death row who didn't belong there."

Robert folded his arms and leaned back in the chair. "Sounds like I — either one of us — is the kind of candidate who needs to run."

"Not for this seat," he replied. "This is a joke. Don't be fooled by what the status quo is doing."

"What's being done is a bullying of poor people, politicians turning their backs on the men and women who put their lives on the line to defend this country. On a state and national level, this is what's going on, and if we don't have voices in government that want to do the right thing, then how will anything change?" Jackson said.

The senator wiped his face with a napkin. "My point has been proven."

Everyone at the table looked around at one another in disbelief. "What is this all about?" Nic asked.

Liza couldn't take her eyes off Jackson Franklin. He was gorgeous with those haunting green eyes and caramel skin. Then when he spoke, he was pretty amazing. Too bad they weren't on the same side. This was Robert's seat and Jackson needed to stick to what he was doing. She'd done the research; he counseled wounded warriors who returned home from the war. He knew what they were going through because he'd been hurt in combat as well. Though, sitting across from him, she couldn't see any wounds, scars, or anything other than a man who looked as if he was going to connect with voters. He would be serious competition for Robert.

Finally, she forced herself to look away and pay attention to what Nic and the senator were saying. His point was proven? Wait. What?

"What I mean," the senator continued, "is you two are the best candidates in the primary. I'm willing to talk to the other crackpots who threw their names in the hat just because they have nothing better to do. But I'm serious about what I said; I don't want to see you two tearing each other down. Both of you have a future in this state and national politics — if you're doing this for the right reasons."

Liza smiled and nodded. She started to chime in, but she felt Jackson's eyes on her. She looked up and they locked eyes. The half smile on his lips sent a ripple down her spine. *Let me stop staring at this man. He's the enemy,* she told herself as she looked down at her iPad. Busying herself with fake note taking, Liza tried not to think about sliding Jackson's shirt off his broad shoulders. Her stylus slipped from her fingers and rolled underneath the table, landing at Jackson's feet. She looked down at his leather shoes and the adage about men with big feet replayed in her mind. "Jesus," she muttered.

Jackson reached down and picked up the stylus, then held it out to Liza.

"Thank you," she said.

He nodded and turned his attention back to the long-winded senator. Two hours later, both sides were leaving with donations and more advice than they would ever be able to use.

When Robert and Liza hopped into his car, he turned to his friend. "Why didn't you just rip your clothes off and hop on that man's lap?" Robert spat.

"Excuse me?"

"The looks you were giving Franklin! I mean, damn, Liza, I know you need to get laid but —"

"You'd better watch your damned mouth, Robert. I don't know what the hell your problem is but I will —"

"Sorry, I'm sorry, but if you were swayed by him after a couple of hours, how am I going to compete with that?"

At the moment, Liza didn't really give a damn. How dare he talk to her like that. Hadn't he just said yesterday how honored he was to have her as a part of his team? Maybe it was the pressure. But if this was the beginning, then what could she expect as things heated up in the primaries and the general election?

"You need to get a handle on your attitude," she said. "Because I'm not going to lose my best friend over words. However, you will not accuse me of BS when the mood hits you. Better take up boxing."

"This is why I love you — you keep it real with me — and, Liza, I'm sorry. I just didn't expect a dumb soldier to be so well spoken. And tell the truth, his little soliloquy made an impact. What if a video of him speaking like that goes viral?"

Liza didn't want to tell Robert that he was right and one look at Jackson on YouTube, Vine, and Twitter would definitely move him ahead in the polls and grab the female vote because he was breathtaking. Not that Robert was a dog, but what woman wasn't attracted to a man who could protect her with hand-to-hand combat?

"You're going to have to connect with women voters. Here's what research shows," she began as she powered up her iPad. "More than half of voters who actually show up on Election Day are women. You can't pander to them, because they are smart. Advanced degrees and careers. You have to show them that you appreciate who they are and will advance their interest in the General Assembly."

"I know that. But . . ."

"Has to be more than lip service. Aren't you glad you have me to help you out with that?"

Robert chuckled. "I need your help with something else too," he said.

"What?"

"Chante."

It was Liza's turn to laugh. Though she wasn't about to break girl code and tell him that her sorority sister was smitten. "Why do you think you need my help?"

"I want to get this right. I think Miss Britt could be the one."

"Really?" Liza said, not attempting to hide her smile. She really hoped her friends would be happy together.

CHAPTER 6

*Two weeks before the Democratic special
  primary*

Jackson stood in front of a group of Army
recruits at West Mecklenburg High School.
As he looked out into their young faces, he
remembered how excited he'd been when
he'd signed up. Their faces mirrored what
he'd felt all those years ago.

Though he hoped peace would reign during their enlistment. But if they did go to
war, they would need support when they
returned. That's what he was supposed to
speak about to these kids and parents today.
Over the last three months, Teresa said his
speeches had connected with voters and
narrowed the gap between him and Robert
Montgomery, who was the front-runner in
the primary. The field had narrowed down
to three: Jackson, Robert, and Mavis Reeves,
a retired schoolteacher. The word was, according to Teresa, Mavis had run out of

money and would be withdrawing her bid in the next day or so.

Jackson was given his cue to speak and he tossed his cards aside. He wasn't about to ask these people for votes. "Greetings, ladies and gentlemen!" he said. "I want to thank all of these young men and women who've signed up to serve our country. Because of people like you, the rest of us enjoy freedom and safety. I was like you, many years ago. I won't say how many, but it was way before the iPhone."

The parents chuckled and the kids looked at one another with shrugs.

Jackson continued, telling them that the Army was not going to be easy. That the path to success would take a lot of hard work, a lot of sacrifice and time away from those they love.

"But you will find yourself with a new family. Brothers and sisters who will have your back no matter what. You will battle together, you will live together, and put your life on the line in the name of America. We all decided to join the armed forces for many reasons. For me, I wanted to go to college and I knew my parents couldn't afford to send me." Jackson hopped off the stage and stood in the midst of the kids. "I got my degree. I went to war. Some people

70

say I'm a hero because I spotted a roadside bomb and saved my platoon. But if you saw your family was in danger, wouldn't you jump into action?"

Two hours later, Jackson was shaking hands and hugging recruits and parents. Everyone he talked to said they'd be happy to support him at the polls. Jackson couldn't have been happier. People met the real him and they liked what they saw.

Meanwhile, across town, Liza was huddled with Nic and Robert going over the latest poll numbers. He had a slight lead over Jackson and a commanding one over Mavis.

"Mavis is going to drop out," Nic said. "She's broke and I hear that she's going through a divorce."

"That has to be tough," Liza said.

"It's thinning the field, so viva divorce," Nic replied. Liza shook her head. She was beginning to despise Dominic. The man was abrasive. Turning her eyes toward Robert, she wondered how much longer he was going take this.

"What about Franklin? He's locked up the military vote, women are charmed by him . . ." Robert shot a glance at Liza and she rolled her eyes.

"I told you a month ago how you could connect with voters," Liza said as she crossed over to the coffeepot.

"And that is a bad idea," Nic called out. "Can you bring me a cup of coffee?"

Hell no. Get it yourself, jackass. "Sure. Do you take it black, like your heart?"

"Funny," Nic said.

"Guys," Robert said, clapping his hands together. "We're all on the same team. And I'm not going to lose."

"That's right," Liza said as she walked over to Nic and handed him his coffee. "So, what's the plan for beating Jackson?"

Nic took a long sip of coffee. "We have to connect with women. Women are into this Michelle and Barack relationship shit."

Liza groaned and sipped her own coffee. "This is horrible. And, what do you mean calling the President and First Lady's relationship shit? For the record, Robert's personal life is something he doesn't want to talk about."

"My mother is something I don't want to talk about. I'm dating a brilliant woman," he said. Liza shook her head; yes, Chante was brilliant, but she wasn't a political tool.

Catching the look in Liza's eyes, Robert said, "But I'm not going to exploit my relationship to win an election."

"Thank you," she said, then glowered at Nic. "I think you need to speak on some issues that are important to women in this state."

"But save abortion until the general election," Nic cautioned. "One thing about Franklin, he's been playing it safe, talking to his base — the military, families. It's time to call him out on the issues. I think he's a paper candidate." Nic tossed a newspaper with Jackson on the front of the metro section in the middle of the table.

As much as she wanted to ignore Jackson's smiling face, Liza picked up the paper and looked at his picture longer than she needed to. After all, the story was only three hundred words, but the color picture of Jackson showed why women were flocking to him. That man was fine.

And those eyes. Soul piercing.

Liza tore her eyes from the picture; Jackson was the enemy. She had to focus on Robert. The Twitter account. They had a hundred new followers, thanks to Liza's work. Now it was time to take another look at the website and see what they needed to do to make it user friendly and optimized for search engines.

"I'm going to work on your Internet presence. We need to get more pictures of you doing things in the community," Liza said. "People need to feel that you are invested in what's important to them." She nodded toward the paper. "That's the connection that they have with Jackson. And, Nic, you need to get an endorsement from a coalition of mayors from around the state. That's going to give Robert a wider base."

Nic nodded and pushed his coffee cup aside. "That is a good idea." He pulled a file out of his saddlebag. "It's already done."

"May I take a look?" Liza asked.

Nic handed over the folder, and as much as she didn't want to admit it, she was impressed. Nic had gotten endorsements from some of the most well-known and powerful elected officials in the city and county. "We need photo ops," Liza said. "A meet-the-candidate gathering where Robert talks about the issues. But we can't make it seem too elite."

Nic nodded. "That's actually a good idea." Liza fought the urge to say all of her ideas were good. She just listened to Nic go on and on about having the event at one of the city's homeless shelters so people would see that Robert cared about the community, and though they wanted donations to the campaign, Robert needed to give to the center.

"Since you want to connect with women," Liza interjected, "you should have the event at My Sister's Keeper."

Both Nic and Robert nodded. "Let's get on that. We need to make this happen as soon as possible." Nic pulled out his phone and started calling staffers and barking out orders to them to get the session together.

Liza had had enough and decided she was going to leave. "I'm gone," she told Robert.

"Wait," he said. "I need to talk to you about something."

Liza rolled her eyes, thinking that he wanted to talk about this event. "Sure." He nodded for her to follow him outside.

"You know Chante and I haven't known each other that long, but I've fallen hard for her."

Liza smiled and clasped her hands together. Though she hadn't talked to Chante in a while, she figured her friend was happy. "That's good to know," she said.

"I'm going to ask her to marry me. And don't say a word about it."

Liza was cautiously excited. There was a part of her that wondered if this was a way for him to capture the women's vote. *No,* she told herself. *He wouldn't do that.*

"I'll keep my mouth shut. But you'd better be sure and mean it!"

"I wish I had met her years ago," he said with a smile on his lips. "We'd already be married and you wouldn't be questioning my motives."

Though she wanted to ask more questions, Liza decided to trust her friend and just be happy for them. "So, when are you going to pop the question?" she asked with a smile. Robert relaxed and returned Liza's smile.

"Soon. I want to sweep her off her feet."

As she clasped her hands together, ideas started flipping through her mind. There was a balloon drop, a champagne toast with a three-point-five diamond engagement ring in the bottom of Chante's glass. Then she thought about an intimate dinner party with a covered dessert dish and the ring waiting for Chante when she opened it. Before she poured any of her ideas out, Liza realized that she was an outsider to their love. She needed to keep her planning to Robert's campaign and let them run their love life.

"I have to get some things together for the event at the shelter and I can't take another moment with Nic, so I'm going to my office. Call me," she said, then tapped him on the shoulder. Hopping into her car, she tuned the radio to the local NPR station. When she heard Jackson Franklin's name, she turned the volume up.

"Jackson Franklin isn't your typical politician, and in this race for North Carolina senate seat forty-five, there are a lot of players in the field. But Franklin stands out," the reporter said. "Here in the studio with us this afternoon is senate hopeful Jackson Franklin."

Liza pounded her steering wheel. *Why isn't Robert on this show? By the time Election Day comes around, people are going to remember the name Jackson Franklin. He's always on the radio, on TV, or in the paper.*

"Thank you for having me on your show." His smooth baritone flowed through the airwaves.

"Why did you decide to run for office?" the reporter asked.

"Well, it was a decision that came to me after seeing the lack of support our troops face when they return home from serving their country. North Carolina is home to several military instillations and it seems as if we're failing our men and women when they come back. But that wasn't all that I found wrong with our state. We're failing our students, the poor, and the middle class. We've turned into a government for hire that only serves special interests, not the people our politicians were elected to serve."

"Whoa," Liza mumbled. "Nic and Robert should be hearing this." She pulled over and called Robert.

"What's up, Liza?"

"Turn to NPR," she said.

"Why?"

"Just do it. And for the record, Jackson Franklin isn't going to be easy to beat. I hope Nic's listening too." Liza hung up, then turned her attention back to the radio as she pulled back on the road.

Jackson was smooth, but not in a rehearsed way. He was persuasive and passionate. *He's connecting with voters*, she thought as she slowed her car and focused on the sound of Jackson's voice. Her thoughts soon turned from what he was saying to how good he sounded saying it. A bedroom voice that would put Barry White to shame. She almost closed her eyes as she imagined his lips against her ear.

"Get it together," she muttered as she returned her eyes back to the road. She snapped the radio off and reminded herself that Jackson was the enemy. Fine, but the enemy.

Jackson shook hands with the reporter as she walked him out of the studio. "Thank you for the interview," she said. "You certainly earned my vote."

"Thank you."

"Do you have time for a cup of coffee?"

Jackson looked at his watch. "Unfortunately, I have an interview with WBTV, but after the primary, I'd love to have coffee."

"And anything else?" she asked seductively.

Jackson smiled and kept quiet. "See you later," he said as he walked out the door. He was used to women flirting with him, but he knew better than to deal with a reporter in a personal manner while he was running for office. He planned to keep his focus, even if he had yearnings and the reporter was fine as hell.

He walked briskly to the WBTV studio and read over his talking points. So far, things had been easy and he was even beginning to like campaigning. Still, Teresa's warning echoed in his head. "This is just the calm before the storm."

CHAPTER 7

The day of Robert's rally for the homeless event, Liza found herself stuck on the phone with Claude. She was beginning to hate this man and his drama. But because she loved the paycheck she got from dealing with his drama, she did her job.

"I don't want to get married," he whined. "I don't want to have a baby, either. I told her that I'd pay for the abortion and everything else if . . ."

"Have you ever heard of a long engagement? Listen, Claude, you can't have this girl selling the story to the media that you wanted her to have an abortion. You made your bed, so sleep in it."

"But you said . . ."

"Claude, I'm trying to keep your reputation intact. I'm pretty sure after she sees that you're dragging your feet on the marriage, she's going to get tired of the relationship and dump you. Then she looks like the bad guy." Liza stroked her forehead, she really did hate leading him to mislead his child's mother. But the NBA had a bad enough reputation and Claude was every stereotype that she wished to fight against. Maybe that was why she rode Claude so hard. *I am not his mama,* she told herself as he droned on in her ear.

"Claude, stop," she finally said as she glanced at her watch. "I was wrong for trying to force you to be responsible, when it's obvious that isn't what you want. Marry her or don't, but you'd better do right by that child or I'll go to TMZ my damned self."

"Liza, I thought you were on my side."

"I don't know if *I can* be on your side anymore," she said. *Money be damned.*

"Are you dropping me because I don't want to be tied down to some —"

"You just aren't someone I want to represent. I could see if you were unable to care for a child, but you simply don't want to. Maybe you should've thought about that before you . . . Look. You need a new publicist, I quit." Liza ended the call, rose from her desk, and shook her head. She was now twenty minutes late for the event. She grabbed her purse and tossed her phone inside, then dashed out the door. Driving to the shelter, Liza hoped for a great turnout

81

because the last polls that she saw had Jackson with a one-point lead over Robert. He'd been doing a number of media interviews and impressing a lot of people. Hell, Liza was impressed as well, but she'd never admit it publicly. Her alliance was with Robert. He deserved this seat because he'd been prepping for it his entire life.

Jackson, in her opinion, was a cause-of-the-moment candidate. Sure, he was hitting the hot topics, but did he have what it really took to be in it for the long haul? What if he got bored? The new district deserved better. Robert had been studying politics for years. He sat on the right local boards and, in Liza's opinion, this seat had his name written all over it.

Once she arrived at the shelter, things were in full swing. Cameras were everywhere and Chante was by Robert's side with a bright smile on her face. *They look so good together,* Liza thought as she headed toward them.

"You're late," Nic said, grabbing her arm before she reached her friends. "I thought you were going to help me coordinate the media arrivals and interviews?"

"Nic, I have a job, you know? Clients who pay me."

"As I recall, you volunteered to do this.

You're supposed to be here for your friend."

She glanced at Nic's hand but stopped herself from pushing it away and making a scene. "Look and listen, Nic. I've had Robert's back for longer than you've known him. So, don't you ever question my loyalty to him! Now, if you're done, I'm going to greet my friends."

He dropped his hand and nodded as Liza strode away. She fumed but pasted a smile on her face as she hugged Robert and Chante.

"Where have you been?" Chante asked. "You missed the excitement."

"What excitement?" she asked, immediately going into crisis mode.

Chante tapped her shoulder. "Nothing bad, but a lot of excited people ready to elect Robert as their next senator. We registered a lot of voters and . . ." Chante held up her left hand. The diamond engagement ring on her finger sparkled in the sun. "Robert asked me to marry him."

Liza squealed and hugged her best friend, then punched Robert on the shoulder. "You sly dog," she teased.

"Hey," he said, "where's my hug and congratulations? I get punched. What kind of sense does that make?" Liza hugged him tightly.

"Congratulations. You two are going to be so happy," she said.

"I know," Robert said when he and Liza parted. He took Chante's hand in his and kissed it. The beaming smile on Chante's face warmed Liza's heart and she pushed her thoughts of the engagement being a political stunt deep down. *Robert wouldn't do that. Maybe love at first sight really does exist.*

"Hey, Robert," Nic called out as he rushed over to him. "Senator Patrick is here."

"Senator Patrick?" Nic nodded and pushed Robert in the direction of the retired and revered senator. Liza and Chante just smiled and waited for the men to leave so that they could dish.

"How did he ask you to marry him? Was it romantic?"

Chante smiled and stroked her ring. "We were unloading the donations that I'd gotten from the office of business clothes for the women and he pointed to this box on the floor. He said, 'Babe, you dropped something.' "

Cornball, Liza thought while smiling.

"I picked it up and I'm thinking someone messed up. Rob was like, open it. And there was this ring. Then he got down on one knee and said, 'Marry me.' "

"Were there cameras around?"

Chante slapped her hand on her hip. "No, Liza! Everything is not a media event."

Liza threw her hands up. "I was just asking."

"I wonder about you sometimes." Chante raised her eyebrow at her friend, then smiled.

"I'm a sucker for whirlwind romances," Liza said. "You have to let me throw you two an engagement party."

"Something small with no cameras or Twitter updates?"

"Of course. I'm sorry I missed it, but I was stuck on the phone with Claude. I had to drop him as a client today."

"Really? Why? I thought he was a profitable client."

Liza sighed and then explained her problem with him. "I couldn't create this fairy tale for him when he didn't really want to be with that woman."

"I can't believe you'd even considered it."

"I couldn't have him getting a reputation as the guy who told his woman to get an abortion. How would the child feel when he or she does a Google search and finds that out?"

Chante sighed. "At least your heart was in the right place. There'll be other clients, maybe ones who aren't slimy bastards."

Liza nodded toward Robert. "I think he needs you."

"He needs us," Chante said as she linked arms with her sorority sister and started in his direction.

The event turned out to be a success for Robert and led all of the evening newscasts. A few of the local blogs had written glowing stories about Robert, and when the *Raleigh News and Observer*'s political columnist called Robert while the trio was at Hometown Delights having drinks, Liza knew the tide was turning in her candidate's favor.

"This is awesome," Liza said. "And I know you don't want to talk about it, but you have to show people your personality and your history."

Chante glanced at him. "She's right."

Robert rolled his eyes. "I don't know why you two think I have to tell a sad-sack story to gain voters."

"Robert," Liza began, "people need to connect with you. They're connecting with Jackson."

At the sound of his opponent's name, Robert huffed. "He doesn't know a thing about politics and I'm getting sick and tired of you comparing me to him."

"Guys," Chante said. "Let's not do this. If Robert wants to leave the past in the past, then that's fine. Let's focus on who you are now."

Liza rolled her eyes and took a sip of her wine. Then a lightbulb went off in her head. Why wouldn't they focus on the person Robert is? People were just as attracted to confidence as they were to heroes.

"Robert, you're right," Liza said with a smile. "You should show people who you really are. Successful, in love, ready to serve."

He gave Liza a high five. "Now you're getting it."

"Guys," Chante said. "Can we table politics and talk about my engagement?"

Robert leaned in and kissed her cheek. "Of course, babe."

"That's my cue to give you two some alone time," Liza said as she drained her wineglass. "I have to go check Google alerts anyway."

"Why don't you take a break," Chante said. "You don't have to be the twenty-four-hour woman."

"She needs a man," Robert said, then poked his tongue out at Liza.

"Whatever, Bob! I'm doing just fine without one." She winked at him and

Chante. "Besides, all the good ones are taken." Liza waved to her friends as she headed for the exit.

After leaving the restaurant, Liza headed for Amelie's, her unofficial satellite office. She loved the nighttime crowd at the bakery and she loved the silence. Taking a seat across from the community bulletin board, she was about to pull out her iPad when a sign caught her eye. The Jackson Franklin campaign was seeking volunteers. Setting her tablet on the table, Liza crossed over to the board and grabbed the flyer. Reading over it, she shook her head. "Stealing Obama's thunder much?" she mumbled as she read the words "yes, we can."

Though she didn't want to admit it, the flyer would appeal to the people who hung out at Amelie's. Jackson seemed to know his audience, leading her to wonder who was on his team. There was no way this soldier was doing this alone. She tucked the flyer in her pocket and returned to her work. She needed to talk to Nic about this man because Jackson Franklin was more of a threat than they'd initially thought. Liza pulled the flyer from her pocket and studied it intently — more accurately, stared at Jackson's handsome face.

Jackson knew a salted caramel brownie at ten P.M. was a bad idea. Still, he had a sweet tooth and he'd been doing interviews all day in Raleigh and Fayetteville. He had to admit that being back at Fort Bragg was more than a campaign stop. It was like being home again. Seeing his former platoon members and their advancements and everything made him happy, but he was sad that he'd lost his chance to continue to serve his country. That's why he had to make sure the warriors who returned home didn't have to battle for help. North Carolina of all states should've been on the front line to take care of the soldiers.

Jackson rubbed his forehead and sighed as the line slowly moved forward. Glancing over his shoulder, he spotted Liza looking over one of his flyers. Suddenly, his need for the brownie didn't seem that strong. He stepped out of line and crossed over to Liza.

"Can I count on you to volunteer?" he asked. Her head snapped up and he heard her gasp.

"I-I . . . Hello, Mr. Franklin."

"Liza, right?"

She nodded and extended her hand. "Why don't you drop out?"

"That's a wonderful greeting," he said, his lips curving into a smirk.

"Mr. Franklin," she said, tilting her head to the side, "Robert Montgomery is an awesome man. He will represent this district and even get some of the things you're campaigning for passed."

"Funny," Jackson said as he dropped her hand. "I haven't heard much substance come from Mr. Montgomery's campaign."

"Maybe you haven't been listening, or you can only hear the words coming from your camp."

The way she poked her lips out and rolled her eyes should've been a turnoff, but there was no way to deny the tightening between his legs would become a full-grown erection if he kept looking at her full lips.

"Would you like to join me for a cup of coffee?" he asked, all the while wondering what in the hell he was thinking. He knew that she was in Montgomery's camp. But, damn, she was fine as frog's hair.

"No, thank you. I have some work to do and I'm more of a tea person."

"Last I heard, they serve tea here as well," Jackson said.

"Do you think I'm supposed to allow you to buy me tea and then I'll spill secrets about Robert and give you the upper hand? I don't think so."

"I don't want to talk about politics. I just

offered to buy a pretty lady tea," he said, then nodded at her. "Have a good night, Liza."

As he walked away, he didn't hear her sigh. Jackson grabbed his place in line and decided that he would have the brownie after all.

Liza hadn't realized that she was weak at the knees until she started walking toward her table and stumbled over nothing, then eased into her seat. What was it about that man that caused her to lose her mind? From hearing his voice to seeing his face, he made her weak.

"He's the enemy," she warned herself. A tea person? Ha! Liza inhaled coffee, probably needed an IV drip of java. And she turned down free coffee?

Sighing, she tried to return to her work. But she kept stealing glances at Jackson, who stood in line ordering a pastry or something. She wondered what his sweet weakness was. Was he a brownie guy or an éclair dude? *Why do I care?* she questioned as she tore her eyes away from his backside. Maybe after the election she and Jackson could be friends. Maybe.

As she watched him walk out the door with his small box in his hand, the thoughts that danced in her head were far from friendly. They were downright lustful. "Go get some coffee," she mumbled as she gathered her things and headed for the register. Slipping her earbuds in her ears and listening to the latest podcast from Demetria Lucas, she wasn't paying attention when Jackson walked back into the bakery and right into her path. Crashing into his hard chest, Liza thought she was going to fall, but his big, hot hands broke her fall. He pressed her against him. And she wanted nothing more than to feel his lips against hers.

"Where's the fire?" he asked.

"You can let me go," she said, though her body just wanted his touch a little longer, and when he let her go, she shivered.

"Are you all right?"

"Yes, I'm good." Liza smiled. "Thanks for being a gentleman."

"That's who I am," he replied, returning her smile. Jackson and Liza walked to the long line and stood there in an uncomfortable silence. "Want a salted caramel brownie?" he asked, breaking the tension.

"Sure," she replied. "But, I would've taken you for an éclair guy."

He smiled again and Liza's heart started beating overtime. How had she not noticed that cleft in his chin? And those eyes. Hypnotic.

"I have to avoid this place. I don't have the metabolism of a twenty-year-old anymore." He rubbed his flat stomach, which Liza was sure hid a six pack of abs. "But after the day I had, I need some sweetness."

Why did he lick his lips when he said that? Why did her body tingle at the thought of him sampling her wetness and telling her how sweet it was? *Stop it.*

"Campaigning is hard," Liza said, and then her eyes traveled down Jackson's body. She squeezed her eyes shut and sighed. "And it only gets harder. Maybe you should quit."

"Ha. That was funny," Jackson said. "I see why you're such a strong member of Montgomery's team."

"And how would you know that?"

He raised his right eyebrow as if to say, *You're not the only one who's researching the competition.* "Anyway," Jackson said as the line inched forward, "why don't we talk about something other than politics and campaigns?"

"I have work to do," she said. "No time to talk."

"If you say so, but isn't it kind of late to

be working?"

She shrugged as she eyed the sweets in the glass so that she wouldn't look at Jackson. "Social media never sleeps. I'm more than a part of Robert's team. I run my own business as well." She met his gaze. "But, you knew that already, didn't you?"

"I know what's on paper, but I'll admit it, one day — after the election — I'd like to get to know you."

CHAPTER 8

Jackson appreciated Liza's lips. The fullness of them, the curve of them, the way they spread when she smiled. But it was that tongue that he wanted to get further acquainted with. It must have been her nervous habit to lick her top lip. She did it more times than he could count. And every time she did it, he got a jolt in his groin. If she did it again, he was going to have to walk away to hide his burgeoning erection.

"Anyway," she said, taking the focus off his desire, "we could get to know each other a lot sooner if you'd just drop out of the race."

"That's not going to happen," he said. "And we're not going to talk about this."

"You know I had to try it." She winked and licked her lip again.

"No one can accuse you of not being persistent." She smiled at him and he just prayed his erection didn't press against his zipper so that she could see his state of arousal.

Finally, they made it to the counter and Jackson ordered two brownies and two cups of coffee. He'd expected Liza to say something, since she'd claimed to be a tea drinker. She didn't. Instead she took her cup and filled it with the dark roast the café offered.

"Tea, huh?" he quipped.

"Oh, hush. It's late and I need a jolt. This is a job for coffee."

If only he could tell her what he needed. He needed her in his arms, her lips pressed against his and . . . sugar. He needed sugar for his coffee. Anything other than sharing a brownie and a cup of java with Liza would be nothing but trouble. He hadn't had a hint of scandal around his campaign and he wasn't going to let his libido get him in a bind right now.

"Do you want to grab a seat in the atrium?" he asked, thinking that sitting with her in a crowd would ease his lustful thoughts.

"My stuff is in the dining room. You can join me there," she said.

He nodded and held his hand out for Liza to lead the way. They crossed over to her table — which was in a secluded area of the bakery — and sat down. A few moments passed before either of them said anything.

"These brownies are amazing," Liza said after swallowing her first bite.

"They're famous for a reason." As much as he knew he should've focused on his brownie, he couldn't take his eyes off her lips as she munched on her treat.

"I'm going to pay for this in the gym tomorrow." She took another nibble of the brownie.

Jackson imagined her in a spandex number doing yoga. That sent his body into overdrive. "Do you ever relax?" he asked, then took a sip of coffee. He was the one who needed to relax, his hormones in particular.

"I did that in college. But after working too hard for someone else, I can't cheat myself now."

"What did you do before you started your business?" he asked.

"Corporate communications for a nasty bank."

"Wow, corporate America, huh? I can see why that didn't last for you."

She nodded and took a sip of her coffee. "Worst three years of my life."

"And running your own business is fun?"

"Demanding, exciting, and a little scary.

But at the end of the day, it's worth it." Jackson could hear the passion in her voice and was turned on by the sparkle in her eyes. His thoughts quickly turned to seeing her waking up in the morning, hair tousled and her lips swollen from his kisses. He sipped his coffee, forcing himself to look away.

"How did you get into politics?" she asked him, looking over her cup at him.

"Thought we weren't going to talk politics, sex, or religion?"

Did sex just drop from his lips? Liza thought as she lost herself in his emerald eyes. Sure. They didn't have to talk about sex, but that was all she'd been thinking about since they sat down and she crossed her legs to ebb the throbbing between her thighs. Why did she want to lean across the table and lick the corner of his mouth? What in the hell was wrong with her?

"You're right. We're not supposed to talk about those things. I guess I'll hear more about your story during the debate."

Jackson shook his head. "Liza, you can power down."

"What?"

"It's just coffee and brownies, okay?"

Liza smiled. "I don't have an 'off' button, sorry," she said.

"Is there a 'pause' button, at least?" Jackson returned her smile.

"Nope." Liza picked up her cup and took a big sip of her coffee. "You never know when you have to be on, so I just don't turn off. That way, I won't be surprised."

"You are a woman in need of a vacation," Jackson said, then downed his coffee.

Heat flushed her cheeks as she thought about what she really needed. His lips on hers, his hands between her thighs and . . .

"Liza?"

Blinking, she smiled. "What?"

"I think you should switch to decaf."

"Whatever. If I could have a few more hours in the day, maybe I would."

Jackson laughed. "When you invent that time machine, I want in on it."

Liza felt herself relax, and as much as she hated to admit it, she liked Jackson. Why couldn't he be running for city council or some other seat? She couldn't get too comfortable. "I'd better get going," she said.

"I was going to head out myself. Allow me to escort you to your car."

Everything in her should have said no. She should've pulled her independent card and told Jackson that she could walk herself to her car alone. Instead, she nodded and allowed him to usher her through the late-night crowd of pastry lovers.

"This was nice," she said, though she regretted it as soon as the words left her lips.

"It was," he replied with a smile, happy to hear that his efforts to talk to her weren't in vain. "Maybe we can do it again sometime."

"Sure, as soon as Robert wins the election."

"Or, after my victory party." He winked at her and Liza's knees clanked together. What was this man doing to her and why was she allowing it to happen? *Because you're nuts and horny! Horrible combination,* she thought. "You're draped in confidence," she said. "I'll send you flowers and cupcakes when you lose."

"And when I win, you'll throw in some champagne and a kiss?"

Liza covered her shock with a laugh. "You are too much."

"Or just enough. It simply depends on how you look at things. Miss Liza, it was nice meeting up with you tonight."

"I actually enjoyed your company as well," she said with a saucy smile. "Too bad we're not on the same team."

Jackson shrugged. "After the election, I'd love to take you out to dinner."

Say no, get in your car, and go home! "We'll have to see," she said. It might not have been a no per se, but she didn't say yes and that made her proud. Jackson tipped his imaginary hat to her and watched as she climbed into her car. When she started the engine, he sighed. Why was forbidden fruit so tempting?

CHAPTER 9

Liza slowly drove out of the parking lot, glancing at Jackson in her rear view mirror. The way that man filled out his suit was downright sinful. Of all the men in Charlotte she could be attracted to, it had to be him. The man she needed Robert to beat in a few weeks. The man she had been looking for dirt on for the campaign but found nothing. Hell, he wasn't even inappropriate with her tonight. And, man, she wouldn't even have been upset about it. Jackson Franklin was too fine for words, too sexy for synonyms. And a gentleman to boot. Who knew this kind of man was still around?

Then, why is he still single? Liza turned on her "Robert for Senate" brainwaves and wondered if she should dig deeper around Jackson's past and find out if he had a secret baby mama, scorned ex, or anything that would knock the luster off his shining star. Though she'd made up her mind that she was going to put Jackson through a Lexis-Nexis search when she arrived home, the thought of his smile and sparkling eyes made her put the campaigning off until tomorrow. Tonight, she was going to dream of the gentleman she shared coffee and brownies with. Liza nearly floated in the house on thoughts of Jackson.

Across town, Jackson studied polls and yawned. Slapping paperwork on the table, he rubbed his tired eyes. He wasn't going to be one of those people consumed with what others thought about him, but he was happy that things seemed to be going his way. In the latest North Carolina state political poll, more than 75 percent of registered Democrats were likely to vote for him rather than Montgomery.

"Great," he muttered, then yawned again. He reached for his iPad and started to Google Montgomery, remembering that Teresa said he should always know what his opponent was doing. When a photograph of Robert and Liza popped up on the screen, he immediately regretted not going to sleep. That woman was beautiful. Standing beside Robert, she had a huge smile on her face, and in the back of his mind, Jackson wondered if there was more to their relationship than business. He skimmed through the article about Robert's campaign stop at the homeless shelter. He couldn't be mad; at least he was addressing a serious problem in the community. A small tidbit near the end of the article caught his eye: Montgomery had asked his girlfriend to marry him at the stop. So, Liza and this guy had finally made it official. His thoughts turned bitter as he flipped to the second page of the article. When he saw the name of Montgomery's fiancée, a smile spread across his lips. It wasn't Liza.

"I'm going to bed," he groaned as he powered down his tablet. Then he headed for his bedroom with Liza's smile emblazed on his brain. Sure, he should've been focusing on the election. But that woman had smiled her way into his thoughts. This was going to be trouble.

Two days later, Liza had a brainstorm for Robert's campaign as she worked with her new client, Peaches Montague, a wannabe rapper looking to build a buzz for her single "Girls of the World." Liza had talked her out of this thug image she wanted to portray, since the single had such a positive and uplifting message.

She told Peaches that her real-life story — a foster child who'd gone to college and wanted to be a voice in the way women were treated around the world — would set her apart from other female rappers. A new-generation Queen Latifah. When she'd furrowed her brows in confusion, Liza had called her the Janelle Monáe of rap and that had made Peaches smile.

After her client left, Liza decided that she needed to tell Robert that he should wrap his message in an idea that voters would get behind. His dip in the polls gave her pause. She wasn't sure if Nic and Robert had plans for a late push, but they needed it if he wanted to win.

She was about to leave her office when her cell phone rang. "This is Liza."

"Elizabeth Palmer, is this how we do?" Chante asked, then laughed.

"No, you didn't call me by my full government name," Liza said with a giggle. "What's up, girl?"

"Other than needing my best friend to help me plan this wedding, I'm great."

"You just got engaged."

"And, a proper wedding takes time to plan and, unfortunately, I have no help. My fiancé is trying to win an election, you know."

"I heard about that. As a matter of fact, I was going to meet him and Nic."

"Forget them, I need you a little more," she said.

"All right, I'll be right over with . . ."

"Salted caramel brownies?"

Liza shivered thinking of the last time she had the decadent treat. With Jackson.

The very man she needed to be game planning against. The very man she wanted to get naked with and kiss all over. "Umm, if I bring those over and you say one word about fitting into a wedding dress, we're going to fight."

"Thanks for the reminder. I actually have to watch what I eat now."

Liza rolled her eyes, thinking that Chante had a wonderful figure and would probably be able to buy any dress she wanted right off the rack. "So, you are going to be one of *those* brides?"

"And you will be too, soon enough."

"I'm good on the dog and pony matrimony show," Liza said with a snort.

"I have a serious question for you."

"Go ahead."

Chante sighed. "Do you think Rob and I are rushing into this marriage?"

Part of Liza wanted to say yes. But she also believed Robert when he said he loved Chante. "Love doesn't have a timetable. Do you feel like you're being rushed into something you don't want?"

"No. Rob is amazing."

"Then keep doing what you're doing."

"All right. And just bring one brownie and we can split it."

"Absolutely not. I'm bringing two. You will eat all of it and I don't want to hear a word."

"Only because you're forcing me," Chante said, laughter sneaking into her voice.

"Whatever, girl. I'll see you in a little bit."

After hanging up with Chante, she headed to Amelie's and ordered the brownies. Though she knew she'd promised her friend that she was going to head her way to help with the wedding plans, she wanted to talk to Robert first about her idea for his campaign. And she had a gnawing feeling about his sudden need to be married.

Or was it the bitterness inside of her rearing its ugly head? Liza would be the first to admit that she didn't believe men when it came to matters of the heart, and as much as she tried to give Robert the benefit of the doubt . . . *Stop it. He loves Chante. He wouldn't use her to gain political points. Would he?*

Pulling up to the campaign office, she smiled when she saw Robert's car. She admired his hard work on this campaign and couldn't wait to see him as the next senator. Liza pushed her doubts aside and thought about the guy she shared political science classes with at UNC and remembered why she believed in him. Walking into the office, she was surprised that there weren't any of the volunteers around. *Weird,* she thought, then immediately remembered there had been an event where they were passing out flyers.

I thought Robert was going to be downtown too? She wandered through the dark halls and headed for his office. Liza paused when she heard moaning. Was someone hurt? More moaning. No one was hurt. Someone was having sex. Really? Grabbing her phone, she was going to snap pictures of the illicit lovers and send them to Nic and Robert. This couldn't be going on in the campaign office. Anger heated her cheeks as she walked into the office and held her phone up ready to snap pictures. Her anger soon turned to disappointment when she saw who the lovers were. Robert. He stood there with some random woman bent over his desk pumping in and out of her as if he weren't engaged to Chante — her best friend. Her sorority sister. The woman she'd just sold a fairy tale to. And Robert had turned her into a liar. She snapped the pictures, then cleared her throat. Robert looked up and locked eyes with his disappointed friend.

"Liza," he said as he dropped his hands from the panting woman's waist. He pulled out of the woman and Liza turned her head, not willing to look at his wayward dick.

"Bob, who is this woman?" his paramour asked as she tugged her skirt.

"Bob? Bob?" Liza parroted. "Get this sack of trash out of here!"

"Liza, you need to calm down. This has nothing to do with you."

"Nothing to do with me?" Liza slapped him three times in a row. "Have you . . ."

Robert pointed to the half-dressed woman. "I'll call you later. I have to handle this."

The woman rolled her eyes and adjusted her clothes. "Don't call me at all. Married bastard!"

She clicked out of the office, and when the door slammed, Liza slammed into her friend. "What was that? What in the hell?"

"I messed up. This is just so stressful and then the wedding. I needed a release and she . . ."

Liza punched Robert in the chest. "You are . . . I can't. Who are you?"

"I'm a man and this has nothing to do

with you. What are you doing here anyway?" he asked flippantly.

"Don't use that tone with me. Maybe God sent me here so I can stop my friend from marrying you!"

Robert shook his head and grabbed Liza's arm. "You can't tell Chante. I messed up but it won't happen again."

"Says the drunk every time he falls off the wagon and doesn't get help. And get your hands off me — I have no idea where they've been. Chante is going to be heartbroken."

"You're not going to tell her. I need Chante."

"You need her so much that you're banging random chicks on your desk?"

Robert rolled his eyes and started pacing back and forth.

"Oh. My. God! Robert!" Liza exclaimed. "Put your pants on!"

Robert grabbed his slacks and pulled them up while Liza focused on his discarded boxers. How could he be one of those men? A man with a woman who loved him but spreading his seed like Johnny Appleseed? Did faithful men exist anymore or were they just a myth?

"Did you at least use a condom? Oh my! Now my girl is going to have to get tested for sexually transmitted diseases. How could you do this to her!" Liza picked up a mug and tossed it at him. Robert ducked and faced his friend as the mug exploded against the wall.

"Why are you in here acting like a jealous girlfriend? I'm not marrying you. Or maybe that's the problem."

"Oh, please, Robert! Don't you dare pull that crap on me! I don't and have never wanted you. I believed in you, thought you were one of the good guys!"

"Mind your business, Liza. This has —"

"Chante is *my best friend* and sorority sister. You asked her to marry you in a public manner and I came here to talk to you about your relationship with her and . . . I hate what you've done."

"Get out. Stop trying to give everyone else a fairy tale because you can't keep a man."

She wanted to spit in his face. What a bastard! If he was trying to hurt her, he had. Liza thought Robert was her friend, but if this was how he handled friendship, she certainly didn't need enemies. Storming out of the headquarters, she nearly bowled Nic over.

"What's going on, Liza?" he asked as she stomped to her car. She didn't reply. Her mission was to get to Chante and show her that she needed to call this damned engagement off.

Teresa smiled at Jackson as he finished up a phone interview with a reporter from the *News and Observer.* "Well, thank you for your time and I hope I've earned your vote as well," he said, then clicked the phone off.

"Great job," Teresa said. "I love how even your clichés sound fresh."

"If that isn't the most backhanded compliment that I've ever gotten."

"Get over it, Jackson. You're leading the polls, people like you, and I don't think we're going to have to go negative, as you wanted. I believe you're going to be the first senator of district forty-five."

"There's still the general election."

Teresa pulled a file from the board of elections out of her desk drawer. "This is the general election. The filing date has passed and there is not a Republican nor Libertarian candidate to be seen. This really is a race between you and Montgomery. Voters haven't really connected with him."

"Well, I wouldn't count him out yet. He has a determined team around him that I'm sure will do everything possible to get him elected."

"Are you talking about the lovely Ms.

Palmer?"

Jackson was surprised that she knew Liza, for about five seconds, then remembered that she knew everything. "Yes."

"You know their history, right? I wouldn't put it past them to use her assets to get knowledge about our campaign."

"She isn't that kind of person."

"Oh Lord, Jackson Franklin, please tell me you aren't seeing this woman."

"No, I'm not. We just ran into each other at Amelie's one night." He declined to tell her any more details.

Teresa shook her head and pointed beyond her office door. "See all those people who believe in you and are working all these hours to get you elected?"

"Your point?"

"Don't let the little head cost you what we've all been working for."

"That won't be a problem. I know what's important."

Teresa nodded. "Good. We don't have much time left. Now, I have a plan to get out the vote. We need to enlist some drivers to get people to the polls and let them know that the voter ID law is not in effect in this election."

"I've heard some people talking about that and there are a lot of folks who are afraid that their rights are being trampled on."

"They are. I know you shouldn't hate anything or anyone, but the GOP is close to making me hate them with the love of Jesus."

Jackson tilted his head to the side. "That's pretty deep."

"I can't stand the way this General Assembly and governor are disenfranchising a community of people."

"I know," he said. "That's why we need people in office who care about people and not the power."

"When you get a few years under your belt, I'm going to remind you of this conversation."

Jackson smiled, then looked down at his watch. "I have to go in to the clinic and check on one of my patients."

"I hate that you guys are going to have to shut down. I've called in every favor that I have and I can't get what you all need."

Jackson rose to his feet and nodded. "See you tomorrow."

Heading to the clinic, Jackson felt a cold dread wash over him. If the clinic closed and he won the election, how would he be able to make a difference in the lives of soldiers returning home from war in need of help? Would all of this be in vain if VA centers were still shuttered?

"Something has to change," he muttered as he turned into the clinic's parking lot.

CHAPTER 10

Liza knew this was going to be an uphill battle when she walked into Chante's place and saw her friend sitting with one of Charlotte's most expensive wedding planners, Jeanne St. Jean.

"It's about time you got here," Chante said when she spotted her friend. "Come on over and take a look at these samples."

Liza couldn't force a smile, couldn't pretend that she was happy to see her making plans for a wedding. A wedding to a man who was a low-down lying cheater.

"Chante, can we talk in the kitchen?" Liza asked.

Chante took note of the look on her friend's face. "What's wrong?"

Liza nodded toward the kitchen. Once the women were inside and out of the hearing range of the wedding planner, Liza grabbed Chante's hand. "You can't do this."

"Do what?"

"Marry Robert."

Chante ran her hand across her forehead. "I don't understand. We just had this conversation and you told me to follow my heart. Why the one-eighty?"

Liza nodded. "That was before I . . ."

"Chante," Robert boomed as he burst into the kitchen. "Don't listen to her."

As Chante looked from Liza to her fiancé, her face was a knot of confusion. "What in the hell is going on?"

"Are you going to tell her or should I?" Liza asked as she pulled her phone out of her purse.

"I really wish it didn't come to this, Liza. I thought you were my friend," Robert said.

"And you thought I was going to let what I walked in on just slide on the strength of our friendship?"

Robert crossed over to Chante and wrapped his arms around her shoulders. "You know I love you," he said. "And I thought Liza was happy for us. I mean, she's the one who introduced us. But tonight she crossed the line and told me —"

"Stop the lies!" Liza exclaimed. "I walked in on him fu—"

"She confessed that she hoped she'd be the one I'd marry."

Liza blinked rapidly. *What?*

117

"Liza?" Chante asked, her mouth dropping open. "Why?"

"Robert, you're a fucking liar." She pulled up one of the pictures on her phone and held her phone out to Chante, who ignored it as she looked at Robert.

"I'm a liar?" Robert said. "Nic heard everything and he's waiting —"

"Oh, I'm sure Nic will say anything you want him to say. Chante, look at the picture," Liza prodded.

She shook her head still ignoring the photo. "I don't understand," Chante said. "I thought you were happy for me, for us. Is this why you've been ignoring my phone calls, why we haven't been hanging out and —"

"Are you kidding me? Are you seriously kidding me? Chante, I *was* happy for you until I found out that he's a cheating, lying bastard." Liza held up her phone and Robert pushed it away.

"She's trying to cover up the fact that I told her I love you, Chante."

"You know what, to hell with both of you. And, Chante, you're not that desperate. You had your own doubts, so don't act like I've done something to hurt you because you want to get married."

"That's not it at all. You're still simmering

in bitterness because Alvin cheated on you and you think every other man is going to do the same. Or maybe you've finally seen whatever you've been looking for in Robert now that he's off the market."

That was it! Liza had been trying to be nice and save her friend from making the biggest mistake of her life. "Do what you want to do, but when you find out who you've put your trust in, don't come crying to me! To hell with both of you!" Liza stormed out of the kitchen, refusing to allow a tear to fall from her eyes. She was hurt, angry, and disappointed in the people who were supposed to be her best friends.

She wasn't going to take this lying down at all! If Jackson Franklin wanted to win this election, then she was going to give him the ammunition he needed to beat the breaks off Robert Montgomery. She started to drive to Jackson's campaign office, then remembered that she had no idea where it was. More than anything else, Liza needed a drink. *Revenge will come tomorrow,* she thought as she headed to Total Wine and More to get a couple of bottles of chardonnay and merlot. Tonight, she'd drown her disappointment and bad feelings in wine. Tomorrow she would reach out to Jackson and deal with the fallout of losing her best friends later.

Jackson yawned as he looked at the recent headlines about the election. The race had tightened as Robert flaunted his engagement with the lovely lawyer. Jackson didn't want to believe that he was that jaded, but he felt as if Montgomery was using his newfound love to get votes. And it seemed to be working.

Powering down his iPad, Jackson crossed over to the breakfast island in the kitchen to brew himself a cup of coffee. He had about an hour before he needed to get ready and head to the campaign office. He couldn't believe the big debate was less than a week away and the election was just two weeks out. Reaching for a banana nut muffin, Jackson was ready to relax for just a minute. Then he heard the doorbell ring.

"Really?" he muttered as he put his muffin down and headed to the door. Looking out the window, he was shocked to see Liza Palmer standing on his doorstep.

When Jackson opened the door, Liza expected to see him dressed in a business suit holding a cup of coffee with the latest copy of the *Charlotte Observer* draped over his arm. What she didn't expect and was not ready for was a shirtless Jackson Franklin.

"Ooh," she said, blinking then quickly turning away from his chiseled abs and tantalizing pectorals. "I-I hope I'm not interrupting anything."

"Just my breakfast. How did you find my address?" he asked.

"It's not as if you're unlisted. You might want to think about that when you win the election."

"As I recall, a couple of days ago, you were sure that I'd lose. And you told me to drop out."

"Things have changed and I have what you need to win," she said. "May I come in?"

Jackson folded his arms and she saw the 82nd Airborne tattoo on his forearm. God, that was sexy. *Focus, damn it!* she thought.

"Why should I let you in?"

"Because I can no longer stand behind Robert Montgomery and I want you to win this election."

Jackson tilted his head to the side. Dirty tricks were a part of politics and he wanted to believe that Liza was different. But why was she on his side all of a sudden?

"I'm not buying this, and I thought we

were running clean campaigns around here."

Liza pulled her phone out and flashed Jackson one of the pictures of Robert and that woman having sex. "This is all you need to win."

"I'm not running that kind of campaign. And I don't know what kind of game you're playing, but I'm not falling for it."

"This isn't a game. This is your ticket to that senate seat."

Jackson leaned against the doorjamb and folded his arms across his massive chest. "You've been his cheerleader since this began and even longer, according to you. Now you want to help me? Darling, I was born at night, but not last night."

Liza focused on his eyes, hoping they'd be less distracting than his muscular arms. Big mistake. They were intoxicating. Hypnotic.

"I thought Robert was someone else. I thought he was a champion I could stand behind. But he's not. People should know that."

"So, you're morally outraged because he had sex in the office with his fiancée, or are you jealous?"

Standing on her tiptoes, Liza gripped his arm. "I'm sick of people thinking that I'm petty and bitter. I can have a man if I

122

wanted to be lied to and played. But I chose to blaze my own path. I'm sick and seriously tired of men lying and doing whatever the hell they want to do! I guess you're one of those men too!"

"Actually, I'm not. Because watching you stand here all indignant and angry, I want to scoop you up in my arms and take you inside to see how mad you really are," he said with a slick smile.

Liza dropped her hand from his arm and stepped back. "Uh, I —"

"Don't worry, I have self-control. And I have sense enough to know that a man sleeping with his woman in his office doesn't make him —"

"That's not his fiancée, and if a man will lie to the woman he allegedly loves, why would he be honest with the public?" Her voice rose and Jackson did usher her inside, fearing that a neighbor would hear her.

"Would you like a cup of coffee to go with that pissed-off feeling inside you?" he asked as he led her into the kitchen.

Liza rolled her eyes and paced back and forth around the breakfast nook. "Don't patronize me."

Jackson poured her a cup of coffee and handed it to her. "Have a seat and let's talk rationally."

"Do you want my help or not?"

"I don't want your help like this."

She sipped the black coffee and rolled her eyes. "Like this? What does that mean?"

"It means, I'm not going to use scandalous pictures to win the election. People shouldn't worry about what others are doing in their bedroom."

Liza flashed the picture again. "Does this look like a bedroom?"

"You know what I mean. Liza, let's be honest, your feelings are hurt. He's engaged to your friend, you caught him cheating, and I'm guessing she took his side. You want to lash out and that's why you're here. If you really want to help me, send a donation to my campaign, vote for me, or" — he closed the space between them and drew her into his arms — "let me kiss you."

"What?" she asked, blinking as he lifted her chin.

"I want to kiss you." Before she could reply, Jackson covered her mouth with his and Liza melted. He was a skilled kisser. Smooth. Tender. Delicious. And his bare chest against her body caused a river to flow between her thighs. Just before losing herself in lust and longing, she remembered why she'd come there.

Pulling back, she took a deep breath and

turned for the door. "Liza," Jackson called out. "Wait."

In midstep, she stopped and looked at him. "What?"

"I'm sorry, I shouldn't have . . ."

"No, you shouldn't have. Instead, you should've done this," she said as she rushed over to him and threw herself into his arms. Liza nibbled his full bottom lip and then gave him a wonton lick across his lip. Jackson moaned, caught off guard and highly aroused.

"Damn."

"Now that we've gotten that out of the way, can we talk business?"

Jackson looked at the clock on the coffee-maker. He now had thirty minutes to get to his event. "I can't now," he said. "How about we meet later for dinner?"

She slapped her hand on her hip. "I know you're going to this voter turnout thing, organizing drivers and a couple of churches to get 'souls to the polls.' You won't have to do all of that if you just expose Robert for the lying piece of —"

"You're really starting to sound like a jealous ex," he said. "Meet me at seven-thirty."

"Where?"

"Anywhere but the Capital Grille. Bad things seem to happen to politicians who eat there."

Liza laughed, despite herself. "There's always Amelie's," she said.

"Sounds good to me. Or better yet, meet me here. I don't think this is a conversation we should have in public."

"Sounds even better," she replied as she walked to the front door. Jackson fought the urge to kiss her again, and from the look on her face, she was doing the same thing. But that kiss was simply amazing and the only reason he wanted to see her tonight. He wasn't going to use her photos or any inside information she had on Robert. What he wanted was to get inside Liza's mind, heart, and soul. Even if she was the enemy's best friend.

CHAPTER 11

Liza sat in her car feeling confused and angry. Angry with herself for being so distracted by a man without a shirt on and not being able to keep her mouth and tongue to herself; she hadn't gone there to kiss that man. But goodness, it felt so good.

What was she thinking? Someone needed to see those pictures and bring Robert down. Had Jackson been right? Was she acting like a jealous ex because her feelings were hurt? The truth of the matter was, she'd been more disappointed by Chante's reaction. Her sorority sister should have known that if she'd wanted Robert she would've had him a long time ago.

If either of them thought she'd be envious of what she now knew was a farce of a relationship, they were wrong and weren't the friends she'd believed they were. As she started her car, her phone beeped, signaling she had a Google alert. She'd deal with that later. Right now, she wanted to see if Robert was worth saving. Pulling into the parking lot of the Montgomery campaign headquarters, she decided that maybe she'd been mistaken and he'd confessed his sins to Chante after she left.

She walked in the front door and was about to bypass the receptionist when Nic appeared out of what seemed like thin air.

"You can't be here," he said.

"Excuse me? Get out of my way, Nic. I need to talk to Robert."

"He doesn't want to talk to you and you're not a part of our campaign anymore."

"Do you guys really want to make me an enemy?" she asked with her hands on her hips.

Nic laughed. "Please, you're a social media stalker. No one is afraid of you. I've dealt with and dismissed more than a few of your kind."

"My kind? Are you serious right now?"

"Very. Now, kindly leave before I call the police to have you escorted from the property."

"You son of a bitch!" she exclaimed. "I promise I'm going to make you regret this!"

Nic grinned diabolically. "You're making threats in a room full of witnesses. Good PR, if I say so myself."

Liza turned and stormed out. She couldn't contain her anger as she climbed into her car. She banged her hand against the steering wheel and cursed. The litany of profanity that flowed from her lips would've made a sailor and a barber blush. Pulling out of the parking lot, she sped out onto Central Avenue and was promptly pulled over.

"Can this day get any worse?" she muttered as the cop walked up to her window.

Jackson's smile belied his muddled thoughts and there was just one woman to blame. Liza Palmer. He couldn't get the taste of her lips out of his mind and he caught himself more than once licking his bottom lip.

"Jackson!" Teresa said, breaking into his thoughts. "Channel Three is here. Where's your head this morning?"

If only she knew. "I'm good. Let's get this interview taken care of and then talk to the drivers and volunteers."

Teresa raised her right eyebrow at him, giving him a "we'll talk later" look. Heading over to the cameras, Jackson got his game on point. He told the reporter that getting voters to the polls wasn't about him winning or losing; it was about the process. A person shouldn't have to skip voting because he or she didn't have a car. "Everyone has a right to make his or her voice heard on Election Day, no matter whom they support."

The red light on the camera went off and Jackson shook hands with the reporter, then sprinted over to the group of volunteers who'd been helping him all day. They greeted him with applause and a bottle of water.

"You were great over there," Natalie said. "The camera loves you and you always know the right things to say."

"Slow down, Nat," he said. "I'm just telling the truth."

"Something that most people don't do and wouldn't know if it bit them on the a—"

"Let's keep calm, everyone," Teresa said. "We need to focus our energy on getting people out to vote."

The crowd cheered. Jackson was about to follow the volunteers to the tent that was set up on the edge of the park when Teresa stopped him.

"What's going on with you today?" she asked.

"Nothing. Well, that's not exactly true. This morning, I had a visitor."

"Oh Lord," she said as she wiped her face nervously. "Is it a pregnant ex? Someone with a video of you taking a bribe?"

"No. It was Liza Palmer."

"Robert's best friend?"

Jackson nodded. Teresa rolled her eyes. "What did she want?"

Jackson sighed and then recounted most of what he and Liza had discussed. Leaving out the part about the kisses and how she turned his blood to lava with her tongue.

"I don't buy that for a hot second. Tell me why she would all of a sudden want to help you? By all accounts they have been friends since undergrad. This is a trick. We have a debate in two weeks and now she wants to bring him down? Please!"

"She had pictures," he said.

"Photoshop, anyone?" Teresa shook her head. "Don't think for one minute that because you and Montgomery are in the same party you have the same morals. Dominic Hall is a nasty little shit and will do anything to win."

"What does that have to do with Liza?"

"Fruit of the poisoned tree. She will do anything they want her to do and that includes distracting you, rookie."

"Listen, even if they are trying dirty tricks, we're not running that kind of campaign. I told Liza that."

"I hope you also told her where she could go and how quickly she could get there."

Jackson smiled and thought it was best that he didn't tell Teresa about his evening dinner meeting with the lovely Liza. After all, he wasn't planning on talking politics with her tonight. If he was lucky, the only thing their tongues would do this evening would be taste each other.

"I'm not worried about Liza," he said.

"Jackson, which head are you thinking with?" Teresa shook her head. "Let's get back to the volunteers before you get this campaign in trouble." As they walked, Teresa's cell phone chimed. "Yes?"

Jackson watched as she talked, her face contorted as if she'd sipped rancid milk. "Are you kidding me? But why? I'll let my candidate know. Typical."

"What was that all about?" he asked when he saw Teresa shove her phone in her pants pocket.

"State board of elections has delayed the primary."

"Why?"

She shook her head again and frowned. "This is how you know you're doing something to rattle the status quo. All of the media appearances that you've made about voter laws and people not knowing what they need to vote has shaken people who need votes in November. So, your dear governor wants to make sure there aren't any misunderstandings."

"This is ridiculous," he said.

"And extremely transparent. He's trying to look as if he doesn't want to disenfranchise voters with his General Assembly cronies."

"We have to make sure people see through this for what it is."

"Not yet. We have to focus on Montgomery and winning the primary. I wouldn't be surprised if . . ." Teresa turned to Jackson. "You can handle this without me, right?"

"Yeah, what's wrong?"

"I've got to check on something. We'll talk later."

Jackson wanted to question her further, but she zoomed away as if she had rockets on the heels of her shoes.

"Where's Teresa going?" Daniel asked. "She seemed like she was on fire the way she shot out of here."

"She just got a call from someone telling her that the primary has been delayed."

"What?" Natalie asked. "But why?"

"Allegedly so the public can be notified about the current voting laws."

Daniel chuckled. "And let me guess, she

thinks there is a conspiracy behind all of this?"

Jackson nodded and Daniel shrugged. "You know," Daniel said. "She might be right."

As much as he didn't want to believe it, Jackson began to think that Liza's visit that morning may have come with an ulterior motive. Pushing the thought of Liza aside, Jackson busied himself with the volunteers as they passed out flyers about the new voter ID laws that would go into effect in 2016 and signed up people to drive voters to the polls. Many of the elderly people they spoke to that morning were angry.

"That damned governor is stepping on everything we fought for during the civil rights movement," a silver-haired woman said as she signed up to be a driver. Jackson smiled at her and wondered if she could still drive.

She winked at him. "Don't be fooled by the snow. I drive better than that girl Danica Patrick. And my Buick can hold about six people comfortably."

"All with seat belts, right?" Jackson asked with a wink.

"Maybe. Are you going to ride with me?" she asked saucily.

"All right, Mabel," another older lady said

as she linked arms with her friend. "You leave that young man alone before you have another stroke." The bystanders around them broke into laughter.

"Gladys, you are what the kids call a hater," Mabel replied, then walked away.

Natalie nudged Jackson. "Looks like you have a few admirers. It's a good thing women vote more than men."

"I'm hoping that everyone will find a reason to vote for me."

"Gladys and Mabel have a few." She poked him on his bicep.

"You're too much," he said. Glancing at his watch, Jackson realized that he needed to get back to the clinic. He had a meeting with one of his clients who'd refused to talk to another counselor because he didn't trust anyone but Jackson. He hadn't told Daniel, but he was going to work with Carlton Wright until he broke down that wall. It didn't matter if he got paid or not. He understood Carlton's pain and the hard time that he was having getting back into the routine of civilian life.

Like Jackson, Carlton couldn't continue his military career because of an injury he sustained in battle. His injury had been more serious than Jackson's and cost him his right leg. He and Jackson had bonded over their battle scars.

And Carlton told him in their last session that he couldn't open up to someone who didn't have a firsthand understanding of not being able to serve his country.

Men like Carlton were the reason why Jackson wanted to win this election. Someone needed to help soldiers like him. Logic told him that in order to do this, he needed to avoid Liza Palmer at all costs.

CHAPTER 12

Liza felt like a stalker. Technically, she was. After all, she'd followed her best friend to her favorite restaurant. Liza knew her best friend's moves and today was lunch at 300 East. Over the years, they had met in this very spot on Tuesdays to catch up. Today, Liza really wanted to know what would possess her best friend to take Robert's word over hers. And, she had pictures. Why wouldn't Chante even look at them? Looking up at the hostess stand, she saw Chante and Robert standing there. With the election so close, Liza hadn't considered the fact that Robert's punk ass would be accompanying the woman he'd betrayed for lunch.

But there they were, looking like a picture-perfect couple. The childish part of her wanted to toss a roll from her breadbasket at Robert's head. But she held her emotions in check as she moved to a table closer to the one that the hostess led them to. She ignored the waiter's look and made a mental note to leave him a twenty-dollar tip. She was glad the restaurant wasn't packed and she could get close enough to them without being seen. It didn't look as if either of them was paying attention to their surroundings anyway. Robert was a great actor, pretending to be wrapped up in Chante as he held her hand. Liza glanced around for a TV news crew. That was probably the only reason he was being so affectionate.

"Thanks for bringing me to lunch, Rob," Liza heard Chante say. "This was a pleasant surprise."

"I just wanted to spend some time with my lady today."

Liza fought back bile. *What were you thinking when you had that trick bent over your desk? Were you thinking about your lady then?* She picked up the menu and leaned in to eavesdrop further.

"I figured you and your campaign staff would be coming up with a master plan to seal your victory."

"The primary has been delayed. That gives us some time to plan our wedding," he said, then leaned in and kissed Chante on the cheek. Liza felt the return of the bile.

Seriously?

"You know, I was thinking about Liza this morning," Chante said.

"Why?" Robert asked, sounding exasperated. "Liza is the last person I want to talk about. We have a wedding to plan and I don't —"

"Why would she pretend to be happy for us and introduce us to each other and then turn on us like this?" Chante sighed and took a sip of her water.

"You learn who your real friends are when you start to be successful and go after your dreams."

Oh, please! Liza thought. She leaned forward, listening intently as Robert laid the charm on. "I guess all the years that Liza and I have been friends, she was using me as a substitute boyfriend and she must not have expected us to fall in love." He kissed Chante's hand.

Liza silently counted to ten so she wouldn't cross over to them and slap the shit out of Robert. She never wanted him. *Ever.*

"But I don't understand why she would wait until now, when you're running for office and . . ."

Robert shrugged. "Let's not worry about Liza. She's a bitter broad and I wish I had seen that sooner. Nic said she came to the office today and made a scene."

"That is just so unlike her," Chante said. "Liza doesn't do public drama."

"I can't explain why she turned on us, but it's just best to keep our distance from her. I don't want her wild accusations to ruin my campaign or our wedding."

Liza almost snorted when she heard him mention his campaign first. She couldn't believe that this was the man whom she'd put her faith in all of these years. The man she thought would make a good husband to her best friend. Snake. That's what he was, a lying snake in the grass, and if Liza had her way, she'd make sure no one else was fooled by Robert-freaking-Montgomery. And if Chante was stupid enough to believe what Robert was saying, then they deserved each other and she was going to wash her hands of it.

Heading for the bathroom, she decided that she'd duck out the back of the restaurant so the happy, yet delusional, couple wouldn't see her.

Part of her wanted to mourn the loss of her two oldest and dearest friends, but Robert started this war and she was going to make sure she won. Heading to her office, Liza felt her eyes dampen as she remembered how much she wanted Robert to succeed and how she wanted him to soar through the political ranks. What a joke that was. She thought he was different, but he was just like the typical lying and cheating politician who couldn't help but share his wayward dick with everyone who wanted it.

She wanted to save Chante from the hurt, but if she wanted to believe Robert, then fine. She could deal with the fallout as well. Jackson deserved to win — didn't he?

I hope I'm not putting my faith in the wrong man again, Liza thought as she pulled into the parking lot of her office.

Teresa's anger was palpable. Jackson wondered if she'd been a boxer in a former life as he watched her pace back and forth, stop, then square up her shoulders and start pacing again.

"Teresa," Jackson said. "You're going to have a heart attack if you don't calm down."

"This is why I need you focused," she said as she turned to him. Pointing her finger in his face, she shook her head. "The General Assembly is trampling on the rights of poor people, minorities, and women. No one checks these bastards and it's not just the Republicans. We have plenty of do-nothing Democrats sitting in Raleigh using the poor as a footstool and a reason to get on the news. I believe in you, Jackson, and I know you're going to make a difference. If we had at least four or five people like you, we could get a coalition together to make real changes. This state has a chance not to be a joke."

Jackson nodded, knowing that both parties had their issues and Democrats weren't doing enough to stand up for military families either. "This state doesn't belong to lobbyists!" Teresa railed. "I'm sick and tired of North Carolina making the news for all the wrong reasons. Fracking, infringing on voters' rights, and let's not forget marriage equality. So, I need you to win and change the minds of the powerful. This is why I believe this rescheduled election is a fraud."

"But, if we use this time as a chance to tell voters what we're really here for, it could work in our favor," Jackson said.

"Or, the powers that be are trying to put their candidate into position."

"And you think that's Montgomery?"

She nodded. "That's why you have to avoid Liza at all costs. She's a tool in their game."

Jackson kept silent. He didn't want to tell her that he wasn't canceling his dinner with Liza, because the only secrets he wanted to uncover from her were Victoria's.

"What if she isn't?" Jackson asked.

Teresa rolled her eyes. "Are you sure this is what you want to do? Do you know how many politicians were brought down by a pretty face or a blue dress?"

"I'm not worried about that," Jackson said. "I'm in this race because I believe people need to be helped and no one in the GA is doing that."

"So, that means you're staying away from Liza. I don't care what she offers, you can't fall for it. Two words: Donald Sterling."

"I don't plan on making racist statements to anyone."

"Just trust me on this. Don't think she isn't looking for something."

Jackson knew what he was looking for and hoped that Teresa was wrong about Liza.

"Jackson, I know you're a grown man and you're going to do what you want to do, but I would feed Miss Palmer with a long-handled spoon."

Jackson was about to reply when his cell phone chimed, indicating that he had a text message. Pulling his phone out of his pocket, he saw that it was from Carlton.

I can't do this.

He typed a quick response, asking him if he was all right and where he could find him.

At the top of the EpiCentre.

"I have to go," Jackson said.

"What's wrong?"

"One of the soldiers I've been working with is in trouble," he said, then dashed out the door. Jackson hopped in his car and sped to Uptown Charlotte. He wasn't sure if Carlton was going to do something crazy or not, but he had to find him. He was not going to let this man kill himself. After double-parking on the street, Jackson ran up the steps like a man possessed, hoping that he wasn't too late.

"How do I get to the roof?" he asked a security guard in the lobby.

"That's a restricted area, sir," the man replied.

"Then tell me, how did a man get up there?" Jackson pointed to Carlton, who was pacing back and forth on the roof.

"Oh, shit," the security guard mumbled, then started talking into his shoulder radio in codes that made no sense to Jackson. Instead of waiting for backup or whatever the security guard had called for, Jackson ran for the service elevator, hoping that it would give him access to the roof. He said a silent prayer of thanks when he saw a sign that said ROOF ACCESS.

It seemed to take forever as the elevator rose. Jackson held his head down and said a silent prayer for Carlton. "Come on, damn it," he groaned as the elevator stopped. Finally, the doors opened and Jackson bolted out like a man on fire. "Carlton!"

The man turned around, his eyes bloodshot red and tear streaks on his face. "I can't do this shit, man. I can't forget what happened over there. I close my eyes and I see those babies. I hear the screams. I feel the heat. My family doesn't understand. I tried to get better. Talking to you helped, but I can't talk to you all the time." Carlton inched closer to the ledge, teetering on his prosthetic leg.

"How is taking your life going to help anyone?"

"It'll make things easier for everybody. Maybe my wife will find some peace. And a whole man who can . . ."

"I'm not letting you go out like this. You did two tours in Iraq and came back. Do you think your wife would be okay with this? I know how you feel. I thought about it — I put a gun in my mouth and I was going to pull the trigger. But I got help. I want you to get help."

"There's nothing . . ." Carlton took a step closer to the ledge. Jackson followed.

"Don't do this!" he exclaimed. Carlton looked at Jackson and shook his head. "Carlton, you're better than this. Your family needs you."

He shook his head. "They'd be better off without me!"

Jackson crossed over to Carlton and grabbed him, pulled him away from the ledge. "I'm not going to watch you throw your life away, soldier. I'm not going to let a brave man like you turn into a coward. I'm going to walk off this roof with you and if you're going down, you're taking me with you! You have too much to live for. Think about the men you saved when you found those roadside bombs. You diffused them."

"Not all of them. The one that left me unable to serve." He looked down at his missing leg, then shut his eyes tightly.

"What about your son? Is this what you want him to know about you?" Jackson sighed as he grabbed Carlton by the collar of his shirt.

Carlton dropped his head and sobbed. "I don't want to be half of a man. How am I supposed to provide for my family when the

Army is all I know?"

"And what will you give them if you kill yourself? More pain and heartache. If you want to jump, you have to take me with you." Jackson wrapped his arms around Carlton's shoulders.

"You have something to live for."

"And you don't? My life changed when I came home. The woman I loved left me for another man. While I was thinking that she'd be my lifeline, I came home to find her in bed with her lover. She wasn't even sorry. She told me that she thought I wasn't coming back and she was going to move on with her life."

Carlton looked up at Jackson. "Damn. How did you hold it together? I mean, I can't believe a woman would be that cruel."

"And you have a good one in your corner. I've seen you and Barbara together. I hear how you talk about her. She loves you and you love her. You can't break her heart like this. Let me get you help. Let's get off this roof, call your wife, and let's go to Presby," Jackson said. Carlton nodded. Jackson wouldn't let the man go as they walked toward the stairs. He wasn't going to give him a chance to change his mind.

When they reached the ground that was the first time Jackson noticed the cameras,

147

the police and firefighters, as well as other emergency personnel. When an EMS worker reached out for Carlton, Jackson blocked him. "Not until his wife gets here," he said.

"But, sir . . ."

Jackson speared the worker with a cold stare. "Do you know what this man has been through? He needs his wife and you're going to wait for her."

One of the police officers stepped between Jackson and the EMS worker. "What's his wife's name? I'll call her and get her here so we can clear the scene."

Jackson gave him the information and walked with Carlton into a half-empty restaurant. Waving for a server, Jackson ordered two glasses of water. He and Carlton sat silently until Barbara rushed through the door. She flung herself into her husband's arms while two officers stood by the door as if they were expecting trouble. Jackson almost felt guilty as he watched the couple sob together. "Carlton," she whispered, "what can I do to help?"

"Just love me, baby. I'm so sorry I did this."

She stroked the side of his face. "I'm glad you didn't do the other thing. I love you too much to lose you now. I'm going to ride to the hospital with you and I'm going to be by your side through all of this."

Jackson smiled as the couple rose to their feet and headed for the door. The police officers followed behind them in silence. As Jackson watched the couple head for the ambulance, two reporters approached him.

"Mr. Franklin, what happened here?" one asked as she shoved a microphone in his face.

"This is a private matter and I have no comment," he said, then dashed across the street to get into his car. Jackson didn't even care about the parking ticket underneath his windshield wiper as he drove away.

CHAPTER 13

Liza sat in her office organizing a media campaign for the chain of urban boutiques she'd just taken on as a client. She had the news on as background noise while she created a Twitter account for Pink Inc. She loved the name of the boutique but wondered if Victoria's Secret would come after them.

"You can't copyright a color," Liza mumbled as she uploaded a picture of the main store in Charlotte's South End neighborhood.

"North Carolina senate candidate Jackson Franklin played a reluctant hero today," she heard the newscaster say. Liza turned around and focused on the picture of Jackson running away from reporters at the Epi-Centre. "According to witness reports, Franklin stopped an unidentified man from jumping off the top of Aloft, the hotel on the fifth floor of the entertainment and retail complex. When asked by a Channel Nine reporter what happened, Franklin said it was a personal matter and drove away. We're going to Liz Straton, who was at the scene. Several busy uptown streets were closed for an hour because of this incident. Liz, what happened?"

The camera cut to the blonde reporter standing on Trade Street. "Erica, security at the EpiCentre said Jackson Franklin arrived here around two P.M. and asked one of the guards how to get to the roof of the building. That's when they discovered the unidentified man standing near the ledge. While the security officer called for backup, Franklin sprang into action. He took the service elevator and went onto the roof. Then he and the man went back and forth for about a few moments while emergency personnel gathered below."

"It was very intense watching those two men up there," a female witness said into the camera. "There was a moment when it looked as if they were both going to go over the edge."

The camera cut back to the reporter. "Police just told me that the man who was on the roof is an Army Ranger who returned home from Iraq about seven months ago. His name is not being released. But CMPD spokesman Robert Lacy said the man's wife rode with him to the hospital, where he will be evaluated."

"Liz, is there any word on the relationship between Franklin and the man?" Erica, the anchorwoman, asked.

"No official word on their relationship, but Franklin does work at a center that counsels servicemen and -women who have been in battle. Franklin himself is a wounded warrior. He's credited with saving his platoon and sustaining an injury that forced him out of the military."

"What a great story," Erica said. "As more details emerge, Channel Nine will update the story online and on the air at ten o'clock and eleven."

Liza shook her head as she flipped the channel, only to find another news story about Jackson and the unidentified man. "This is great," she said to herself. "I wonder how Robert is going to top this." She picked up her phone and called Jackson. When his voicemail picked up, she was fifty shades of disappointed.

Jackson was sick of his phone ringing. So, he'd turned it off for an hour and sat in the quiet darkness of his office. As the seriousness of Carlton's situation hit him, Jackson shivered. What was going to happen when the center closed and someone like Carlton didn't have anyone to turn to? Jackson wished he had a bottle of whiskey or vodka in his desk drawer. As he was about to stand up, his office door flung open and Daniel rushed in.

"I've been calling you, Teresa's been calling you. Have you seen the news?"

Jackson shook his head. "I've been avoiding that."

"You're a hero."

"I hate that word."

"I know saving Carlton was second nature to you. But the press from this is the push you need to get to Raleigh."

"I'm not using what happened with Carlton for votes."

"Of course not. But people see who you are."

"I just hope Carlton can heal in private. Hope there will be a place like this for him to turn to when he's feeling as if he has nothing to live for." Daniel smiled and Jackson was confused. What in the hell did he have to be happy about?

"The center isn't going anywhere."

"What?"

"Your story, your selflessness, and the fact that you haven't tried to turn this into a political ad has donations rolling in."

Jackson shared Daniel's smile. "That's amazing news."

"Tell me about it. You need to call Teresa. She seems to think that you're making some horrible, life-altering decision right now."

Jackson chuckled. "Tell her that she doesn't have anything to worry about."

Daniel nodded, then gave Jackson a salute. "I'll pass that message along and I will see you at the campaign office."

Jackson shook his head as Daniel left. Then he decided to turn on his phone. The beeps and vibrations of his smartphone alerted him to the fact that he had missed a lot while he'd unplugged. Listening to his voicemail messages, when he heard Liza's voice he instantly felt a budding anticipation. Dinner was still on and he was going to see Miss Liza. He didn't care what Teresa thought, but he would keep her warning in the back of his mind. Still, he didn't want to believe Liza was a modern-day Mata Hari.

While he knew caution was important, he couldn't stop thinking about that kiss. The softness of her lips and how saucily she took his tongue into her mouth, making his knees quiver. He had serious doubts that a woman like Liza, who valued her reputation and was in the business of saving other people's reputations, would allow herself to be used in political muckraking. And she definitely didn't seem like the kind of woman who would use her body to get . . . what? What could she hope to get from Jackson's campaign? Donor list? Hints of a scandal? Or maybe she simply wanted to give the appearance of something underhanded going on.

One thing he knew for sure, if she wanted to expose Montgomery, she would have to do that on her own. There was no way in hell that he would allow himself to get caught up in that nonsense or use those pictures.

Dialing her number, Jackson wondered if this dinner date would be a mistake.

"This is Liza." Hearing her voice replaced his doubt with yearning.

"Hi, Liza," he said. "I'm returning your call."

"Well, Mr. Hero, I'm glad that you decided to call me back."

"I hate that word."

"What word?"

"Hero. I really believe anyone who knew him would've done the same thing."

"Spoken like a true . . . well, you know what I was going to say. Are we still on for dinner or do you have interviews lined up?"

Jackson laughed. "You really think I'd use this for political reasons?"

"Well, if you were my client . . ."

"But I'm not."

"It would be something I'd suggest."

"We're talking about a man's life."

"I don't know what to do with you."

Oh, I could think of several things, Jackson thought, then licked his lips. "What do you eat? Are you like most pretty women who only order a salad and then scarf down a burger when no one is looking?"

"Ha," she said. "I have a pretty healthy appetite. But I don't eat pork or a lot of red meat."

"Cool. I'll order something from your favorite restaurant, and I hope you don't say Ruth's Chris. Then we can eat on my balcony."

"What do you have against Ruth's Chris?" she asked with a giggle.

"I'm just over high-priced steak dinners," he said. "You seem to eat a lot of those when you're on the campaign trail."

"Then I guess it's lucky for you that steak is my least favorite type of red meat and I was actually thinking of something light and a very chocolate and rich dessert."

"I like where this is going. Hometown

Delights has one of the best chocolate cakes I've ever tasted."

"No. Anywhere but there."

"Now, how could you not like . . ."

"Long story. I used to love that chocolate cake from there, but I have bad memories of it now."

"Then éclairs from Amelie's?"

"Sounds delicious to me."

"So, we've agreed on dessert, but what's for dinner?" he asked.

"I'll tell you what, if you take care of dessert, I'll bring dinner."

"Sounds good."

"See you soon," Liza said. Jackson ended the call with a smile on his face. Though he knew this really had the potential to put a wrinkle in his campaign, if Teresa was right. Deciding that he needed to call her so that she didn't track him down and find him with Liza, Jackson dialed her number.

Liza had a warm sensation rippling through her body as she recalled her phone call with Jackson. There was something about his voice that made her nerves stand on end. *Focus,* she ordered herself. *This is about loading Jackson with the bullets he needs to beat Robert. I won't allow this man to kiss me and I won't kiss him either.* Liza called over to Hometown Delights and ordered the New Orleans chicken, rice pilaf, mixed vegetables, and a bottle of sparkling cider. The cake from that restaurant may have reminded her of her epic failure at playing matchmaker, but she didn't have to boycott the whole menu. And though their wine selection was one of the best in the city, cider was safe. The last thing she needed was to be intoxicated around Jackson. Just looking into those green eyes was enough to make her drunk with want, need, and desire.

"Maybe I should just e-mail him the pictures and skip this torture," she groaned as she glanced at her watch. "No, I'm a grown-up. I can handle this." Just as she was about to head out the front door to pick up the meal, her cell phone rang. Looking down, she saw that it was Chante.

"Hello?" Liza asked after answering on the second ring.

"Liza," her friend said. "I think we need to get together and talk."

"That sounds like a good idea. I really hope we can . . ."

"Liza, I have an opening Tuesday morning and I hope that you can explain yourself."

"Explain myself? What do you mean?"

"I thought you were a friend to me and

Robert, but for you to betray us in this way, it isn't right and I just don't get it."

"You're delusional," Liza blurted out.

"Then Robert is right. I was so hoping that he was wrong. You're jealous and you've been harboring this long crush on him."

"I have a bridge in Brooklyn and some ocean-side property in Idaho. I don't want your lying-ass man."

"You know how close we were in college? We used to talk about those sisters who claimed they had each other's backs until one got something the other one didn't have. I thought we were better than that."

"And if you believe anything different, then there really isn't anything left to say and no need for us to meet."

"Fine." The line went dead and Liza wanted to jump through the phone and shake some sense into her former best friend. She didn't realize she'd been crying until a fat tear splashed on the back of her hand. She truly loved Chante and the last thing she wanted was to see her friend get hurt. But Robert was going to destroy her. Wiping her eyes, Liza blinked rapidly, telling herself that Chante made her choice and she was going to have to live with it. She tried to shake off her feelings about Chante as she headed for the restaurant. Liza tried to formulate a plan to bring up the pictures to Jackson again. He said he didn't want to go negative, but exposing Robert for the lying creep he was would be a service to the voters. As she pulled into the restaurant, Liza texted the photos to Chante. If she didn't believe her, maybe she'd let the pictures speak for themselves, that is if she hadn't blocked her number.

After picking up dinner, Liza headed for Jackson's telling herself that this was not a date. This was business.

Jackson spread a white tablecloth across the steel table on his balcony and silently reminded himself that this was just dinner; it wasn't a political meeting and it surely wasn't a date.

"Why couldn't this just be a simple date?" he muttered as he set a citronella candle in the center of the table. Reaching into his pocket, he retrieved his lighter and lit the wick. "Because it isn't." He headed inside and grabbed the éclairs. After setting the table, Jackson heard the doorbell ring. Glancing at his watch, he was appreciative of Liza's timeliness. Crossing over to the door, he smiled at the thought of the woman on the other side. When he opened the door and drank in her image — curve-hugging ivory jumpsuit and holding two bags of food in her hands, he was ravenous. But it wasn't the aroma of the dinner that stirred his appetite. It was the way Liza's breasts peeked through the fabric of her suit and silently cried out, "Kiss me."

"Welcome," he said.

"Thanks." She walked inside as he stepped aside and allowed her to enter. "I'm sure I didn't tell you this morning, but you have great taste."

"You're talking about my place, right?" He winked at her.

"Yes. Very tasteful and will photograph well when you're senator."

Jackson wagged his finger. "We're not doing that. We're having dinner."

"All right." She shrugged. "Just dinner."

"Give me your cell phone."

"Excuse me?" She furrowed her brows in confusion.

Jackson held his hand out. "Your phone. I already know you never power down, so I'm enacting a no-phone policy at dinner."

She shook her head. "Can't do it. I have clients and . . ."

"The world will work just fine without you for the next two hours."

"And where is your phone going to be?"

Jackson pointed to his breakfast nook.

161

"Right there, on a date with yours. I'm not a twenty-four-hour candidate. I do take a break."

"What do cell phones do on a date?" she asked with a wily grin on her face.

"I guess we'll find out after dinner," he said when he took her phone from her. After setting it on the counter alongside his own, Jackson turned to Liza and led her to the balcony. A warm breeze blew across them as Jackson pulled out a chair for her and set the food on the table.

"So, what are we having for dinner?" he asked as he opened the bags.

"Chicken, rice, mixed veggies, and I brought a nice bottle of . . ."

"Bordeaux? Chardonnay? Sauvignon blanc? I keep those on deck."

"You know your wine, huh? Actually, I have sparkling cider."

"You have to know a little bit of everything these days," he said. "And you can save the apple juice for yourself."

"Apple juice? Really?"

"So, cider is what whets your appetite?"

She licked her lips and smiled. Jackson hoped she didn't see the effect she was having on him. "I'd love a glass of sauvignon blanc," she replied, hoping she wouldn't regret her decision.

"I'll grab a bucket of ice, two glasses, and then we can eat."

"Sounds good," Liza said, then crossed her legs. Jackson gave her one fleeting look as he headed inside to grab the wine and ice.

Liza closed her eyes, caught her breath, and wished that she could get her mind right. She was there to give him those pictures of Robert and that woman, then convince him to use them so that he could win. Yes, he wanted to be Mr. Positivity, but Liza knew what he was up against and the kind of tricks that Robert and Nic would use to win. She was putting her pitch together in her mind when Jackson returned to the balcony. He looked so smooth. He looked so satisfying. What was she doing? She didn't come here to be seduced by this man. She came to hand him the election. She came to get the ultimate revenge on her former friend, on the person who was supposed to have her back and her support. But he ruined that when he decided to lie on her and to her best friend. Too bad Chante fell for the lies. Was she that desperate to be with Robert that she'd lost her mind?

"Get it together," she mumbled.

"What?" Jackson raised his eyebrow at her.

"Bad habit of mine; I talk to myself."

"You know, there's a word for that."

Liza sucked her teeth as Jackson set a wineglass in front of her and poured. "Anyway," she said, "you have a great view up here."

"That's one of the reasons why I bought this place. The view and the silence."

"And I had you pegged as a guy living in the suburbs with a huge yard and a tractor."

Jackson looked out at the twinkling lights of the city. He'd wanted to be that guy once, when he thought he was coming home to the woman he'd planned to spend the rest of his life with.

He'd planned to have a lush green yard where the kids would play and their dogs would roam. Jackson sighed. Did he want to tell her any of that?

"In a different life, that would've been me. But the suburbs are for families and whatnot. I'm good in my little corner of uptown."

"And I guess you're enjoying the bachelor life too much to think about settling down or getting a family home in Huntersville?" She took a sip of her wine.

"I thought I would've given up this bachelor life a long time ago, but here I am."

164

She set her glass aside. "You broke her heart and you're punishing yourself for it?" Liza probed. "That's noble and tragic."

"You ever think that I got my heart broken?" Jackson asked as he reached for the bottle of wine.

"Nope. I believe you're the heartbreaker."

"That's where you're wrong. I went to war, came back to find that I'd been replaced. Didn't even get a stereotypical 'Dear John' letter."

"Ouch. That's just wrong."

"Wrong was coming home from the airport alone and catching her in bed with her lover." Jackson didn't even try to keep the bitterness from his voice. "But, I hope she's happy with her decision."

"No, you don't," Liza said. "That would make you perfect, and no one is that much of a saint."

"I wouldn't say I'm a saint, because I did spend a few months very angry. Still, you can't turn feelings from love to hate without losing a part of your soul."

"Wow. That's deep. I wish I had that clarity when my ex and I called it quits."

"What did you do?"

Liza shrugged and took a slow sip of her wine, then said, "Had him run out of town on a rail."

"Are you serious?"

She nodded. "I gave that louse everything and he cheated on me."

"Still bitter?"

"No."

Jackson raised his wineglass to his lips. "I beg to differ. You have to just look at it this way: he got out of the way for the right man to come along."

"And you know this because . . . ?"

"You're sitting here with me, aren't you?"

"Well, I guess you have a point."

Jackson sipped his wine and smiled. "And I'm sure my ex is sitting in a corner suffering."

"She has to be because she messed up when she let you walk out of her life."

Jackson lifted his glass to Liza's and they toasted. Smiling, Liza leaned in to him and kissed him on the lips.

Oh, my, God. What am I doing? she thought as she felt his tongue slip between her lips. He tasted good. He was a hell of a kisser and Liza was out of her mind. This hadn't been why she wanted to have dinner with him. This was the last thing she wanted to do — well, maybe not. Kissing this man made her body tingle, made her wet, made her want to climb up on the table and allow him to feast on her.

Jackson pulled back. "I think we'd better eat before the food gets colder," he said.

"Yeah, that's a good idea," she replied breathlessly. "Jackson, I really don't know what came over me and why . . ."

"I like kissing you, Liza. You have a wonderful set of lips that make me forget that I swore I'd never fall for another woman again."

"And you make me forget a lot of things too. I actually didn't come here to kiss you and drink your delicious wine. I came here tonight to hand you the keys to winning this election."

Jackson groaned. He knew this was going to come up, but he didn't expect the kiss first. "Liza, I'm not talking politics or elections with you."

"I want you to win, Jackson. I know how —"

"What did he do? Everyone knows that he was your best friend, and for you to just be here ready to *give me the keys* to win this election doesn't seem right."

CHAPTER 14

"Robert isn't the man I thought he was and I don't think the voters deserve to be lied to," Liza railed. She folded her arms underneath her breasts and rolled her eyes. She told herself that she was going to present facts to him and force him to understand why he needed to strike first to win this election.

Jackson raised his eyebrow. "I know you said there's never been anything between you and Robert, but you're acting like a very jealous ex."

"I'm a little tired of hearing that bullshit. Robert's engaged to my sorority sister who used to be my best friend. She's sipped the Kool-Aid and believes everything he says, including that I'm jealous of their relationship. I introduced them. What sense does that make?"

Jackson shrugged. "Sorry I said that. But I'm not looking to run a dirty campaign."

"But Robert will. I know for a fact that they have been looking for dirt on you for weeks."

Jackson folded his arms across his chest. "Can't find what's not there."

"Nic and Robert aren't above making stuff up, and I have something real for you."

"I'm not going to use it," he said with finality. "This is about winning fair and square, not with dirty tricks and whatever you have on your former friend."

"What if he wins? How would you feel then? You would've allowed a liar to head to the General Assembly and all of the things you wanted to accomplish would go on being ignored."

"Liza, if I don't win, then it will be because the voters didn't want me to represent them."

She rolled her eyes. "Or because you were outplayed by Robert and Nic. I don't want them to win when I know you're in this for all the right reasons."

"Forgive me if I don't believe you. Because if I'm not mistaken, it wasn't that long ago that you were telling me to drop out because Robert was the best man for the job."

"That's when I was drinking the Kool-Aid. I've learned the hard way how wrong I was."

"I've broken the main rule of this dinner," he said. "There was supposed to be no talk of politics, and we've spent the last few minutes doing just that."

Liza drank the last of her wine and stared at Jackson. "Just what did you think was going to happen here tonight?"

"Two people having dinner, sharing good wine and maybe a bit more of this." He lifted her chin and kissed her again. Slow. Deliberate. Passionate. The empty bottle of wine fell off the table as he leaned in and reached for Liza. A wineglass crashed as their kiss deepened and she moaned. Her mind flooded with lust-filled images of Jackson's head between her thighs, his hands palming her breasts as she came all over his face. Shivering, she pulled back from him. *Breathe,* she told herself. *Just breathe.*

"Whoa," she said once her heart rate returned to its normal pace. "So, you just planned to kiss me senseless all night?"

"You started it this morning when you burst through my door and showed me how to kiss you. Do you know how hard it was for me to focus after that?"

"I-I umm," she stammered. "Well."

"It was harder than that. Much harder, until I had to focus on something else."

"Saving that soldier?"

He nodded. "Men like Carlton are the reason why I'm in this race. The day I decided to run was when funding was cut at the center where I work."

"Let me put a fund-raiser together for you guys. I know . . ."

Jackson held up his hand. "No need. We got quite a few donations today. People see how important the center is, and they have given us enough money to keep our doors open for now."

"That's awesome," Liza said with a bright smile. "But, how long will that last?"

"I don't know."

"You really should think about letting me host a fund-raiser," she said again. "People get really hot about something, but then cool off really quickly."

"We'll have to see about that," he replied. He knew she was telling the truth. He just hadn't allowed himself to think that far ahead. Liza caught the pensive look on Jackson's face and shook her head.

"You don't trust me, but you want to kiss me every chance you get. You know that doesn't make a lot of sense."

"I simply want to keep business and personal separate. Liza, I bet you're great at your job, but you did it for Robert for a long time. Imagine how that will play out in the media."

She snorted. "So, now you care about what the media thinks. At least you're starting to think like a politician."

"I want to win, but not in a sleazy way."

"Exposing Robert for the liar he is isn't sleazy."

"If he had been stealing money, taking bribes, or anything like that, I'd be all over it. But this . . . I can't do anything with his personal life."

"When you throw your hat in the public arena, you don't have a personal life anymore. Look at what just happened with you."

"That isn't the same as someone snapping pictures of a private moment in my office. Suppose someone has pictures of you and I kissing?"

"Well, being that neither of us made a big production about getting engaged, it really wouldn't matter, now would it?" Liza rolled her eyes as she rose to her feet. With all of the wine and kisses, she was a bit wobbly as she strode toward the balcony's railing. Jackson quickly caught up with her and wrapped his arms around her waist.

"Don't worry," she said as she turned around to face him. "I wasn't going to jump."

"I know. I just wanted to hold you."

"You want to do more than hold me, and I'm willing to let you."

Jackson was taken aback by her boldness, but at the same time, it turned him on. "And just what are you willing to let me do?"

She took his hand and placed it between her thighs. "I want you to start by touching me here." Her voice was like a sensual note from a saxophone, telling him of pleasure to come. He knew this was the last thing he should be doing right now. But he stroked her womanly core with his thumb.

"You want me to touch you like this?" he asked, rubbing her back and forth. Liza moaned. Shivered with delight and was keenly aware of how love starved her body was. Could he bring her to climax with his thumb? Had it been so long since she'd been touched this way by a man that all it would take would be a thumb?

"Umm," she moaned as he continued to rub her hardened nub. With his free hand, he untied the halter of her jumpsuit. Discovering that she didn't have a bra on and had the most perfect breasts that he'd seen in real life made him harder than the bricks on the balcony.

"We should take this inside," he moaned.

She nodded in agreement. Liza needed this man inside her. She needed to feel the touch of his hands all over her naked body. In a swift movement, Jackson scooped her into his arms and carried her into his home. He had every intention of heading to his bedroom and properly laying her on the bed and tasting every inch of her. But the softness of her skin made him so anxious that he couldn't make it past the sofa. He lowered her onto the leather sofa, then peeled her clothes away and parted her thighs. He had to know if she was as sweet as he dreamed that she was. Running his fingers against her thighs, he thought silk had nothing on the softness of her skin. He lifted her legs and placed them on his shoulders as he dove into her wet valley. And yes, she was sweet. And wet. Her sticky wetness covered his face as he lapped and sucked her precious bud. Liza cried out with zeal as she experienced the most earth-shattering orgasm. Her thighs shook as she clenched the back of Jackson's neck. "Yes! Oh. My. God. Yes!"

He was far from finished tasting her as he pressed his finger inside her hot pot while he suckled her hardened nipples. Liza came again, harder. With more intensity than before. There was something about Jackson's tongue that seemed to hit every hungry spot of her body. And she wanted — needed — more. Urging him silently, she pressed her hips into his hand and his finger went deeper. Her thighs began to shake as he touched her G-spot. "Umm, Jackson!" she cried as he flicked his tongue across her nipple while twirling his finger inside her G-spot. Her pleasure poured down her thighs. Jackson pulled his mouth from her succulent breasts and planted his face between her legs, lapping up her sweet release. Liza's voice went hoarse as she cried out while Jackson licked and sucked her juices and her throbbing bud. Jackson could've feasted on her all night, but his erection had other plans. He needed to be inside her, needed her walls holding him as they ground against each other. Jackson wanted her so bad that it hurt. But he had to at least make it to the bedroom, where he had a condom and of course the bed. Easing back from her, Jackson smiled at the sated look on her face.

"Let me take you upstairs," he said, his voice a husky whisper. "I need you, Liza."

She blinked and nodded as if she couldn't speak at all. He extended his hand to her, and as she rose from the sofa, he got a full glimpse of her naked body. One word stuck in his mind: magnificent. From the curve of her hips to the tips of her toes, she was a beauty, a living goddess. And for the night, she was his. Lifting her into his arms, Jackson rushed up the stairs to his bedroom, wishing he'd had candles burning so that he could watch the light of the flames flickering against her skin as he made love to her.

Next time, he thought as they entered the bedroom. Jackson lay her across his king-sized bed, and for a moment, he simply stared at her naked body.

"What?" she asked when their eyes met.

"You're beautiful."

She eased toward him on her knees and reached up to unbutton his slacks. "It's really not fair that you're standing here fully dressed and I'm just laid bare," she said with a seductive smile.

"Then by all means," he said as he assisted her with removing his clothes. After he was stripped out of his clothes, it was Liza's turn to marvel at his physique. Lean, six-pack of abs, strong thighs, and that erection. It made her mouth water with anticipation. She reached out and stroked him, causing Jackson to cry out in delight. When her lips captured his penis, Jackson's knees went weak. She licked, sucked, and kissed him with such passion and enthusiasm that he had to temper his building climax. "Stop, stop, stop," he moaned. "I feel like I'm about to explode. I need to be inside you."

She pulled back with a wily smile on her lips. "Great, because I need to feel you. Deep inside."

He reached into his nightstand drawer, pulled out a condom, and Liza took it from his hand. "Allow me," she said as she tore the package open and rolled the sheath in place. Jackson eased into the bed and Liza climbed on top of him.

"Always have to be in control, huh?" he asked as she guided him into her wetness.

"You'll enjoy it," she said as she ground against him. They moved in a slow motion, Liza reveling in his thickness filling her wetness. He felt so good. And he knew how to thrust his hips into her and touch her most sensitive spots. Tossing her head back, Liza couldn't believe how hard and fast she reached her climax. Her love-starved body could barely handle the sensations running through her. But Jackson wasn't about to stop. Gripping her hips, he flipped her on her back.

Bringing his lips to her ears, he flicked his tongue against her lobe. "Now, let me show you how good it feels to let go." Jackson thrust into her, making Liza's pleasure increase tenfold. He gripped her hips as he slowly ground against her, touching all of her sensitive spots. Liza wrapped her legs tightly around his waist, pulling him in deeper. He had been right — she loved the way she felt as she let go and allowed him to control her body. She lost count of the number of orgasms that she'd been treated to after Jackson reached his own climax and drew her into his arms. "Amazing," he breathed.

"Yes," she said as she followed a bead of sweat down his bicep with her index finger.

He stroked her forehead and smiled at her. "I think this is the first time I've ever seen you powered down."

"Oh, stop," she whispered. Liza inhaled his sexy scent. She didn't want to move or power up. If this were a perfect world, she would stay in Jackson's arms for the rest of the year. It felt so good to be held. Closing her eyes, she sighed.

"What's wrong?" Jackson asked.

"This was so impulsive," she quietly said, but didn't move from his embrace. "I just want you to know I don't normally do things like this."

"Neither do I," he said. "But you were so damned irresistible. I'd like to think that this wasn't a one-night stand."

"It wasn't. But this isn't why I agreed to have dinner with you."

"Yeah, you wanted me to slip into sleazy politics and get back at your friend —"

"Former friend," she interjected.

"Friend, former friend, whatever. Liza, I don't want you to be my political rival or my deep throat . . . you know what I mean."

"I know that if you want to win, you're going to have to put your Clark Kent ideals to the side and realize this is a nasty business."

"Clark Kent ideals?"

"Truth, justice, and the American way. That only works in superhero movies and not even there, because even Superman has a dark side. Did you see *Man of Steel*? Even when Superman got pushed too —"

"Liza, hold up," he said. "After what we just shared, *this* is the conversation you want to have? Do I need to remind you that we have a lot of other things to talk about?" He reached for her hand and placed it on his growing erection. "This is a space where we don't talk politics, revenge, or fictional supermen."

"Right," she said as her fingers danced across the tip of his erection. "I'd have to say you're pretty super yourself."

Jackson covered her mouth in a hot and

lusty kiss, his tongue teasing her full bottom lip as she stroked him with a smooth motion. Breaking the kiss, she locked eyes with Jackson as she prolonged his pleasure with her skillful strokes.

"Liza," he moaned, then licked his lips.

"And if you're super, then I have to say, I'm pretty wonderful," she replied with a wink. Jackson reached into his nightstand drawer and grabbed another condom.

"And modesty certainly isn't one of your superpowers, is it?" Before she could answer, he covered her mouth with his.

Hours later, Jackson and Liza were sated from their lovemaking and the sky was starting to lighten. Had they been at it all night? Jackson brushed his fingers across Liza's forehead as she slept. She was beautiful, close to being angelic. But he knew that she was far from an angel. How was he going to convince her that she needed to let her anger toward Montgomery go and how was he going to continue to see her when he wanted to win the senate seat? He hated the doubts that were creeping into his mind while he looked at her. Suppose this had been a setup? But Jackson hadn't done anything wrong; he wasn't married nor was he engaged. Of course, people had ideas about politicians and sex. Like, they

shouldn't have it. That was completely illogical to him. It wasn't as if he was running to be a Baptist preacher. Shaking his
head, Jackson wondered if a honey trap had
taken him in or if he'd jumped into politics
without thinking how his life was going to
change.

Liza's eyes fluttered open as Jackson sat
up in the bed. "Oh my," she whispered as
she looked at the sky. "I didn't mean to
spend the night."

"I'm kind of glad that you did," he said.

She stroked his chest. "Me too. But leaving is going to be a bit difficult," Liza said
with a yawn.

"You sure know how to stroke a man's
ego," he quipped.

"That's not what I mean." She thumped
him on the shoulder. "What if there's a
photographer roaming around out there?
You can bet that Robert would use any
picture of you that someone fed him to
bring you down."

Jackson groaned. "Let it go, Liza. I'm not
playing dirty politics. I'm not going to let
you try to plant fear into us seeing each
other. Unless there is something you need
to tell me."

She sat up and glared at him. "What are
you trying to say, Jackson?" Her right

eyebrow shot up at his accusation.

"I'm not trying to say anything. I was asking a question," he replied.

"Don't you think it's a little late to be thinking about what my motivation was to be here last night?" she retorted.

"What I'm saying is I hope what you and I share isn't a game."

"And just what is it that we share? One night where we had a little too much wine?"

"So, that's all you want this to be?" He shrugged. "All right."

"Isn't that what it was to you?" Liza was trying hard not to put emotions into what she and Jackson had done. It was just sex. Amazing, mind-blowing, and phenomenal, but just sex. She almost braced herself to hear those words from Jackson. When he stroked her cheek, she knew he was going to. . . .

"I don't know why you have such a low opinion of men, but I'm not in the one-night stand business. Especially not with a woman like you."

"A woman like me?" she quizzed.

"One taste won't be enough. One kiss was enough to make me yearn for you when I should have been focused on the election. I see your face when I prep for the debate. So, yeah, I want more. I just don't want the ugliness of politics to be the reason we're together or to come between us. You know Robert's secrets and the like because he was your friend for years. You have every right to be mad about what he's doing to your sorority sister, but I don't give a damn. And I don't think a man's personal life should determine whether he's fit to lead or not."

"That's where you're wrong. If a man can lie to the woman he plans to marry, what does campaign promises mean? Not. A. Damned. Thing!" She pounded the bed with her delicate fist and Jackson laughed.

"Why are you patronizing me?" Liza demanded.

"Who hurt you? I mean, this is more than an ex who cheated."

She chewed her bottom lip and sighed. Figuring that she was already laid bare, she had nothing else to lose. "My father."

"What?"

"My father taught me that trusting a man was dangerous. Leads to disappointment and distress. I lost my mother when I was really young, about eight."

"How did she die?"

"She got her heart broken," Liza said, her voice sounding far away. "My dad worked for a computer company. Traveled and claimed he was working hard to provide for us. It had been just the three of us — so we thought." Liza closed her eyes and shivered. Jackson instinctively drew her into his arms, stroking her smooth forearms.

"Maybe that's why I never loved Robert as more than a friend. He reminded me of my dad."

Jackson wanted to hear her story but didn't want to push her. Her face wore deep emotions that tugged at his heartstrings. Maybe he shouldn't have pressed her about her feelings and why she wanted revenge on Robert so badly. Her private pain was hers. Still, as she spoke, he listened intently.

"My mama gave up everything to be a wife and mother. She was smart, so smart — except when it came to love. She loved my dad more than she loved herself. They met in college, back when women were expected to go to school and get an MRS."

"An MRS?" Jackson asked.

"A husband. Believe it or not, women used to teach their daughters that without a man they weren't worth a damn. Imagine a world where women dumb themselves down to gain the attention of a man because their mothers told them that's what they were supposed to do." Liza sighed, knowing that world still existed and she saw it firsthand when she was at UNC. "My mother could have been a professor, a principal, anything. She loved education and wanted to teach. My dad wanted her to give up her teaching position after I was born. Said that his wife should be at home raising his children and keeping dinner warm for him. She agreed. And tried to have more children, but she suffered three miscarriages in a row. My father actually blamed her." Liza shook her head. "Said she wasn't taking care of herself, called her lazy and a bad mother."

"I'm sorry," Jackson said, kissing her forehead.

"Anyway," she said, her voice regaining its coolness. "Dad came home from a business trip and told my mother that he was leaving. He might as well have been saying he wanted chicken instead of fish for dinner. Then he said he had a new family, a fertile woman who would give him the son he deserved."

"Liza." His heart ached for her.

"My dad rejected us and my mother couldn't take it. She pretended that everything was all right. But that day she sent me to school . . . I should've known something was wrong. She gave me Oreos."

Jackson furrowed his brows in confusion. Liza flashed him a sardonic smile. "She wasn't one to give me sweets. She'd always say I was hyper and sweet enough and then she'd cut up an apple for me. But that day, she gave me a huge package of Oreos. I was just a cookie-loving kid, so I was happy. When I got off the bus that afternoon, I didn't think I'd ever be happy again. My mother was dead."

"I'm sorry," he intoned, holding her tighter. "That had to be . . ."

She brought her finger to his lips. "I've said enough and I don't want to talk about it anymore. That's why I depend on me. And I like to hold people accountable. I wish I could've sent my dad to prison for murder."

Jackson ached for her and he wished he knew the right words to say. But these were battle scars he was ill equipped to handle.

"Let's have breakfast," he said.

Liza nodded. "That sounds like a great idea. I've given you enough of my sob story."

"Nah, you've given me insight."

"And that isn't a story I normally share," she said, shivering as she thought about the parts she left out. "Promise me that you won't throw this up in my face when we have our first or second argument."

"I'd never do that." He stroked her cheek. "Make a promise to me."

"What's that?"

"One day, you'll stop painting men with that same brush of pain."

Liza wondered if Jackson would prove all of her notions about men wrong. Then she remembered her faith in Robert. One day, the other shoe might drop and she'd find out that Jackson was no different. "One day," she said wistfully.

After taking a quick shower and dressing, Jackson and Liza headed to The Original Pancake House for buckwheat pancakes and crepes. "I don't get crepes," Jackson said as they drove to the restaurant.

"Because you don't have to worry about carbs and calories."

"You think so?"

Liza rolled her eyes. "Normally, I'm in the gym this time of morning. But, I think I got a great workout last night."

"And I can't wait to do that workout again," he said as they pulled into the parking lot.

Liza smiled because she wanted the same workout again herself. But, she wasn't going to let him know that right now. She still had hope that Jackson would wake up and realize that in order for him to win this election, he was going to have to loosen up those tight moral standards he had.

As they walked into the restaurant, neither

of them noticed the photographer across the street snapping shots of them.

CHAPTER 15

After being seated and ordering their breakfast, including a pot of coffee, Liza studied Jackson. He was a beautiful man with haunting eyes. He caught her stare and smiled.

"What's on your mind?" he asked.

"Why are you in politics? You really seem too good for this."

"I believe more should be done for people who have given up their lives, health, and families to serve this country. Our servicemen and -women shouldn't come back to North Carolina, of all places, and have to deal with no health care, no jobs, and wind up homeless. Then there are the poor of this state who are being ignored by the fat cats in Raleigh. It's not enough to just vote and protest. Sometimes you have to change the system from within."

"Not about the power at all?" she asked, then took a sip of her coffee.

"Liza, I had no intention of ever going into politics. Then I found out that the center where I worked wasn't going to get any more funding. I couldn't just walk away and allow the men and women who needed help the most to be ignored."

"It's going to take more than military families to win this district."

"Thought we had a deal," Jackson said, then took a sip of his coffee.

"Excuse me?"

"When we're together, we don't talk politics. That's not where . . ."

"Jackson, I know you think I just want to use you as a tool of revenge against Robert, but I would love to see someone like you win this senate seat and . . ."

The shrill ring of Jackson's cell phone interrupted her. "This is Jackson," he said when he answered.

"I thought you were smart," Teresa snapped. "I thought you said you were using your big head to think about all of the people who believe in you."

"What are you talking about and why are you calling me so early?"

Liza shot him a puzzled look.

"Are you having buckwheat pancakes at The Original Pancake House?"

"Teresa, are you having me followed or

190

something?" he asked, turning to look out of the window.

"I'm not but it seems Nic is. I just got e-mailed a picture of you and Liza heading into that restaurant. I'm sure this is going to end up on a blog somewhere or maybe this was the plan all along. And you fell for it. Damn it, you were supposed to be smarter than this."

"Let's talk about this later," he said.

"I don't trust her and you're a fool if you do."

The line went dead and Jackson turned to Liza. "You're not the only one with pictures," he said.

"What are you talking about?"

He told her what his campaign manager had just shared with him. Liza slammed her hand against the table. "I told you that Nic and Robert weren't above dirty tricks. Now are you willing to listen to me?"

"Nope. Two people having breakfast doesn't make a political scandal."

She rolled her eyes and held back her comments. Liza knew what those pictures could do, and she also knew that Nic was the kind of person who'd allow a rumor to spin out of control. And how Robert would use those pictures to further drive the wedge between her and Chante. How could Jackson be so calm about this?

"I have to go and start some damage control," she said. Jackson shook his head and smiled as she rose to her feet. He continued to sip his coffee.

"Please sit down."

"You don't get it, do you?" she asked as she returned to her seat. "Everyone isn't as honest as you are."

"And leaving without eating isn't going to change anything that's going to happen in the next fifteen minutes," he said matter-of-factly. "I believe the voters will focus on the issues and not worry about pictures from either side."

Liza smiled and shook her head. "You really do believe in Santa Claus and the Easter Bunny, don't you?"

"And don't forget Superman as well."

Liza placed her hand on top of Jackson's. "Too bad I didn't meet you before all of this. I could've whipped you into shape and shown you the ugly truth about politics."

Before he could reply, the waiter returned to the table with their breakfast orders.

Worry kept Liza silent as she and Jackson ate their savory dishes. For her, the crepes could have been paper. What was Robert's plan and how did pictures of her with Jackson fall into that plan? What would Chante think? How would Robert spin this story to make it look as if she'd betrayed them again?

"What's wrong?" Jackson asked when he noticed her frown.

"Nothing — nothing that you want to talk about anyway."

Jackson leaned over the table, placing his fork beside his plate. "Are you more worried about what this picture means for you or . . ."

"There you go being patronizing again." She stabbed her food with her fork.

"I was simply asking a question. And I'd never patronize you. What harm do you think those pictures are going to do to you?"

Liza leaned back in her seat and pushed her plate away. "My reputation is all I have. Robert knows that and I know he's trying to discredit me. Especially with Chante. I tried to show her the pictures of him and that skank, but she wouldn't even look, and then he goes on and on about me being jealous of the two of them. I thought I had a reason to be happy for them." She continued to toy with her food since her appetite had disappeared.

"Maybe you need to let Chante learn her lesson without your help."

Liza's right eyebrow shot up. "And what kind of friend would that make me?"

"Sometimes, you have to allow people to make their own mistakes," Jackson said. "If the friendship is real, you guys will find your way back to each other."

Liza wiped her face. "Besides Robert, Chante is my oldest friend and I miss her. But I have to wonder what kind of friendship we had if she believes that I would try to ruin her happiness because Robert said so."

"Have you talked to her without him around?" Jackson asked, touched by the pain in Liza's eyes.

"Nope," she said. "Chante seems completely under his spell."

"Or maybe she loves him. People get past infidelity, you know. What if Robert has come clean with her and —"

"He hasn't done that because she's still accusing me of stealing her happiness. No, being jealous of her joy or some shit like that. If Robert were the man I thought he was, I'd be leading a parade for this marriage. But he's going to break her heart."

"Maybe that's a lesson she needs to learn."

"Don't you think that's a little harsh? If you knew that you could save someone from heartache, you'd just let it happen because they need to learn a lesson?"

"We're talking about grown-ups," he said.

"Nothing that's done in the dark stays hidden that long anyway."

"Are you going to be a flashlight?"

Jackson rolled his eyes and picked up a strip of bacon. "Nope," he said before taking a huge bite of the salty meat.

"You can't fault me for asking," she said as she picked at her crepes. "I wish I had been warned before I found out about my ex."

Jackson stopped chewing. "So," he said after swallowing, "when you were head over heels in love with your ex, you would've listened to anything that anyone said about him that didn't match with what he said?"

"You think you know everything, huh?" she quipped.

"I know human nature and I know that your friend isn't going to receive your message, pictures or not."

Liza pulled out her cell phone to see if Chante had responded to her text message. Nothing. "Well, at least she can't say she didn't know when she catches him with another woman on their fifth anniversary."

"You sent her the pictures?" Jackson shook his head. "That was *not* cool."

"Throwing away more than ten years of friendship over a lying, disgusting —"

"You introduced them and you didn't

think he was horrible when you did that."

"But I have proof. I walked in on . . . You know what, it is what it is. Now I have to worry about what he's going to do with the pictures he has of us."

Jackson downed his coffee and wanted to brush it off as not being a big deal, but that call from Teresa made him realize that this could be the beginning of a political scandal. What was he supposed to do? Stop getting to know one of the most enlightening women he'd met in a long time?

"Liza, you're one of the most unique and driven women I've met in years. And in the words of Maxwell, I want to get to know you."

Liza's cheeks heated from his compliment. "That's a nice thing to say," she replied. "But how can we do that when you have an election to win?"

"People make time to do what they want to do all the time, no matter how busy they are."

Liza smiled. "I'm sure your campaign manager isn't going to like this and probably thinks that I'm trying to get inside information from you."

Jackson nodded. "She does."

Liza blinked. "Jackson, you know that I'm not trying to do that, but don't you think you need to take things a little more seriously? I've heard of the legendary Teresa Flores. She's not someone who will keep working for you if you don't follow her edicts. She gets results, and I know these photos aren't going to make her happy. Maybe it's best that we . . ."

"I love Teresa and I know she's doing her best to get me in this senate seat. But no one is going to tell me what to do in my personal life. If it's not immoral or illegal, it's no one's business."

"Except for the public's and the voters'. I really don't think you get it, Jackson. Once you hop into the public arena, everything you do is open to scrutiny, judgment, and some twisting by your foes."

Jackson squeezed the bridge of his nose just as his phone began to vibrate with text messages. He saw there were messages from the same reporters who'd been lauding him as a hero yesterday. Now, they wanted to know why he was cavorting around town with Liza Palmer. Then came three messages from Teresa. She needed him to get to the campaign office right now.

"We have to go," he told Liza as he pulled his wallet out and left enough money on the table to cover the tab and a tip.

"If this is about the picture, do you think

it's wise for us to be seen together? I'm going to take a cab back to your place and grab my car. You leave and I'll try to diffuse this from my end as much as I can."

"Liza, don't get involved in this," Jackson said. "And I'm not going to stop seeing you."

"If you want to win, it might be for the best. Besides, we can always have last night."

Rising to his feet, Jackson wanted nothing more than to pull Liza into his arms and tell her that one night would never be enough and that he didn't give a damn about an election. But he did give a damn and he wanted to win. He wanted to win so that he could fight for the military families, for the disenfranchised voters, and the poor people who didn't have a voice in Raleigh.

He stopped himself because what Liza had said made sense. And he could hear Teresa telling him that he was thinking with the wrong head.

"I'll call you later," he said, then walked out the door.

Liza sat at the table and closed her eyes for a moment. Then she called a cab, and as she waited, she typed her name and Jackson's into the Google search engine. The first link that popped up was the blog she hated the most, QC After Dark. That gossip site was one of the worst, behind Media-TakeOut, in her opinion. Clicking on the link, she read the story with a frown on her face:

NC senate hopeful Jackson Franklin was seen cavorting around Charlotte with one of his rival's biggest supporters. Cameras spotted Franklin and Liza Palmer, a PR and social media maven, heading into The Original Pancake House very early this morning. Palmer was recently dismissed from Robert Montgomery's campaign after she and Dominic Hall, the campaign manager, had a loud argument in the headquarters. Hall told QC After Dark *that Palmer threatened to ruin Montgomery by any means. It looks as if Palmer plans to keep that promise.*

"I'm going to kill Nic," she muttered as she watched a yellow cab pull up in front of the restaurant. Her phone rang and she wasn't surprised to see that it was Robert.

"What in the hell do you want?" she snapped.

"Liza, you need to stop meddling in my life or you're going to seriously regret it," Robert hissed.

Liza laughed. "Are you really threatening me? You've lost what's left of your mind."

"Chante believes those pictures were Photoshopped and after seeing who you're hanging with now, she's convinced that you're acting like a jealous girl who couldn't get what she wanted. Now, we can leave this between us or I can go public and tell the state how you and Franklin are trying to sabotage my campaign because I didn't want to marry you."

"You slimy son of a bitch."

"I'm going to win and Chante will be at my side. Stop playing games, Liza, and go back to sending tweets."

"You know what I'm finally starting to figure out? You're a piece of shit and you don't respect me or any other woman because you're mad at your crackhead mother. So, you want all of us to suffer. That's why you hung out with those hood rats in college and it's probably why you were screwing one in your office. You know Chante is way too good for you and I never wanted anything more than your friendship. Now, you can shove your self-serving bullshit where the —"

"Liza, all you had to do was mind your business. I was under pressure and I needed a release. You should be glad that I don't want to treat Chante like a spare piece of ass. You said you believed in me. What else have you been lying about over the years? And for you to turn to this wannabe Rambo.

When I win, remember that you could've been a part of my team."

"Fuck you, Robert!" she shrieked. The only thing that stopped her from tossing the phone across the restaurant was the stares of the patrons who'd heard her outburst. Sighing, she rose from the table and headed outside to the waiting taxi. She had to make Robert pay — without herself suffering. But when she arrived at Jackson's to pick up her car, she saw that the damage had already started. Three news trucks were roaming the parking lot like fat land sharks. Two cameramen paced up and down the sidewalk with cigarettes hanging from their lips. Liza rolled her eyes. *They act as if the man sent a selfie of his penis to a fifteen-year-old on Twitter,* she thought as she paid the driver her cab fare. Stepping out of the car, she fell in with a group of Johnson and Wales students, silently praying that the cameramen wouldn't see her. Just when she thought that she'd made it, she heard someone say, "Isn't that the Palmer chick?"

She hated the media! The two cameramen rushed over to her with two reporters in tow. Seconds later microphones were shoved in her face.

"Miss Palmer, Miss Palmer," a reporter called out. "What's going on with you and

201

candidate Franklin?"

"I don't have a comment right now," she said, attempting to shield her face from the camera and keep her calm.

"Are you still working on Montgomery's campaign?"

"No comment," she said, then pushed past them, ignoring the questions being lobbed at her. Liza knew she couldn't go to her car until the media left. After all, video of her leaving Jackson's complex would add more fuel to the smoldering fire. She hated Robert right now. Wanted him to simply drop dead. She walked up the street for about five blocks and happily entered Starbucks. Though she probably needed tea, she ordered a venti cup of Italian roast and skipped the cream and sugar. She sat in a corner and glanced at the people walking down the sidewalk. Why couldn't she be an anonymous banker? What if she had stayed in corporate America? Her life wouldn't be such a mess. *And this too will pass,* she thought as she toyed with her cup of coffee. After four refills on her coffee, Liza got tired of hiding. Tired of acting as if she'd done something wrong. She was Liza Palmer. She handled scandals; she didn't cause them or run from them. It wasn't as if she was sleeping with the president. And Robert had one more time to try and spin that yarn about her being jealous because she wasn't his fiancée and she'd hurt him. Why had she turned a blind eye to his dark side all of those years ago? He'd been a brilliant student, but a player when it came to women. He'd treated women with a cold disregard after getting what he wanted from them. Maybe that was why he focused on the hood rats. Just like with her father, he wanted to mold his woman into what he expected her to be for his image. She'd seen it but ignored it because he was her friend. Because she needed someone to believe in. She walked out of the coffee shop and decided that she wasn't going to hide anymore. And she wasn't going to give the media the show they wanted either. Arriving at Jackson's place, she was glad to see that the media was gone. She hopped into her car and drove home. It was time to plan her rebuttal.

CHAPTER 16

Teresa's eyes blazed with anger as she looked at Jackson. "What were you thinking? I told you she was bad news! You think those cameras showed up by accident?"

"No," Jackson said. "But I don't think she had anything to do with it."

She rolled her eyes. "You slept with her and now you think she's just an innocent woman who wants nothing more than the best for you."

"I never said I slept with — that doesn't matter. Look. This picture shows two people going to breakfast. We haven't done anything wrong and it has nothing to do with my campaign."

Teresa slid her iPad over to him. On the screen was the QC After Dark blog's story about him and Liza. "Look at the comments."

Jackson was surprised at how many people had latched on to the story, had opinions about his sex life and were just cruel to Liza. "You're going to have to make some kind of statement," Teresa said. "See how you go from hero to sex addict in twenty-four hours?"

"Sex addict? Really?" Jackson said with a chuckle.

"That's what the voters will see. You're single and you can't control your libido — why should they trust you in Raleigh? All anyone you rub the wrong way will have to do is stick a pretty girl in your face and *boom*!"

"You're overacting right now."

"No," she said as she began to pace. "You're underacting to the fact that people judge your every move. Oh, look, here's an update." She shoved her phone in his face, showing him a news alert from Channel Nine. "Guess who was seen leaving your residence? Now there is no doubt that you two are sleeping together — at least in the public's eyes."

"So, what are we supposed to do?" he asked.

Teresa, for once, was at a loss for words. Walking over to the TV in the corner of the conference room, she turned the power on and they watched the mid-morning newscast. Of course, there was a breaking news alert.

"Though the primary election has been pushed back, it is not quiet in the campaign for North Carolina's new senate district. Video emerged this morning showing two rivals heading to breakfast. Liza Palmer, a public relations expert and until recently a member of Robert Montgomery's political team, and Jackson Franklin, the other democratic candidate running for the senate seat, were seen together at a Charlotte restaurant. Montgomery released a statement this morning saying that Palmer had been released from the campaign and was trying to team up with his opponent to share inside information about his campaign," the anchor said. Robert appeared on the screen.

"I thought Liza Palmer was a friend. We've known each other for years, but it seems that she has fallen into the trap of power. She decided that she wanted to play the game of seek and destroy. I was hoping that my opponent, Mr. Franklin, would honor our pledge of a clean and positive campaign, but I see that he has dishonored what we agreed to by teaming up with a vindictive and vengeful woman. Is this the kind of person we want in the General Assembly? We have too many people in Raleigh who don't keep their word to protect, serve, and put the citizens first. Sending Franklin there to represent this new district would be like keeping the status quo in place."

"Turn it off," Jackson said as he fumed.

Teresa shut the TV off and took a seat beside Jackson. "I'm sure you and Liza had an innocent breakfast. Now, how do we convince the public of that?"

"Knock, knock," Liza said from the doorway.

"Oh, great!" Teresa exclaimed, then headed to the window. "Why are you here?"

"Calm down," Jackson said, trying not to smile at the alluring woman standing in his doorway. She looked ready for action in her pink business suit and white heels.

"Teresa, let me say that it is an honor to finally meet you in person. I simply wish it was under better circumstances," Liza said as she strode over to her. Teresa ignored Liza's outstretched hand and closed the blinds.

"Again," Teresa said, "why are you here? I'm sure you know the media will be all over this nonstory."

"I'm here to offer my help, as I offered to Jackson before."

He shook his head. "I don't want your kind of help, Liza."

"Even with him all over the news painting you as the liar when we have concrete evidence that *he* is?!" Liza shouted.

"What evidence?" Teresa asked.

Jackson shook his head at Liza. "No."

Ignoring him, she pulled out her phone and showed Teresa the scandalous photos of Robert and the woman in his office. Teresa shrugged. "We can't do anything with those pictures. That's actually between him and the woman he plans to marry."

"Even after all of the things he said on the news? I heard it on the way over and I don't think it's fair that he gets to start these rumors about Jackson and get away with it."

Teresa folded her arms across her chest. "Let's be honest, *Miss Palmer*. This is more about your reputation and not Jackson's. Tell me what your game is and why I shouldn't just toss you out of here and have your picture placed with security as someone to keep off the property?"

"I'm not going to lie; I want to clear my name and I also want Jackson to win this seat. Robert is not the man I believed in all of those years ago — hell, even a week ago."

"And who's to say that this isn't a ruse to get Jackson to go negative and prove your buddy right?"

Liza and Jackson sighed in unison. Teresa shook her head. "How sweet. But would you answer my question?" she snapped.

"Do you really think I'd risk my reputation for Robert? What do I have to gain by looking like a lunatic while he's sitting in Raleigh? I've worked too hard to play a game that would cost me everything. And I'd never give up who I am for a man."

Jackson crossed over to Liza, understanding her outburst, and wrapped his arm around her sagging shoulders. "Liza isn't the problem," he said.

"Maybe," Teresa replied, softening a bit. "I have an idea. The two of you need to have a press conference."

"What?" Jackson asked.

"The public needs to know that Liza is *not* affiliated with our campaign. So, we hold a press conference and let everyone know that she isn't doing all of that stuff that Montgomery said this morning. And it reeks of Nic. I really despise that man. He has a lot of people fooled. But he's dirty and, Liza, that's why I thought you were. If I was wrong, I apologize. But if I happen to be right, God help you. I believe in Jackson." She shot him a look, then shook her head. "And that's why I'm not leaving this campaign. But the longer we keep quiet, people are going to believe that Robert is right. Liza, this is your forte, isn't it? Get a statement together and let's call the media."

"But I thought I wasn't a part of the campaign," she said.

"You're not, but I'd be a fool not to allow you to use your specific skill set to help us get the focus back on what's important. The issues."

Jackson smiled at Liza and dropped his arm. "I guess we have work to do."

She reached into her oversized purse and pulled out her iPad. "Then let's get busy," she said.

Jackson forced himself to ignore the twitching in his groin at the way she said "get busy."

About three hours later, Jackson had a new admiration for Liza — and it had nothing to do with the curves he knew were underneath that tailored pants suit. She was really good at her job. She'd crafted a statement that didn't read as if it was canned. It was as if she'd captured what Jackson would actually say. No wonder her clients ranged from professional athletes to millionaire CEOs.

"This is good," Teresa said as she read over the release. "Too bad you can't be a part of our team."

"I have the key for you to win," Liza said. "But just like Jackson, you believe in truth, justice, and the . . . whatever. I want to help."

"Darling, after today and what Montgomery went on camera and said, you can't help us at all. Unless you want to give a really nice donation."

Liza sighed and sucked her bottom lip in. Then she looked from Jackson to Teresa. "I want Jackson to win, and if this press statement helps and I need to make a donation, then I will."

Teresa smiled brightly. "That sounds like a plan, because as good as you are with what you do, Montgomery pissed on any help you could give us. Make sure you make your check out to the Committee to Elect Jackson Franklin."

Liza smiled sardonically as she reached into her purse and retrieved her checkbook. "Yeah, he made a mess of anything I could do to help you guys without looking like a total stalker." She made out the check and handed it to Teresa.

"But you want Jackson to win?" she asked.

Liza nodded. Not only did she want Jackson to win, she wanted to spend another night wrapped in his arms with his lips pressed against hers. However, that was none of Teresa's business.

"If that's the case, then you should walk away from Jackson," she said.

"Teresa," Jackson said.

She squeezed her temples. "I don't know how to explain this to either of you. Whatever is blooming here — It. Can't. Happen. Not right now. If Liza didn't know Montgomery, I'd be all for it. Wouldn't care who you spent your time with. But you were Robert's cheerleader for a long time. This isn't going to look good and it will lead to a lot of questions that take the focus off the issues. The public is easily sidetracked by bullshit like this."

Jackson and Liza exchanged perplexing glances. Silently, they told each other that last night hadn't been a one-night stand. But how would they see each other when the media would be on their tail?

Jackson wanted to pretend that after today's statement things would return to the issues and his personal life would be his to have again. But he wasn't that naïve. He knew that every reporter in the state would be looking for a chance to find him and Liza together. That would be breaking news. Then there was Liza's business and reputation to consider. She'd worked too hard to allow rumors and innuendos to bring her down. Jackson wanted to proclaim what she would mean to him after getting to know her better. But was that the public's business? Hell no. What he wanted to share with Liza was something that didn't need to be publicized on the evening news. She touched him in a way that he hadn't felt in years. And what was most important, he felt as if she was a woman he could trust. Then again, he'd felt like this before and come home to watching the love of his life riding another man as if she had graduated from the school of Bronco Billy.

"Seems like we're going to lead the five o'clock broadcasts. So, we have a couple of hours to work everything out," Teresa said as she looked from Jackson to Liza. "I'd love it if you two just didn't look at each other like you wanted to head straight to bed."

Jackson wondered if it was that obvious. "I'm going to get some coffee," he said. "Can I get either of you ladies anything?"

Teresa crossed over to Jackson and tapped him on the shoulder. "I'll get the coffee, you two do whatever," she said, then headed out the door.

Jackson turned to Liza and smiled. "I guess we have to avoid eye contact," he said.

"When the cameras are around, yes. But I

think we're alone now," she replied with a wink. Jackson crossed over to her and drew Liza into his arms.

"Then let's do this thing we've been wanting to do since you walked in the door." He brought his lips down on top of hers and kissed her slow, long, and deep. Her tongue danced with his in a sexy tango that made him harder than concrete. He cupped her bottom, pulling her closer as their kiss deepened. Liza nibbled on his bottom lip and Jackson moaned. Her mouth was magical. Just the thought of some of the things her mouth did last night made him even harder. Pulling back before he took her right there on the table, Jackson stroked her cheek. "You know this complicates things."

She sighed. "I know. I guess we'll always have last night."

"And tonight. I just don't want you to think that every time I invite you out and you end up at my house I'm trying to take advantage of you."

"After all of this, you want me come over tonight?" She shook her head. "Jackson, if you want to win this election, you and I can't . . ."

"My personal life has nothing to do with the election. And that's one of the reasons why I never would've used those pictures of

Montgomery and that woman."

Liza sucked her teeth. "You're giving voters way too much credit. People don't separate private and public anymore. Once you decide that you're going to be a politician, you give up privacy. From what you post on social media to the woman you want to spend the night with."

"Liza, I'm not a teenager hiding from his parents. If I want to see you, I will. And I do want to see you — every inch."

She trembled with desire as he brought his lips to her ear. "And," he said, "you're going to come over in something as alluring as that jumpsuit you wore last night. I like peeling your clothes off."

The heat from his breath almost made her want to peel her clothes off right then, to hell with the media, the rumors, and everything else. She wanted Jackson with every fiber of her being. "I could take a cab over. Because I don't want to do anything that would cost you an election that you deserve to win."

Before Jackson could respond, Teresa returned with the coffee. "Is all the sexual tension gone now? I just saw Channel Nine's truck pull up. Remember, we're telling them that you two aren't involved —

politically. Anything else would just be a lie."

Jackson winked at Liza, then straightened his tie. "We're good."

"I'm going to check my makeup," Liza said. "Where's the bathroom?"

Teresa headed for the door. "I'll show you." As she and Liza walked out of the conference room, he wondered how he was going to keep his feelings for Liza under wraps.

When Liza walked into the restroom to touch up her lipstick, she hadn't expected Teresa to follow her. "Miss Palmer," Teresa said, "I want to believe that you don't mean any harm to Jackson."

"I don't."

Teresa threw up her hand. "Whatever this is that's going on between the two of you, if the media or your former friend find out about it, it's not going to end well for Jackson. He has some good ideas and he's in this for all the right reasons."

"I know," she replied. "I really want the best for him."

Teresa folded her arms across her chest. "Then stay away from him, at least until the election is over. I mean, if you really care."

"I just said the same thing to him," Liza

said. "But, Teresa, he made me see that whatever we do has nothing to do with the election and as —"

Teresa rolled her eyes. "You do this for a living and you know that this is not going to be a secret in Charlotte. It's a slow news cycle and then there is Nic. He's going to be looking for anything to bring Jackson down."

"I have what you need to bury Robert." Liza sighed and dropped her head. "Teresa, you're right."

"And that picture of Robert, as disgusting as it is, can't come from this campaign. Then we are no better than they are."

"True. It's just a little sad that he gets off scot-free and Jackson has to live in a bubble."

"That's the life of a politician. But everything done in the dark comes to light. Montgomery isn't going to win, because he's running for the wrong reasons."

Liza leaned against the sink. "And you really believe that?"

"I've been running campaigns for twenty years now. Aside from our current governor, I've seen a lot of power-hungry candidates get torn down because of their greed. Your friend — sorry, ex-friend — won't be any different. The truth will come out and vot-

217

ers will make the right decision. Now, fix your lipstick and hold on to your feelings until the election is over."

Teresa walked out of the bathroom and Liza wondered if she should take her sage advice.

CHAPTER 17

When Liza walked into the conference room, she saw all of the local stations had made it to the press conference and there was even a camera from a TV station from Raleigh. *People love a scandal,* she thought as she stood beside Jackson, forcing herself not to look at him. But being this close to him made her insides quiver. She thought about how she'd spent the night in his arms. Somehow, they would have to make it through this press conference and go their separate ways. She stole a glance at him as he chatted with a perky blond reporter. Liza wanted to roll her eyes. But why? Was she jealous? How was she laying claim to a man who was about to be off limits to her?

"We're ready to begin," Teresa said. "Mr. Franklin has a debate to prepare for and I'm sure Miss Palmer has her business to run."

And Blondie needs to get behind the camera

and out of Jackson's face, Liza thought as she plastered a plastic smile on her face.

The cameramen hoisted their cameras on their shoulders and the reporters piled their microphones in the middle of the table. All eyes focused on Liza and Jackson. She'd never been nervous in front of the media, but today her heart was beating like an African drum.

"Good afternoon and thank you for coming so that I can address a nonissue," Jackson said, flashing his trademark smile. "I want to thank Robert Montgomery for pledging to run a clean campaign and thank him for doing so, until today. It was sad to see my opponent on television this morning and listen to the half-truths and innuendos. Were Liza Palmer and I in the same restaurant for breakfast? Yes." Jackson paused. "But, how many other people were in that restaurant this morning? To imply that there is a vast conspiracy against him is ludicrous. Was everyone in the restaurant plotting against him? I know that we have a debate coming up and people may not be paying attention to the election right now, but let's focus on the issues. Do we really want to send a man to the General Assembly who jumps to conclusions without all of the facts? How is that any different from the people we have in office now? I look forward to debating Mr. Montgomery on the issues and not whom I have breakfast with. It is clear that Miss Palmer and I had breakfast together. Who can resist The Original Pancake House?" Jackson laughed and so did the reporters.

"So," the blond reporter began. "What did you and Miss Palmer discuss at breakfast?"

"Crepes and pancakes," Liza said with her camera-ready smile plastered on her face. "It's not a secret that I worked on Mr. Montgomery's campaign. I think he has been preparing for political office since we were undergraduate students at the University of North Carolina. We had a disagreement on some issues and thought it best to part ways. I'm not involved in any campaigns, because I have a business of my own to run. I was never paid by Mr. Montgomery's campaign and who am I to turn down crepes?"

"Are there any questions?" Teresa asked. "Mr. Franklin and I have some campaign work to do and Miss Palmer has her business to run. And, let me add, she is not affiliated with the Franklin for Senate campaign."

The group of reporters was disarmed by the statements that Liza had prepared, as

221

she knew they would be. That's why she kept it fun, light, and told the truth. She hoped the story would play out that sometimes breakfast is just breakfast.

Match point, jackass, she thought as she watched the cameras get packed away. Liza thought it was best for her to leave with the media. She was surprised that Jackson followed all of them outside. He shook hands with reporters, and when the trucks began pulling out of the parking lot, Jackson turned to Liza.

"That went well," he said. "Are we still on for dinner and dessert?"

"Jackson," she said, turning her eyes away from him, "I don't think that's a good idea."

"What did I tell you?"

"Do you want to be the first senator for district forty-five?"

"You know I do. But how does having dinner with you tonight change any of that?"

"The game was changed when we had that press conference and said we don't have anything to do with each other. If you think that doesn't change anything that happens between us, then you're wrong."

"We just told the press that you don't have anything to do with my political campaign. That's the truth."

Liza closed her eyes and tried to pretend

that she didn't hear Teresa's voice in her head.

"I want you to win this election because you are the best man for the job."

"Okay," he said. "Glad to have your vote. Now, can I have more?"

"And what more do you want?" she asked with a wicked gleam in her eyes.

"You know exactly what I want more of, and tonight, I'm going to get my just *desserts.*"

Heat flushed her face. "This is dangerous."

"It is not. Are you married? Are you involved in illegal activities?"

She rolled her eyes. "If only it were that simple."

"Later," he said, fighting back the urge to blow her a kiss. Liza walked away and Jackson watched until she climbed into her car. His mind wandered to her legs wrapped around his waist and . . .

"Franklin? You want to come in and work on your campaign?" Teresa called from behind him.

Turning around, he saw that his campaign manager wasn't very happy. "Let's go to work," he said.

Once they were inside the building, she turned to him and shook her head furiously.

223

"You have to leave thoughts of Liza Palmer in the wind."

"Teresa."

"I'll admit that I was wrong about her — she's not trying to take you down — but that's when things get complicated. The media is going to be looking for any hint of something shady. That includes another breakfast meeting or watching her leave your house looking like a carbon copy of yesterday."

Jackson folded his arms across his chest. "I find it hard to believe that my personal life makes a big difference in where I stand on the issues."

"And Bill Clinton never had sex with that woman. John Edwards was just hanging out with that videographer and the baby wasn't his. Anthony Wiener . . ."

"I get it. But those men had something that I don't: a wife."

She nodded. "True indeed. But I don't trust that Nic and Montgomery won't use this woman to sully your reputation indirectly. Imagine someone having naughty pictures of you and threatening to use them. How would you handle it? Wait, don't answer that. I know what you would do. You'd explain it to people and hope they understood. You're an honorable man. I don't hold your opponent in such regard. I think any man who would cheat on a woman like Chante Britt — and get caught by a social media maven — is a damned idiot. But he'd throw you and everyone else under the bus to save himself. If those pictures come out, we can't have anything to do with them, and being around Liza is going to cloud how innocent we are when it comes out."

"When?"

"Stuff like that doesn't stay hidden for long. We're talking sex and politics. One thing Robert did today was paint a target on his back while he was trying to paint one on your head." Teresa smiled. "I tried to tell Nic a long time ago that when you start digging graves for people, be sure you don't fall in first. He has this idea that he's smarter than everyone else in the room. I've never voted for a candidate who hired that sleazebag to run their show."

"You and this Nic guy have history, huh?" Jackson picked up a folder from the center of the table and looked at the latest poll numbers that Teresa had printed off.

"It doesn't matter," she said. "All that matters is getting you elected. The margin between you and Montgomery is narrowing and I wonder how the events earlier today will change these numbers."

Jackson didn't say anything as Teresa began going over the upcoming campaign events and debate preparations. Maybe he was fooling himself thinking that he could make a difference. The main thing he'd wanted he'd gotten: funding for the center. Was he ready to give up his personal life in order to be a public servant?

"I meant to give this to you at our meeting this morning, but we had to put out that fire," she said, then handed him a letter. Jackson smiled when he saw the return address was from Fort Bragg.

Dear Sarge,

When I first joined the Army, I thought I'd never see war. I thought I was just doing this so I could go to college. You made me understand what wearing this uniform means when you told me about the four tours you did in Afghanistan. I knew then that service wasn't just about what I could get out of it. The last time I saw you was when you got your Medal of Honor for saving your brothers in battle. Then, the other day while I was wasting time on the Internet — not while on guard duty! — and I saw this YouTube video of you on the roof talk-

226

ing a man down. I was like, damn! Sarge really meant all that stuff he said about leaving no man behind. I'm not rich. But I had to send you some money for your campaign. You are the hero this state needs. And I don't care about you not liking the term. You. Are. My. Hero.

Sincerely,
SGT Riley Cooper
82nd Airborne

He blinked back the tears in his eyes. Cooper had been a hotheaded private and now he was a sergeant. Jackson felt like a proud father hearing from one of the young men he'd trained all those years ago.

Teresa handed Jackson Riley's three thousand-dollar donation. It was that moment right then that Jackson knew he couldn't quit or do anything to risk his chances.

Liza walked into her office, but she didn't turn the television on. She didn't really want to see the news coverage because seeing Jackson on TV would do nothing but set her body on fire. Still, the professional inside her knew she needed to see how the story was playing out. Rubbing her eyes, Liza told herself this wasn't a story but her life. A life Robert was trying to make a part of political theater because he couldn't keep his dick in his pants.

Now, she was mad. Picking up her office phone, she called Chante. If her friend wanted to be stupid, Liza needed to know if the heffa had seen her text message.

"Hello?" Chante answered.

"Chante, it's Liza."

Her friend's sigh echoed in her ear. "What could you possibly want? Great performance you put on today. Caught you and your coconspirator on the news."

"You really think Robert is telling the truth?" Liza scoffed.

"I know you, Liza. And as much as you tried to pretend there's nothing but crepes between the two of you, I know better."

"If you know me so well, then you have to know I'm telling the truth about Robert."

"What I know is, you're bitter and you think that every man in the world is like your father or Alvin Thorne. You introduced me to Robert, and for you to do what you did to him, it makes no sense. I thought you wanted me to be happy and get a life outside the courtroom."

"Chante, if you're going to believe the lies Robert told you because you want to be married so badly, then go ahead. But those pictures I sent you don't lie. That's the man you've pledged your life to and he doesn't give a hot damn about you."

Chante sighed again. Liza could feel her friend faltering. "Maybe you shouldn't have done such a great job of selling Robert to me, because I love him, Liza."

"Then I guess you've decided that love makes you stupid. Chante, if Robert had been the man I thought he was, the man who pretended to care about you and the people of this district, then I wouldn't have those pictures."

"Like you couldn't have Photoshopped them," she said in a small voice.

"No matter what Robert tells you, Chante, I'm not trying to hurt either of you. But I don't want to see you make a mistake and wake up in twenty years realizing that you married a fraud. Or finding out that you have some incurable disease because of his wayward dick. But you're a grown woman."

"Just be honest. You don't want to see Robert happy."

"Chante, I don't want to see you hurt," she replied. "Yet, every time I try to tell you about your *man,* you want to throw my past in my face."

"Liza, you introduced us. You said Robert was the best thing since sliced bread. Now he's the devil and a liar?"

"This is your bed and you're going to have to sleep in it. I tried," Liza said exasperatedly.

"Liza, what really happened between you and Robert? Last week the two most important people in my life were the best of friends. I had been looking forward to planning my wedding with you. Making that stuff we talked about while we were in college come true. You're my best friend and I just want you to stop this. . . ."

"Have a nice life and I pray that Robert shows you his true colors before you walk down the aisle."

"So, that's it?" Chante asked.

"You've already decided that I'm the bad guy here, so I'm going to move aside and let the chips fall where they may. If you need me, you know how to reach me." Liza hung up the phone and fought back an ugly cry.

She and Chante had become instant friends when they were pledging their sorority. Chante had been the legacy who'd wanted to prove herself to her new sisters. Around the third week of pledging, Liza had been ready to quit, wondering what was the purpose of being a member of the oldest black sorority in existence. Chante had been the one to encourage Liza to stick it out and showed her the true meaning of sisterhood. Liza mourned for the loss of that friendship, that sisterhood.

Tears wet her cheeks and Liza said a silent prayer that Chante would come to her senses. Her iPad chimed, alerting her that she had a Google alert. Opening the message, she wasn't surprised to see that it was about her. When she saw the source was QC After Dark, she started to ignore it. After all, the gossip site had written about her earlier today. She clicked the link anyway, curious to see if they'd updated the story since her press conference with Jackson.

What she saw made her jaw drop: *Was Liza Palmer a Hush-Hush call girl?*

"What the . . . ?" She read on, her blood boiling as she saw the lies:

A source has uncovered documents that link Liza Palmer, the social media and PR maven, to the Hush-Hush call girl agency that was broken up in 2007. According to documents, Palmer worked for the high-end agency and the so-called South Park Madam.

Liza stopped reading the lies and wanted to call her attorney. Then she laughed scornfully. Chante was the person she'd call with this kind of stuff and she had just given her friend the kiss-off.

Folding her arms across her chest, Liza knew who leaked the story and she wanted to drive straight to Robert's campaign headquarters and choke the life out of him and Nic. When that woman had approached Liza after her release from federal prison, she'd refused to work with her. The former madam had reached out to her so that she could rehab her image. But Liza had said no. She had no intentions of turning a sex peddler into a saint.

It would've been a lucrative account, but Liza had her principles, and to see this story online enraged her beyond words. Part of her wanted to toss her iPad directly into Nic's face and break his nose. Because she had no doubt that he was behind this. *And Chante is questioning my loyalty. Robert told Nic about this and now they're using it all out of context.*

She turned on the TV and wasn't surprised that she was the lead story. Not wanting to hear the lies, she shut the TV off and groaned. How was she going to combat this?

When her cell phone rang, Liza was shocked to see that it was Chante.

"What?"

"I just saw the news and I know that mess isn't true."

"Then ask your fiancé why he's spreading rumors."

"You think Robert was behind this?"

"Think? Chante, I told two people that the South Park Madam wanted me to help her when she got out of prison. You were one of them."

"He wouldn't. . . . Can I talk to you and not see what I'm going to say as a headline?"

"That's Robert's MO, not mine."

Chante expelled a sigh. "He's changing. In ways that I don't like, and I'm willing to believe that he would do anything to win this election and . . ."

"You're starting to question the engagement again, huh?"

"Liza, I've missed having you in my corner. At first, I thought this was kismet. Thought this was my chance at a great love. That's why I didn't want to believe anything you said about him, when I knew you were telling the truth."

"Chante, love makes us do crazy things. Think about how many times you and Gabby tried to warn me about Alvin."

Chante laughed. "And you didn't listen."

Liza started to say they didn't have pictures of him with other women, but she held her tongue. "I'm going to confront your man and since you're my attorney, I need you present."

"Sure, but how does me being your attorney make a difference?"

"You can remind me of the charges I'll face if I break his face!"

"He and Nic are at Capital Grille."

Liza did laugh heartily. "Are you going to meet me there?"

"No, I'm going to come to your office and pick you up. If Robert did this to you, I don't want anything to do with him. I understand politics is a nasty game, but to out and out lie on you, I can't let that go."

"Then let's go."

"I'll see you in about fifteen minutes," Chante said.

When Liza hung up the phone, she smiled. Glad that her friend had gained control of her senses again. She couldn't wait to see Robert's face when she and Chante walked into that restaurant.

CHAPTER 18

Jackson watched the newscast in silence. This was the last thing he'd expected to see or hear about Liza. Teresa shook her head and grabbed the remote control. "A call girl?" she bemoaned.

"No one said she was a call girl," Jackson replied.

"But that's what people are going to think." She started pacing. "I wonder if this was part of Montgomery's plan? To throw his friend under the bus."

"How do you know he's involved?"

"Too many unnamed sources and this type of rumor is just too personal."

Jackson pulled out his cell phone and walked out of the room. He needed to know if Liza was all right. He didn't believe what was on the television, but he knew she had to be mad as hell.

Voicemail. *God, I hope she doesn't do anything crazy,* he thought as he hung up the phone and pressed it against his forehead. He wanted to find her, not to ask her about the rumors, but to hold her. He knew this was going to be hard for her to overcome, especially since her reputation was a huge part of her business. And to think that her friend had done this to her — so much for a clean campaign. Wait, technically, this had nothing to do with him. Who was he kidding? He would be linked to Liza and this rumor would haunt them. More importantly, the woman he cared about was hurting.

Wait. He cared about her? How could he not? She was sexy, sweet, driven, and the best kisser he'd met in some time. "Jackson," Teresa called from the doorway. "We need to release a statement. I'm getting calls about Liza and I thought we made it clear that she wasn't a part of our team."

Jackson rose to his feet. "Not yet," he said. "I need to see her first and make sure she's all right."

Teresa shook her head, muttering in Spanish that he was going to lose because he was allowing the wrong head to think for him.

"Hey," Jackson called out. "I can speak Spanish too, you know! And I'm using my brain, thank you very much."

"Whatever," Teresa retorted. Jackson

grabbed his keys and headed out the door. He drove over to Amelie's to grab a couple of salted caramel brownies and two cups of coffee. Chocolate always made things a little better. At least that's what women always said.

After getting the order from the bakery, Jackson realized that he didn't know where her office was located. Sitting in the parking lot, he Googled her name. Of course, the first links all led to the stories about the South Park Madam and Liza's alleged ties to her. Finally, he found Liza's website with her office address listed. He wasn't surprised that her office was in uptown. Driving around the parking lot of her office, he looked for her car. After he saw it, Jackson decided to head up to her office. He was quite disappointed to find the door locked and no sign of Liza. He waited for a few minutes, then felt like a stalker and headed back to his car, wondering where Liza had run off to.

Liza felt like one of Charlie's Angels as she and Chante walked into the Capital Grille. They spotted Robert and Nic sitting at a table in the corner sipping champagne and reading files. Liza assumed they were going over debate preparations or their next character assassination. Chante strode over to the table with Liza at her heels and slammed her hand down on the table. "Robert!" she exploded.

He looked up at her, shock registering on his face as he spotted Liza. "Babe, what's this all about?"

"This is about you lying and spreading rumors about people you're supposed to care about."

"I think you can see that we're busy here," Nic said, then sneered at Liza. "How are you doing, Miss Palmer?"

"Don't speak to me, you slime," Liza shot back, then rolled her eyes.

Nic clutched his chest. "I'm hurt." He nodded toward Robert. "Can we dispose of this quickly?"

"Dispose of this?" Chante snapped as she clutched a glass of water.

As much as Liza wanted to see her girl toss that glass of water in Nic's face, the last thing they needed to do was cause a scene. Liza touched her shoulder and shook her head. "Not here."

"Liza, what have you done now?" Robert asked.

"So, you're allowing Nic to let you go dirty?" she snapped.

"Liza, you need to leave. Chante, I don't

know why you're entertaining the alleged call girl."

Forget making a scene. Liza grabbed the glass of water that Chante had let go and tossed it in Robert's face. "I really can't believe I had so much faith in you and believed that you were the right man for this job. You're not qualified to be a dogcatcher."

Robert laughed as he wiped his face.

"Smile, Liza," Nic said as he snapped a few pictures with his phone. Chante slapped his phone away.

"Robert, are you behind these lies?" Chante asked.

"What are you talking about?" he asked, then laughed. "You're listening to the wrong person if you think anything Liza is saying is truthful."

"Liza isn't saying a word and I asked you a question. Are you and this man," she spat, pointing her thumb at Nic, "behind the story about Liza and the South Park Madam? You and I both know what's being implied is a damned lie."

"We are not responsible for what the media reports," Nic said coolly. "Is it our fault that a reporter did his or her job and found out that your friend deals in smut?"

Liza tensed as she was about to douse Nic

239

with the other glass of water sitting on the table. "Go to hell, Nic."

"Seems you know the direct pathway," Nic said. "I'm glad you're no longer associated with our campaign and you're so damaged Franklin's camp isn't going to want to touch you. It's a pity, because you're good at what you do."

Chante followed her friend's eyes to the steak knife on the table. "Now, Liza, that knife is only going to earn you an assault charge."

"Chante, you're being ridiculous right now," Robert said. "And you're allowing her to do what she does —"

"And just what is that, Robert?" Liza snapped. "I've been nothing but a good friend to you and this is the thanks I get?"

"You've been riding my coattails for years and I tolerated it because I felt sorry for you. I'm done with that now. And, if you were smart, you'd just walk away."

"You felt sorry for me?" Liza shook her head and slumped her shoulders for a moment. This was the man she'd considered her best friend, the man she'd wanted her sorority sister to marry, and the man she'd thought was meant for greatness.

Wrong. She. Had. Been. Wrong. "I guess your mother's crack habit did affect you.

Because you're obviously out of your damned mind. If I were you, I'd be shaking in my boots. You think that you're the only one with dirt? The difference between you and me is that I don't want to hurt you. But if you think I'm going to stand by and be a casualty of your political ambitions, you're wrong."

"I don't have time for this or your rantings," Robert said as he stood up, still damp from the water she'd tossed in his face. "Thanks to you, I have to change my clothes before my next meeting." He turned to Chante. "We'll talk about this later." His voice sounded like a wolf's growl.

Chante narrowed her eyes at him. "No, Robert, we're going to talk about this now or you can forget about the fund-raiser at the law firm."

Grabbing her arm, he gritted his teeth at her. "You're in this with her? You bitches are trying to ruin me."

"Bitches?" Liza and Chante said in concert. They turned to each other.

"I know he's not talking to us," Chante said.

"I know that's right," Liza replied. "Because the only bitches I see in here are Nic and his punk ass."

Chante snatched her engagement ring off

and tossed it in Robert's face. " 'Cause, who wants to marry a bitch?"

"Chante, wait," he said, sidestepping Liza and trying to block Chante's exit. "We need to think about this. You and I are getting married. We have people who —"

"No," she said, pushing against his chest. "You want me to make sure my partners donate to your campaign and I'm not doing it. I don't fund liars!"

"Don't do this to me. You know I need this." He tilted his head toward Liza. "Whatever she said to turn you against me is a lie and —"

"It's not what Liza said, it's what you have done. I don't know what to believe anymore," Chante said, tears bubbling up in her eyes. "You said all of these weeks that Liza was the problem. That she was the one who was causing problems for you and your campaign. That she wasn't happy for us and was jealous of me. I believed you and almost lost my best friend. Have you given up everything that matters so that you can have a little taste of power?" She shook her head and pushed away from him.

"Bastard," Liza muttered as she and her friend stormed out of the restaurant. Once the women were alone, Chante turned to Liza and let the tears flow.

"I'm so sorry," she said in between sobs. Liza hugged her friend.

"It's all right. We were both wrong about this man and we just have to figure out what to do."

"I know what I want to do. I want to walk into that restaurant and slap the sh—"

Liza shook her head. "There is a better way, but the first thing I have to do is clear my name and make sure this rumor doesn't hurt Jackson's campaign."

Chante raised her eyebrow. "So, what's really going on with you and Jackson Franklin?"

A heated blush rose to Liza's cheeks. "Nothing."

Chante thumped her friend's shoulder. "Don't give me that! I know that look. You and that man have a little thing, don't you?"

"We are just friends," Liza said, not meeting her friend's gaze.

"Whatever. So, when you two were seen having breakfast, you were just leaving his house?"

"Maybe."

"Wow. He is very attractive, but what was all that about you two not having anything to do with each other?"

"What was said was, I'm not a part of his campaign, and that's the truth. Besides, he's keeping his word about not going dirty in this race."

"Good for him. But how do you know that?"

Looking at Chante, she wondered if she should come clean about why she'd actually gone to Jackson's place. "He gave me his word."

Chante rolled her eyes. "He's a politician. He's going to say anything you want to hear."

"Jackson isn't like that," she replied quickly.

"Mmm, you're defending him, smiling when you talk about him. Sounds like a crush to me. Be careful, Liza. Seems as if politics has a way of changing people."

"Or simply showing us who they really are. What if I've been wrong about Robert all of these years? Ignored the red flags and unleashed him on your life and the people of this district?"

"You talk about him as if he's a malignant virus. Wait, he is. But that's neither here nor there. The election isn't over and Jackson could be trying to use you to get the upper hand in another way. Pillow talk about Robert's plans and . . ."

"Our pillow talk isn't about . . ." Liza brought her hand to her mouth as Chante

244

clapped her hands.

"I knew it. I knew it!"

"Keep it down," Liza said. "It's not something we're broadcasting. Especially now."

Chante shook her head. "I can't believe that Robert would allow such a rumor to get started about you. This isn't something that you can recover from easily. Slut shaming is sport with the media and Robert knows this."

"I'll come through it," Liza said. Then her phone chimed. Thinking that it was another Google alert, she started to ignore it, but she pulled her phone from her purse.

Where are you? And I hope I don't need bail money.

"Text from your *boyfriend*?" Chante teased as she noted the smile on Liza's face.

"He's not my boyfriend," she replied as she typed her response to Jackson.

On my way to my office. I didn't do anything this time, but I can't say that I won't tomorrow.

I can. I'm waiting for you at your office with salted caramel brownies and cold coffee.

See you soon.

"I hope he doesn't disappoint you, because the last thing we need is to be two bitter chicks," Chante said.

"Bitter? Really?"

"Maybe that's a little much, but I'm truly tired," Chante said, then shook her head. "And you wonder why I focus on work so much. Court cases rarely disappoint me, but this thing here with Robert has reminded me why I . . ."

"No," Liza said. "I'm supposed to be the one buried in work, not you. You're the one who's going to have the Claire Huxtable existence, remember?"

Chante fanned her hand and laughed. "And you were supposed to live the Whitley Gilbert life."

"Well, Alvin was as nerdy as Dwayne Wayne," Liza said, then rolled her eyes. "I've finally learned that the past can't dictate your future, no matter how recent."

"I'm not ready to receive that lesson yet. I can't believe that I was tricked by . . . I'm sorry, Liza. I was so cruel to you because I believed everything that man said. I thought Robert really cared about me and bought the dream he was selling me. On paper, it looked as if I was on my way to that *Cosby*

Show life."

Liza stroked her friend's shoulder. "It's going to be fine. He'll get his."

"And how dumb am I going to look when I go into the office and ask my partners not to give Robert a dime after doing all that lobbying on his behalf." Chante sighed. "I see why you work for yourself and alone."

"No one else can tolerate me," Liza said with a wink as they climbed into Chante's car. "Do you want me to go to the office with you and help make this cancellation easier?"

"No offense, but people think you were part of the South Park Madam's brothel. . . ."

"She never had a brothel!"

"I'm just saying, you would probably make those stuffed shirt assholes double their donation to Robert."

"Anyway."

"Besides, you have something pleasant waiting for you at your office. Don't get caught up in my drama. I'll find a way out of it."

"Okay, but you know this is what I do. I've just got to figure out how to fix my own mess for a change."

"Too bad good old Marie Charles cleaned up her act and moved to Paris. She'd be happy to knock you out of the headlines."

Liza sucked her teeth and quietly wished that the former headline-grabbing socialite was up to her old tricks and would knock these rumors out of the news.

After Chante dropped Liza off at her office, the two promised to get together later and figure out how to cut Robert out of their lives and their social circles. More than anything, Chante and Liza needed to figure out how to take Myrick, Lawson, and Walker out of Robert's back pocket.

Liza's mind wandered to the pictures as she stood outside of her office. Why not fight a rumor with the truth? She had actual proof that Robert was an immoral, lying, cheating dog. Didn't the public deserve to know? Maybe she could . . . Jackson's piercing gaze stopped all thoughts of hunting down chickenheads and hootchie mamas. Suddenly, she wanted to fling herself into his arms and kiss him as if they were the only people in the world and all they had to worry about was his place or hers.

She wanted to be in a world with Jackson where elections were already won and rumors of her being involved with a call girl ring had already been dismissed. "Hi," she said breathlessly.

"Are you all right?" he asked as she unlocked the door to her office.

"As all right as I can be," she said, then held the door open for him to follow her inside.

"Swanky digs," he said as he looked around the pale blue and pink office. "This is where all the magic happens?"

"You could say that," she said as she offered him a seat on the blue velvet loveseat in the corner of the room. "It's usually not this quiet."

"Quiet might be a good thing," he said, then handed her a brownie. "You didn't confront Robert, I hope."

"Well," she said as she peeled the plastic off the brownie, then took a big bite.

"Were there cameras around?"

She swallowed and shook her head. "No. But Chante was there and she's seen the light or the truth as it is."

"Which is?"

"Robert is a low-down snake in the grass and we were both wrong about him. The sad thing is, she had her partners at the law firm all geeked up to have a fund-raiser for him. And that's all he's worried about. He doesn't give a damn about their relationship or how he's hurt her or me."

"Do you think you're going to get past

these rumors?"

She polished off her brownie and shrugged. Jackson reached out and wiped a spot of caramel from her chin, then kissed the sweetened spot. Liza shivered and silently admonished herself for getting so distracted by that man's lips.

"Jackson," she said. "You know what Robert is trying to do."

He inched closer to her, nearly planting her on his lap as he gripped her chin and stared into her sparkling eyes. "I don't give a damn what Robert is trying to do. First of all, I don't believe you have ties to the South Park Madam. Second of all, you and I are not working together. I came here because I knew this had to upset you. Your reputation is important to you and how you make your living."

"And that slimy son of a bitch knows that as well. What if everyone recovers from this episode except me? Robert has already distanced himself and his campaign from me. You and I made a big show of not working together. Everyone is in the clear except me."

Jackson brushed his lips against hers. "Soon enough, everybody will know that these rumors are nothing but innuendo and lies."

A tear slid down Liza's cheek. "It's just hard to rationalize that someone you believed in so much could turn out to be such an ass. Kind of like dealing with my father all over again."

"This isn't your fault and don't start thinking about the things that shaped you in the past. You've overcome a lot of things. You'll rise above this and be stronger than ever."

"You have a lot of faith in me," she said with a smile.

"You're Liza Palmer. I get the feeling that people who bet against you end up on the losing side of things." She brought her lips to his and kissed him slowly.

"I could get used to having you as a cheerleader," she said as they broke the kiss.

"Maybe you should get used to it," he replied as he stroked her hips. Liza smiled and her face brightened. She had no idea why she felt as if Jackson Franklin was about to become a full-time figure in her life, but she liked the feeling.

CHAPTER 19

Jackson and Liza sat in the quiet stillness of her office for more than an hour before his cell phone rang. He knew it was Teresa. They had debate preparation scheduled and he was late. Though he knew he had to be ready to battle Montgomery in their upcoming debate, he didn't want to let Liza go. The loveseat where they'd been lounging had been so comfortable. He even noticed that she'd dozed off as they sat there.

"I guess the real world had to interrupt at some point," he said as he reached for his phone.

"Well, you do have an election to win. And I, for one, hope you crush Robert in the debate. He's going to try to outslick you with his lawyer bullshit."

Jackson brought his finger to her full lips. "Remember our agreement? We don't talk about politics."

"That's just ridiculous," Liza snapped. "I

know that you aren't going to use the ace in the hole, but you could at least . . ."

"Liza, I'm not changing my mind about you and your involvement with this election. Robert will expose himself and I don't want him to use you as an excuse."

She rolled her eyes and decided not to tell him that she was going to find the woman in the photo with Robert and let her tell her story to the media. "Fine," she said. "Don't let me interrupt your plans." Liza leapt to her feet and crossed over to the door. "The real world awaits."

Jackson stood and smirked at her. "You're very sexy when you get indignant. How long are you going to be here tonight?"

As much as Liza wanted to continue playing the role of the angry political advisor, Jackson's smile disarmed her and she said, "I'll be here pretty late. Should I order dinner?"

"Sounds like a good idea," he said. "I'll bring the wine." Jackson blew her a kiss before heading out the door. Once he made it to his car, Jackson tried to turn his focus to the debate. He knew he wasn't supposed to take this personally, but after what Robert did to Liza, this was personal and he didn't like him.

He could almost hear Teresa telling him

to get it together and focus on the issues. Part of him wished that he could just take the pictures Liza had and use them to his advantage. But that just wasn't who he was and why should he put that woman in the spotlight because Robert made a bad choice? This was the part of politics that he didn't like at all. This was what turned the average person against the men and women in office. It was self-serving and wrong. He hadn't wanted to be that kind of candidate, and no matter what, he wasn't going to be. However, things were getting pretty sleazy. Linking Liza to that madam was underhanded and wrong.

Arriving at his campaign office, Jackson made the effort to focus on the issues and push Liza out of his mind.

"Thanks for showing up," Teresa said sarcastically when Jackson walked in. Then her face grew serious. "Is Liza all right?"

"She's upset. I'm sure she thinks that her business is going to take a hit because of this allegation about her being tied to the South Park Madam."

"And I wonder how it's going to hit us," Teresa said as she handed Jackson a file.

"Why would this . . ."

Teresa shot him a silencing look. "I know

you and Liza have something going on and it's not going to be long before the media put it together with the help of Montgomery and Hall. That's why we have to win this debate and put the focus back on the issues."

"Let's get started, then," Jackson said.

After about two hours of going over the issues and preparing for the questions they were expecting, they called it a night. Jackson yawned, looking at the clock. It was nearly eight P.M., and though he was tired, he couldn't wait to see Liza again.

"I know you're not going to listen to me about Liza," Teresa said. "But please just be as discreet as possible. If the wrong people see you two together again, it's going to be difficult for us to overcome — again."

"I'd like to think that the voters have more to worry about than who I'm dating," he said.

"So, you two are dating. This is so dangerous, Jackson. Even if she isn't trying to get information about our campaign to help Montgomery, we can't ignore these rumors swirling about her and the effect that they would have on our campaign. I don't like this and I'm going to tell you just what I told her. If what you two have is real, then you can wait until after the election to explore it."

"Wait, you told her what?" Jackson asked. "My personal life is my business."

"Again, you are such a rookie. You are public property now. Being a single candidate puts everything you do under a microscope. Why do you think Robert got engaged so quickly?"

"From what I understand, that's about to implode in his face."

Teresa smiled. "Let's hope that it gets some coverage and takes the focus off you and Liza. Let's just hope no more rumors get started."

"I'll see you tomorrow."

"Jackson, just remember that you have a lot of people in your corner and you need to think about what winning this seat would mean to them."

"I know what my responsibilities are," he said. "I intend to do what I have to do not to let my supporters down."

"Even if that means letting Liza go?" Teresa didn't stick around for Jackson's answer. It was as if the confused look on his face said it all.

By eight-fifteen, Liza was beginning to think that she was going to have to eat all of the Chinese takeout she'd ordered alone. She'd already polished off an order of crab rangoon as she convinced herself that Jackson was busy preparing for the debate and hadn't stood her up. As she opened a container of fried rice, her mind returned to the conversation she and Teresa had had earlier that day. Suppose she'd convinced Jackson that he needed to stay away from her until the election was over. Or maybe she'd told him that Liza was toxic to their end game.

It wouldn't be the first time that a man had put his ambitions over her. She was halfway through the rice when she decided that she and Jackson were over and her focus needed to go back to rehabbing her image since Robert had thrown so much mud on it. As she logged on to her social media accounts, tears welled in her eyes. *There's no fool like a fool for love,* she thought as she read some of the comments on her Facebook page. People asked if she had been a call girl. People wanted to know if she'd really been a partner with the South Park Madam.

"This is some bull," she gritted as she started to delete some of the more vicious comments. She angrily shoveled a forkful of rice into her mouth.

"I hope there's something left for me,"

Jackson said from the doorway. Liza looked up and tried not to beam as he smiled at her. "Sorry I'm late."

"I'm sure you had a lot of work to do," she replied as she crossed over to him. Jackson drew her into his arms.

"Why didn't you tell me about your tête-à-tête with Teresa?"

Liza sighed. "Because I didn't think I needed to. Actually, I was going to take her advice, but . . ."

"While I can appreciate the good nature behind what she said to you, keep in mind that I'm a grown man capable of making my own decisions. She's my campaign manager, not my mother or my social life coordinator."

"She does want you to win this election, and with everything that happened today, maybe she was right. Technically, we have to sneak around to eat takeout and we have to make sure no one is pointing a camera at us when we embrace."

Jackson pulled her closer. "I'd much rather kiss you than listen to all the reasons why we shouldn't be together right now."

Before she had a chance to protest, his mouth covered hers in a fluid motion and their tongues danced slowly. Liza's body heated up like a campfire on a hot July afternoon. He reached for the zipper on the back of her tunic, but before he zipped it down, he pulled back from her and stared into her brown eyes.

"Any cameras around?" he quipped.

"Not a one," she said, then unbuckled his belt.

"Then," Jackson said as he took her hands into his and nudged her legs apart with his knee, "I think we should take advantage of these fleeting moments of privacy."

Jackson nibbled her bottom lip as he let her hands go and unzipped her tunic. Her skin was soft and warm against his fingertips. She wanted to feel him against her naked skin and take him deep inside her hot valley. But Jackson had his own ideas about how things were going to go as he walked her over to the loveseat in the corner. He peeled her clothes off slowly, while keeping his on. Jackson loved the image of her against the velvet cushions. He dropped to his knees and stroked her thighs. Liza shivered and closed her eyes as his fingers danced against her wet folds of flesh. When he replaced his fingers with his mouth, Liza moaned and gripped his shoulders. His tongue flicked across her throbbing bud as his hands covered her breasts, massaging her hardening nipples.

Liza cried out his name as he deepened his sensual kiss. When Jackson made her reach climax, Liza howled in pleasure. He licked her sticky sweetness from his lips as he rose to his feet and stripped off his clothes. Liza locked eyes with him and smiled. She sat up on the loveseat and wrapped her arms around his waist.

"You taste so delicious," he moaned as she stroked his erection.

"I'm glad you think so. It's my turn to taste you," Liza said as she brought her lips to the tip of his hardness.

"Yes," he cried as her lips captured him. Her mouth was hot and wet and Jackson's knees threatened to go out on him. Deeper and deeper. The near explosion of his desire prompted him to pull back from her oral pleasure. "Woman, you are amazing."

She chuckled and stroked his powerful thighs. "You're not so bad yourself. I need you, Jackson."

He pulled her to her feet, then wrapped his arms around her, kissing her slowly and deliberately. Liza wrapped her leg around his waist and Jackson's erection twitched with anticipation and desire.

"Protection," he groaned. Liza nodded in agreement. He leaned her against the loveseat and reached for his discarded slacks.

He pulled a condom from his front pocket and Liza took it from his hand.

"You were pretty confident, huh?" she asked as she opened the package.

"Let's just say I come from the school of being prepared," he said with a wink. Liza took his thickness in her hand and stroked him until he was throbbing with desire. She slid the sheath into place and Jackson reached down and lifted her into his arms. He brought her lips level with his, then kissed her hard and deep as she wrapped her legs around his waist. He thrust into her, making Liza moan in delightful pleasure. She matched his strokes and ground against him while he clutched her buttocks. Throwing her head back as the waves of an orgasm began to wash over her, Liza screamed Jackson's name.

He fought the urge to come, wanting to prolong her pleasure, wanting to watch her face as she was flushed with pleasure. But when she tightened her walls against his erection, Jackson howled and reached his climax. His knees nearly buckled but he managed to hold her up until they made it to the loveseat and collapsed.

"That was so good," she said breathlessly. "So good."

"I think we need a new word to describe

what that was."

"Umm," she said as she traced a bead of sweat across his chest. "Spectacular?"

"That's a good one. And an apt way to describe you as well." He held her closer, enjoying the rhythm of their heartbeats. Her skin, damp with sweat, was soft to the touch and he couldn't stop stroking her thighs.

"You're trying to get something else started, huh?" she asked as his fingers danced across her inner thigh.

Jackson smiled. "Who's going to turn down more spectacular?"

"Maybe we need to move this to another location," she said. "I'd hate for the cleaning ladies to walk in on us like this."

"That wouldn't be good," he replied. "So, my place or yours?"

"I think my place is closer," she said. "And hopefully not under the watchful eye of the press. I'm actually unlisted."

Jackson thought about the story that had been leading the news all day. "Maybe we should head back to my place."

Liza frowned, but knew he was right. "Then let me stop by my place and grab some clothes first."

"And I'll pour some wine so we can relax and . . ."

"Have round two?" She winked at him as

she dressed, and they headed out the door. Liza felt like a teenager sneaking out of her office looking around to make sure no one saw her. It was pretty ridiculous, she thought, since she had done nothing wrong and Robert was the one who had the most to hide.

"Is the coast clear?" Jackson quipped. "We really don't have to do this."

"Do what?"

"Sneak around like criminals or secret lovers," he said. Jackson ran his hand across his face. "I had no idea that you had to give up so much of your personal life. Then again, when I walked into this campaign, I didn't have a personal life."

"Really?" she asked. "So, you were just all work and no play?"

"You're one to talk," he replied. "I remember that first night we had coffee and brownies, you told me how much you work."

Liza stopped and faced Jackson. "Then I guess we're two sides of the same coin. The problem is we weren't supposed to like each other." Silently she added, *But I could see myself falling in love with you.*

"It's a good thing we don't follow the rules," Jackson said, then pulled Liza into his arms. "I'm glad we met, even if you were on the wrong side in the beginning."

She stroked his cheek. "And for the first time ever, I'm glad I was wrong. And why don't we make it my place instead? Like I said, I'm unlisted."

Jackson took her hand in his, then kissed her fingertips. "Sounds good. Now, let's get out of here and stop acting as if we're doing something wrong."

They walked out of the office building, not worried about cameras or scandals. And Jackson followed Liza to her home, ready to spend the night with her wrapped in his arms.

CHAPTER 20

As Liza drove to her town house in Dilworth, a tony neighborhood just minutes from Uptown Charlotte, she didn't think about the media following her, just the fact that Jackson was behind her. Smiling as she pulled into the private driveway, she wondered if things would change between them when the excitement of the election wore off.

A chill moved through her. Why was she scripting the end when they'd barely gotten things started? "Get it together," she admonished herself as she shut her car off.

Jackson pulled in behind her as she exited the car. He got out of the car and smiled at her. "Nice neighborhood," he said.

"Thanks. Let me give you a tour." Liza walked to the door and opened it. She flipped the lights on and Jackson was immediately taken by her unique style. The walls of the living room were painted a sexy shade of red and the leather furniture in the room was black with a crimson accent. Above her fireplace was a painting of a woman sitting on top of the world with a stiletto dangling from her big toe.

"Nice," he said, nodding toward the portrait.

She grinned as she glanced at the oil rendition. "This was one of the only things my ex gave me that made it past the breakup and purge."

"Who's the artist?"

"Celina Hart. She's so dope. Her work is amazing."

"Can't say that I've heard of her, but I will definitely check her out." For a moment, Liza and Jackson just stood in the middle of her living room in a tense silence. Liza's laughter calmed the mood.

"Why are we standing here as if we haven't seen each other naked before?" she asked.

Jackson shrugged. "I guess it's the whole being on your turf now. I get the feeling that you don't invite a lot of people into your inner sanctum."

She nodded. "You're right. I guess that means you think you're special now, huh?"

"I already know that." He drew her into his arms. "And you're pretty damned special too." He brushed his lips across hers and

Liza felt as if she was going to melt in his arms. Damn, he knew how to make a woman feel good. And Liza liked the feeling. But her fear wasn't far away. She knew men left. Would she be able to handle it when this thing with Jackson came to an end?

"What's that look?" he asked.

"What look?"

He took her face into his hands. "We all have something that interrupts a moment. And whatever was going through that pretty little head of yours, let it go."

"So, you're a mind reader now? Suppose I was just thinking about what kind of wine I have chilling?"

Jackson nibbled at her bottom lip. "I know it's white," he said as he slipped his hand underneath her bottom. "Since you think I'm a seer, let me see if this was what you were thinking." He brought his lips to her ear, flicked his tongue across her earlobe. "You were wondering if I'd kiss you here." He brushed his lips up and down the column of her neck. "Then," he said as he slipped his hand inside her tunic, "you wanted me to touch you here."

Liza moaned as his fingers danced across her erect nipples. "Yes," she breathed. It took everything in him not to rip her blouse off, because the way she said yes made him harder than a hardware store full of bricks.

"And you know the last thing you thought," he said as his other hand tugged at the waistband of her slacks.

She shook her head, her breathing shallow in anticipation of his next move. He unbuttoned those pesky pants and slid them halfway down her hips. Jackson smiled at her barely there lace thong. Had to love a woman who didn't have an affinity for granny panties. He rubbed his index finger against her crotch. Liza felt weak with desire, heady with need, and ready for action.

"You want me to taste you right" — he wiggled his finger against her throbbing clitoris — "there."

"Umm," was the only reply she could muster as he dropped to his knees and pulled her to his lips. He pushed the crotch of her panties to the side, then captured her sweetness, sucking and licking her until her knees quaked. Liza cried out his name as she felt her orgasm take hold. His tongue was magical, and his lips were tantalizing and a torture tool. Because the more she came, the more he licked and sucked. The more he licked and sucked, the more she came. It wasn't long before Jackson had peeled her pants away, and as shaky as her legs were, Liza was simply amazed that she hadn't fallen on her face. He led her to the ottoman near the fireplace and laid her on top of it, facedown. He stroked and massaged her buttocks, then kissed the cheeks.

"I bet you're sweet all over," he intoned. "I intend to find out." Jackson traversed her body with his tongue, spending time sucking and kissing her toes, and then he flipped her over. The look on her face turned him on like a light switch. She reached for his shirt, pulling the tail from his pants, but he grabbed her hand and held it above her head.

"Come on, let go," he whispered as he spread her legs with his free hand. "I've got this." His fingers brushed against her mound of femininity.

"Yes, yes you do."

He slipped his finger inside her wet folds of flesh as he kissed her neck. Liza writhed under his touch. Those lips and that finger sent her into sensory overload. She felt as if she exploded from the inside out.

"That was a good one," Jackson said, pulling his lips from her neck.

"I don't know how much more I can take," she breathed.

"Oh, you can take a lot," he said. "Where's

the bathroom?"

Liza furrowed her brows. "The bathroom?"

"Yes. And what kind of tub do you have?"

"What are you about to do now?" she asked as he rose to his feet and held his hand out to her. Liza took his hand and pointed him toward the stairs. Liza led him into her bathroom and watched as he filled the garden tub with water.

"Don't you think it's time to take off your clothes, Mr. Franklin?" Liza asked as she stepped into the half-filled tub. He licked his lips while watching Liza lather up a bath sponge.

"I think you're right," he said as he stripped. Jackson joined Liza in the tub and took the soapy sponge from her hand. Gently, he rubbed the sponge across her breasts and she shivered. Jackson dipped the sponge between her thighs, stroking them gently as she reached back and shut the faucet off.

Liza wrapped her arms around his neck as he lifted her leg around his waist. As much as he wanted to thrust deep into her wetness, he knew they had to be protected. Pressing his luck and willpower, he pulled her closer, feeling the heat of her desire teasing his erection. He kissed her slowly, their tongues dancing a slow tango. She moaned as his hands stroked her back. His touch made her wetter, hotter, and ready for him to give her every inch of his throbbing erection. She took the sponge from his hand and stroked it across his chest. His nipples stood on end and Liza circled them with her fingertips. A low groan escaped his throat as she pressed against him and kissed his neck. Yes. He had to let her go and grab a condom or he would simply bury himself inside her.

"Condom," he said. She nodded and Jackson set her on the edge of the tub. He reached into his pants pocket, pulled out the prophylactic, and made quick work of opening the package and sliding the condom in place. He returned to the tub, where Liza had already slipped into the water. Joining her in the large garden tub, he backed her against the wall and spread Liza's thighs apart and molded her against his body. She tightened her thighs against him, urging him to thrust inside. As he thrust inside her, they both sighed and slowly ground against each other, making the water spill over the edge of the tub. She held him tightly, needing to feel every inch of him, wanting to ride him slow and long. Jackson loved her long strokes, fought with himself to keep his climax at bay. He loved seeing Liza sated and calm.

He could feel her on the verge of exploding. Her muscles tightened around his erection, making it harder for him not to come. Then she moaned, slow and deep. He snaked his hand up her back and rested it on her neck. "Come for me, let me come with you," he breathed into her ear.

"Mmm, oh-kay," she moaned. And they both reached their climax and leaned back in the now tepid water. Her back rested against his chest as they soaked.

"You are just full of surprises," Liza said when she finally caught her breath.

"And what makes you say that?"

"You read my mind perfectly and did everything I wanted."

Jackson chuckled and stroked her arms. "You're pretty damned amazing, Liza."

"Me or the sex?"

"The sex wouldn't be amazing if you weren't. I hope you realize that I want more than just your body."

She sighed, mad that she was allowing her insecurities to come to light in the afterglow of their lovemaking. "I'm sorry," she said. "Then again, I'm not really sorry. I don't want to be taken advantage of or hurt."

"I'm not going to take advantage of you

and I'd never do anything to hurt you."

"No one intentionally hurts other people unless he's a psychopath. What if these rumors about me don't go away? What if being with me will cost you this election? Do you think Robert isn't going to use this to his advantage?"

Jackson placed his finger to her lips. "There you go breaking the rules again. We're not bringing politics into our time together. You and I know that this rumor is bullshit and . . ."

She pulled back from him and rose to her feet. "I really love that you believe in the people. But I don't share your faith in the general public. Do you know how many times Twitter has killed people and everyone believed it?"

"It's not your problem," he said.

"Oh, but I am a problem?"

Jackson rose from the tub and ran his hand across his face. "Really?"

"You said it." She folded her arms across her breasts and tilted her head to the side.

"And you're twisting my words. Why do you want to pick a fight with me?"

Liza dropped her head, then reached for a towel. Jackson took it from her hands and tossed it over his shoulder. "Are you going to answer my question or not?" he asked.

"I'm not picking a fight with you, but if you don't win this election, I don't want you to resent me. And if I'm the reason why you lose, you will resent me."

"Whether I win or lose has nothing to do with you. And remember, I'm the mind reader, not you."

She snorted and reached for the towel. "That's easy for you to say now."

Jackson allowed her to take the towel from his shoulder. "If I win or lose," he began as he pulled her against his chest, "we're going to be fine."

"Okay," she said. Jackson wasn't convinced.

"Liza, I need you to chill. I need you to relax, and I need you to stop trying to act like you're looking for an escape clause."

"Escape clause?"

"You keep acting as if you expect me to just walk away from you."

Liza stroked the back of her neck. "Do you want a cup of coffee?"

Jackson brushed his fingers across her cheeks. "I want you to answer a question for me," he said. Liza looked up at him and her face reminded him of a lost little girl.

"What?" she asked, her voice low and throaty.

"Do you always expect the worst?"

"I . . ." Words failed her. Did she expect the worst? Yes. That had been her life. Especially when she thought things were going well. Why would things be any different with Jackson?

"I guess it's up to me to prove you wrong," he said. "And the last thing we need is coffee. I'd prefer to simply go to bed."

She smiled sheepishly. "I'm sorry," she said.

"You don't have to apologize." He took the towel and dried her shoulders. "Just stop judging me because of what he did."

"I'm not judging you, per se," she said as she placed her hands on top of his. "I just like to be prepared so I'm not blindsided."

Jackson shook his head and draped the towel across her shoulders. "That's no way to live."

Liza stepped back from him and grabbed a second towel from the linen shelf. "Let's just go to sleep. You should probably try to get some rest since the debate is tomorrow."

"Do you plan on attending?" he asked as he wrapped the towel around his waist. "I'd love for you to be there."

"Are you sure that's a good idea?" she asked as they headed down the hall to her bedroom.

"Why not?" he asked.

Liza pursed her lips, then turned the lights on in her room. Jackson smiled at the calm colors adorning her walls: pink and lilac. The queen bed in the middle of the room obviously doubled as her office. Her MacBook sat open on the nightstand and her TweetDeck account was open. Jackson got dizzy watching the tweets scroll across the screen. "You really don't sleep, do you?" he asked.

"I have to keep up with what's trending," she said, then crossed over to the computer and closed it. "Especially if I had a client who may be getting the wrong kind of attention on social media. The wrong tweet can ruin someone's life."

Jackson shrugged and climbed into the bed. Liza joined him and fluffed a pillow. She stopped herself from grabbing her laptop, which was her nightly ritual, to schedule tweets and Facebook posts for her clients. They'd be all right for one night. She was going to try this living-in-the-moment thing. Glancing over at Jackson, she smiled at how comfortable he looked lying there with the towel wrapped around his waist.

"Want to watch TV or . . ."

He pulled her into his arms. "I want to relax. You should try it sometime. Let me give you your first lesson. First, you turn the lights off."

"I don't like sleeping in the dark."

"Turn the lights off."

She got out of the bed and hit the switch to turn the lamps off. "Happy?" she asked as she climbed back into bed.

"It's a start," he said. "Next, you get back into my arms."

"This relaxing thing seems pretty good," she said when she rested her head on his chest. He stroked her arm.

"Finally, close your eyes," he whispered against her ear.

"I'm not sleepy," she replied.

"I didn't say go to sleep," he said as he slipped his hand between her thighs. "I said relax."

"How am I supposed to relax when you're doing that?" Liza moaned and Jackson squeezed her thigh gently.

"Keep your eyes closed," he said as he continued to massage her thigh. "Breathe in slowly."

She followed his directive and took slow, deep breaths. His hands made her forget rumors, debates, and anything else that had been stressing her. It felt so good. So good. And before she knew it, Liza had fallen fast asleep.

CHAPTER 21

The next morning, Liza treated Jackson to a home-cooked breakfast of eggs, sizzling turkey bacon, and French toast. But when he walked into the kitchen in his slacks and no shirt, she didn't want to eat the food she'd cooked; instead she wanted to pour maple syrup on his chest and lick it off. *Have mercy,* she thought as she turned away from him.

"Good morning," he said.

"Morning. I hope you like French toast." She busied herself making a pot of coffee and warned herself not to focus on the carnal desires flowing through her brain.

"It smells delicious in here. I guess this is a better idea than heading to The Original Pancake House again."

Liza reached for two coffee mugs as she nodded. "I'm sure Robert is looking for some kind of drama to pop off so that he can use it in the debate tonight."

"Are you going to be there?" he asked as she handed him his mug of coffee. "You never answered me last night."

"I don't think that's the best idea. There's no need to add fuel to the fire. You need to be focused on the issues and not worrying about the next rumor that's going to be started about us."

"That's your bag. I'm not worried about what Robert and his team are going to try to say. There are real issues that people are concerned about. I get e-mails about them every day. That's the difference between me and Robert."

A lightbulb popped on in her head. "What are you doing with those e-mails?"

He shrugged. "I answer all of them and, hopefully, I'm guiding people in the right direction."

"You should use those in your debate. You should show Robert and the voters that you're in tune with the people and what their needs are. Do you plan on doing any commercials?"

"That's really not in the budget," he said, then took a sip of coffee.

"Unofficially, I can help you. A few YouTube videos and just one to go viral will make you the front-runner that no one will be able to catch up with."

Jackson shook his head. "I thought we made a deal?"

"Then just take my idea and let Teresa handle it. Jackson, I believe in you."

He set his coffee mug down and crossed over to her. Drawing Liza into his arms, he kissed her forehead. "Thank you."

"It's not the most . . ."

He silenced her with a deep kiss. Liza closed her eyes and saw a future with Jackson. She saw a white gown, heard promises of love and believed them.

Those thoughts scared the living hell out of her. She broke the kiss and smiled at him, hoping her eyes didn't betray her inner turmoil. How was it possible that she was falling for this man so quickly?

"So, what did I do to deserve that?" she asked.

Jackson stroked her cheek. "You're just you," he said. "And I think you're starting to relax a little."

"After last night, I think I like relaxing." She kissed his chin. "But are you going to at least shoot one video?"

Jackson rolled his eyes. "Remember the rules?"

"Whatever." Liza pushed him playfully and grabbed her cup of coffee. "Why don't we just pretend that it was your idea?"

"Anyway, Liza. Why don't we just talk about how awesome this breakfast is going to be?" He winked at her and headed over to the breakfast bar.

"Don't set your standards too high," she said. "Cooking has never been my forte."

He dug into his eggs and discovered that Liza wasn't telling the whole truth. But then again, who couldn't cook eggs? Turned out that the whole meal was delicious.

"And you said you couldn't cook," he said as he reached for a strip of bacon from her plate.

She smacked his hand. "Greedy!"

"Next time, cook more." He grinned and broke the strip in half. He held out the bacon to her and Liza took it into her mouth — licking his fingertips at the same time.

"I must admit, your fingers made that bacon taste a lot better."

Jackson looked at the clock on the stove. "I'd better get going. Teresa and I have some debate prep to do." He rose to his feet and Liza tilted her head.

"Forgetting something?" she asked, then pointed at his bare chest. "That's the picture that we need to see on the news this morning. Candidate for senate seen leaving alleged call girl's house shirtless."

"That's not funny," he said. "No one said you were a call girl."

"I bet if you win the debate, they will." She took their empty dishes and dropped them in the sink. "I'm sorry, I guess this isn't me relaxing."

"No, it isn't. But we're going to work on that later," he said with a wink.

"I think your shirt is in the bathroom."

When he headed upstairs, Liza grabbed her cell phone and checked her e-mail. She wasn't surprised to see that there were more than ten Google alerts about her. Most of the articles she'd seen before, but when she saw a story where the South Park Madam had issued a statement about her, Liza read it in disbelief.

South Park Madam denies involvement with social media professional.

"Yes!" she shouted as she read the denial. Liza almost wanted to find this woman and hug her and give her a kiss.

Jackson rushed into the kitchen, his shirt half buttoned. "What's wrong?"

"Finally something is right!" She shoved her iPhone underneath his nose. "Looks like I'll be at the debate after all."

Jackson gripped her wrist to keep her hand from waving. "Calm down, Liza," he said. "I can't read this if you keep waving your hand."

"The South Park Madam said she doesn't even know me."

"That's great news and I told you that this would work out."

"I can only imagine how Robert is feeling right now. I told him that he wouldn't win by playing dirty and not to make an enemy of me."

Jackson buttoned his shirt and then kissed Liza on the cheek. "Let me remember that as well." He took her hand in his as they walked to the door. "The next few weeks are going be hectic, so if you don't hear from me, I want you to know I'm going to be thinking about you."

Liza nodded. While she understood the election was close and he had to focus, she couldn't help but miss him already. "Maybe you should just focus on the election. I want you to win because you're the best man for the job." She stood on her tiptoes and gave him a quick peck on the lips.

"See you later," he said, then walked out the door. Liza watched him as he backed out of the driveway and wondered if there was something she could do behind the scenes to help him win the senate seat.

As her phone rang, she decided that she was going to find the woman who was in

Robert's office that day. He had a lie, but she had the truth!

"Hello?" she said when she retrieved her phone from the breakfast bar.

"Liza, it's Chante." Immediately, Liza didn't like the sound of her friend's voice.

"What's wrong?"

She sighed. "Robert."

"What did he do now?"

"He went to my partners about the fundraiser and basically said that I'd fallen victim to your lies and he still wanted their support. So, this morning I get a call from Taiwon, that asshole, who said I need to keep my personal business out of the office and then he threatened me with suspension."

"What?! Why?"

"Taiwon seems to think Robert is going to be a great senator for the business sector of this district and doesn't think Jackson has what it takes to make a difference in Raleigh. He won't even take my proposal to the partners that we give a donation to both. I'm willing to bet that Robert's making a deal with the big cash donors. I'm really starting to loathe that man." Chante groaned. "I know this all could've been avoided had I just listened to you and . . ."

"It's okay," Liza said. "I'm just confused

about who's the bigger ass, Taiwon or Robert. You know what, though, I have an idea. Since Robert wants to spread rumors, let's spread some truths about him."

"Are you talking about that trollop?" Chante asked.

Liza wanted to laugh. Who called a woman a trollop in the twenty-first century? "Yes, I'm talking about the woman in the pictures. Before you, Robert was known to date rats. And from the way big-booty Judy went off when I walked in on them, she is more of a rat than a trollop. But she was really mad about him being in a relationship. Who knows what Robert promised her."

"Whatever. I'm not sure about outing her. You know how these things turn out. The man is forgiven and the woman is called all kinds of names for the rest of her life."

"You're forgetting a few things: we're not talking presidential sex, we're not talking John Edwards, and Robert is a black man. The media loves to see the rise and fall of a black man in politics. And for once, I actually want to see this story as well."

"But do we really want to take it this far? Wait, don't answer that and I'm going to pretend that I don't know anything about any of this."

"What if I put you on retainer and you

represent her in case things get hairy? I'm going to put her story out there."

"I can't believe I'm agreeing to this. Bring me my check along with a salted caramel brownie from Amelie's or there is no deal."

"You drive a hard bargain, counselor. I'll see you in about thirty minutes."

After a quick shower and two more cups of coffee, Liza was dressed and ready to bring Robert to his knees. Part of her mourned for the man she thought he was, and on the drive to Amelie's, she almost talked herself out of the plan. She wanted to see if Jackson's Pollyanna view of politics was right. For his sake, she hoped that it was. But the realist inside her wasn't going to leave his beating Robert to chance. People deserved to know the unfettered truth about Robert freaking Montgomery.

Standing in line at the bakery to get the brownies she'd promised Chante, Liza strengthened her resolve. Robert tried to ruin her with lies; she'd bury him with the truth and then tweet about it. It was the only fair thing to do. He knew that if she had the call girl stigma attached to her, it would destroy her business. And there was no way in hell that she was going to allow Robert to beat her. She just hoped Jackson would understand.

■ ■ ■ ■

Jackson, now freshly showered and dressed in a pair of black slacks and his 82nd Airborne T-shirt, sat in his campaign headquarters surrounded by three advisors and Teresa — who wasn't excited about Jackson's opening statement.

"This is boring," she said flatly. "Who wrote this?"

"I did," Jackson said. "This is what my campaign is about and it's the truth. What do you suggest?" He was starting to get frustrated. He couldn't remember the last time he had someone pick out his clothes and what kind of bottled water he should drink at the podium. Smart Water, the image consultant had said, gave him an air of pretension. Hell, he thought it was damned good water. So, he'd agreed to take the Deer Park.

But he wasn't about to let anyone change his words. Jackson knew he wasn't flashy. He hadn't been running as the shiny suit candidate and he didn't plan to do so in this debate.

"What I suggest is you put away the political cliché handbook and be the man people met at all of those campaign stops. Be the man who had a bunch of scared parents watching their kids march into Uncle Sam's army smiling and feeling secure." She tossed his speech back at him. "This is bullshit. This is boring. This isn't going to get you elected, and it damn sure isn't going to beat Montgomery."

"I think we need a break." He wasn't sure how much longer he could hold back his dissatisfaction.

"No," Teresa said. "We need to focus. Something we should have been doing over the last few days, but it seems as if your head was someplace else."

"Is this about me having a life?" Jackson snapped.

Teresa slammed her hand on the desk. "I've spent months breaking my back for you. Making sure this campaign was everything you wanted it to be — clean, fair, and honest."

"What are you saying?" he demanded. "Haven't I done everything that I'm supposed to do?"

"I don't think you get this. You don't realize how much people believe in you and I'm watching you piss it away."

"We need a break," he said again, wondering where Teresa's hostility was coming from. He shooed the other advisors out of the room, then turned to face Teresa. "What in the hell is your problem?"

"My problem?" She snorted. "I'm not the one with the problem. You're in and out of Liza Palmer's office and house as if people aren't watching you. As if Robert and his ilk don't have a kid with an iPhone following you around Charlotte looking for tarnish."

"So what? I've been seen with Liza? And?"

"You're still naïve. It used to be cute. Scandal is going to get people interested in the election, and the side that underhandedly throws the most dirt is going to win. That's not going to be us — because you think that's wrong. You think Robert Montgomery isn't going to bring up your personal life tonight? I bet you invited her, didn't you?"

"I did."

"Dumb. She can't be your girlfriend now. She can't even be your friend."

"What does that have to do with the election?"

"Everything. You're forgetting that there are conservative Democrats as well. Your relationship with Liza is going to ruin everything."

"Is this about the South Park Madam rumors? She came out and said —"

"Who believes the pimp?" Teresa asked.

"Look, Jackson, I'm not just being a hard-ass. I believe in you. I want you to win. But you're not making this easy for us."

"So, what am I supposed to do?"

"I'm going to ask for the last time, cool it until the election is over. Can you just take a cold shower or something?"

Jackson stroked his forehead. He knew he needed to focus on the election, but Liza was quickly becoming just as important to him as the senate seat. But he knew damned well if Montgomery won it would mean more suffering for the military families, for the wounded warriors, and the poor people in the district who end up losing to developers would end up with nothing.

But would Liza be there come Election Day or would she write him off as another man who'd abandoned her?

"You and Robert don't believe in the same thing," Teresa said, as if she was tapping into Jackson's brain. "If he wins, you won't be the only one to lose."

"You're right," he said.

"We've had this conversation before. Is it going to register and stick this time? We're getting too close to the finish line to let those losers win."

Jackson nodded. He'd already warned Liza that he was going to be busy. Maybe she would understand and know this had nothing to do with her.

CHAPTER 22

Liza shook her head as Chante finished one brownie and started another. "Do you know how good it feels not to have to starve myself to fit in a wedding dress?" she asked between bites.

"I don't know why you were doing that anyway. You were going to be such a beautiful bride."

"Whatever. I wonder if I can get my deposit back from the designer. What the hell was I thinking? There were signs."

"What do you mean?"

Chante pushed her half-eaten brownie aside. "He'd come home smelling like perfume, and every time I said something it was always 'I was at a campaign stop.' Or some old lady had hugged him. Then he'd finish with a flourish. I didn't believe in him and was allowing others to fill my head with lies. He was the liar. I'm beginning to see why he won so many cases. Robert outlawyered me most of the time. I believed him for a while."

"And when did you start questioning him? Because it sure did feel like you believed him for a long time."

Chante sighed. "At first, I did think you were stirring up trouble. I mean, after Robert proposed, it seemed as if you just disappeared and I needed you. The little nuggets that he dropped in my ear made sense, and every time I called you and got your voicemail, what he was saying became easier to believe."

"You do realize that I was working on his campaign and I run my own business. But wait, little nuggets? Before I caught him with that girl?"

She shrugged. "Maybe he knew that you'd be the one to catch him and he was going for the preemptive strike. And you'd never been that busy before. I guess he knew the right buttons to push."

Liza nodded. "Still, was Robert saying all of this from the beginning or after the photos?"

Chante toyed with her brownie. "I might have mentioned to him that I thought things had gotten weird between us. And . . ."

"You asked him again if there had been anything between us?"

She nodded and popped a piece of brownie in her mouth. "Robert told me more than you've ever told me about you two. And at the time, I thought he was telling the truth."

"What did that son of a bitch say?"

"It doesn't matter. I know he was lying."

Liza shook her head. "No, I want to know."

"Well, you know I've never kept it a secret that I thought you and Robert were more than friends. He told me that a long time ago you came on to him."

"That lying dog!"

"Keep your voice down."

"I've never come on to Robert, not even after getting plastered at the East End Martini Bar."

"He's a very convincing man," she said. "And that's what scares me about him winning this senate seat."

"Just think, I thought his charm and persuasiveness would be the best thing about him. Who knew that he was going to use that against me?" Liza rose to her feet and paced back and forth. Then she stopped and faced Chante. "You know why Robert and I were so close?"

Chante shook her head. Liza sighed. "I thought that my dad was probably a lot like him when he was younger. I never got a chance to know my dad because when my mother couldn't have more kids, he left us for another family. I stayed with my aunt until I went off to college. Dad sent money but I haven't seen him since I was eight years old."

"How did Robert remind you of your dad? That's been one thing we've never talked a lot about."

"I always thought they had the same smile. I even thought he was my brother for a little while. Then I met his family. Once upon a time, I hoped he'd lead me to my dad. Then I realized it wasn't going to happen and I thought Robert was my best friend."

"Some friend," Chante said. "I just can't get over the fact that he spread that call girl rumor about you. Who does that?"

"Had I known he was such a jackass, I never would've introduced you two. I just thought it would've been great to bring all of my favorite people together and create our own little family unit."

"Aww, Liza," Chante said, then offered her friend a sad smile. "Too bad it didn't work out."

She waved her hand. "I know it sounds corny. I'm an adult, I should be over my daddy issues, but I'm just a big sack of . . ."

"You're fine, Liza. And I'm sorry I allowed Robert to get in my head when you've always been one of the most honest and trustworthy people I've ever known. You're my sister and I love you."

"So, are you going to help me bring the bastard down?"

Chante held out her fist to Liza. "With pleasure!" The ladies bumped fists and giggled, sounding as if they had been transported back to college. But this was a serious matter. Something that they had to handle swiftly and discreetly.

"How are we going to find this *woman*?" Chante asked. "I'm sure she didn't tell you her name or give you her phone number."

Liza pulled up a picture of Robert and the woman on her iPad. Chante rolled her eyes at the image. "Have you ever watched that show *Catfish* on MTV?" Liza asked.

"Nope. Why?"

"The guys who host that show use Google to search faces. And I've used it a couple of times when I've gotten clients out of some sticky situations. I'm willing to bet that this girl has a Facebook or Instagram account. It's hard to stay hidden these days. And Robert should've remembered that when I told him I had pictures." Shaking her head,

Liza began doing the search.

Chante was about to respond when the door to her office swung open and Taiwon stalked in. "Are we working or having girl talk?" he asked smugly.

Chante leapt to her feet. "I'm actually meeting with a client, Mr. Myrick. Is there something you need that is super urgent and you couldn't be bothered to knock on the door?"

Liza wanted to give her friend a high five because this Myrick man was rude and needed to be slapped.

"I didn't realize you were actually working," he said, then headed out the door.

Chante closed her eyes and counted to ten. "I want to be a partner, I want to be a partner," she chanted.

"Is it worth it?" Liza asked. "I mean, you could always open your own firm. Because if that's something you deal with every day, I don't know how you do it. I'm guessing he's one of the partners."

"That's one thing I've always admired about you. One day you decided that you didn't want to work for someone else and you opened your firm. I need security. I need a little safety and making partner here is going to give me that. Taiwon is one of the managing partners and I need his vote.

But I can do without his attitude. Such a diva."

"Why don't you start living? You're too good to be working here with jackasses like tall, dumb, and jerk face."

"All of the partners aren't like Taiwon. If they were, I would've left a long time ago."

Liza crossed her legs as she watched the software do its thing. "They don't deserve . . . Hot damn! Here she is." She turned her iPad around to show Chante the Spokeo page that showed the woman from the picture. Dayshea Brown, who lived on Parkwood Avenue. "Now that we have a name, all we need to do is find her Facebook page."

"What if she doesn't have a Facebook page?"

Liza shot up her eyebrow in disbelief. "Who doesn't have a Facebook page these days? Other than you?"

"Point taken," Chante said as she crossed over to Liza and looked over her shoulder as she searched. Seconds later, the image of Dayshea Brown filled the iPad screen. She was doing the infamous duck lip kiss face, dressed in a too tight T-shirt showing off her ample breasts.

"And that is what he wanted to have sex with while I was at home waiting for him,"

Chante hissed. "I feel like I need to be dipped in Clorox."

"I told you he's attracted to hood rats. Sort of like that Kanye West song."

"Eww, you know I don't listen to that crap. What's the name of the song?"

Liza shrugged. "I don't remember, but that's beside the point. Let's focus on finding this girl and getting her to tell her story."

"Maybe we should wait until after the debate," she said.

Liza nodded. "Knowing him and Nic, they are going to try to have Robert look like some saint. We know that isn't true and the voters should know that as well."

"And then this girl will come out and tell everyone about her romp with Robert. How are we going to deflect attention from me, who people think he's still going to marry?"

Liza chewed her bottom lip. "Well, you can tell everyone that the engagement is off because he's a dishonest and dishonorable man. One statement."

Chante pursed her lips and rolled her eyes. "You and I both know that won't be enough."

"I can make it enough," Liza said.

"You're good, but you are no Judy Smith."

"Whatever! Remember the NBA player who's wife was arrested for fighting at the

NC Music Factory? Why do you think that story disappeared?"

"Because no one really gives a shit about the NBA in this city? I'm not saying that you aren't good at your job, but this is sex and politics. These stories don't just disappear," Chante said. "Still, I trust that you will keep the media off my back." She looked down at her left hand and stroked her empty ring finger. Chante closed her eyes and thought about the ring that Robert had given her. "That bastard."

"You should've kept the ring, we could have pawned it," Liza said. "It had great clarity."

"Shut up. How much do you think I would've gotten for it?"

Liza shook her head. "Too late now. So, are we going to go to her place or not?"

"Why not? Leaving this office means that I can avoid whatever Taiwon wanted." Liza and Chante headed to the parking deck and drove to the north Charlotte neighborhood.

"What if she's at work?" Chante asked as she navigated down the street.

"Five dollars says that she isn't." Liza held her hand out to her friend. "Make sure I get my money."

Chante pulled into the driveway of the house that the GPS had led them to. The front door was open and the volume of the TV could be heard from the yard.

"I want my money," Liza said as she and Chante headed up the steps. "Hello?" She tapped on the torn screen door. Dayshea walked to the door, her head covered by a greasy satin cap and holding a cigarette in her left hand.

"Who the hell are you bitches?" she asked as she tightened the belt around her robe.

"Dayshea Brown, I'm Liza Palmer."

She gave Liza a long, hard once-over. "Oh, yeah, I know who you are. You walked in on me screwing your old man. I know you didn't come here looking for trouble." She squared up behind the door and Liza grinned.

"Honey, he was not my man and I'm here because I have questions."

"I don't have time for this! It's almost time for *The Young and The Restless* and I'm not missing my stories because you have questions." She sucked her teeth and rolled her eyes. "Anyway, you need to be asking him questions because I . . ."

Chante pushed Liza aside. "Is Victor Newman still raising hell?"

Dayshea laughed. "Don't tell me you watch my show. What do you want?"

"The truth about you and Robert,"

Chante said. "How did y'all meet? What did he tell you about himself?"

Dayshea glanced at the thin gold-plated watch on her wrist. "Look, honey, I don't have a whole lot and sometimes money is tight. So, I do things I'm not always proud of. But I don't fuck married men. That's just wrong." She turned to Liza. "It's not my fault your husband lied."

"Damn it, for the last time he is not my husband. He wasn't even my boyfriend."

Dayshea rolled her eyes. "I couldn't tell. You went off like he was your man and that's the kind of drama I don't need in my life."

"Actually," Chante said once Dayshea allowed them to walk inside, "he was supposed to be my husband."

"Damn!" Dayshea exclaimed, throwing her hands up. "I can't fight both of y'all. Was paid to —"

"You're misunderstanding us," Liza said, throwing her hands up. "We're not here to fight you. We're here to help you."

"You got money?" Dayshea asked.

Liza and Chante looked at each other and smiled. "We have an opportunity for you to make way more money than you were given to let Robert . . . well, you know," Liza said.

"What do y'all bougie gangsters want

from me?" Dayshea asked as she folded her arms across her chest.

"Your side of the story. Your truth. Robert used you and lied about who he is," Chante said. "And let's not forget that he lied to me and I was sitting at home planning a wedding. And eating celery when I wanted chicken and waffles."

"Wait," Dayshea said. "You left him?"

Chante nodded. "But I don't blame you. He was the one who promised me that he loved me and would be faithful."

"And if a man lies to the woman he loves, he can't be trusted," Liza interjected.

"Is he important or something?"

"He wants to be. But we can't let that happen," Liza said.

Dayshea dropped her arms and shrugged. "And I'm supposed to stop this somehow? By telling people that we had sex?"

"That he paid you for sex," Chante replied.

"As a matter of fact," Liza asked, "who paid you?"

"Why don't y'all sit down?" Dayshea pointed to a ratty sofa near the TV. "We can talk after my show goes off."

Chante and Liza sat on the sofa and silently prayed that nothing would crawl out of it.

■ ■ ■ ■

Jackson finally saw Teresa smile. They'd finally agreed on the wording of the opening statement and the crafting of the story that he was going to tell about why he was running for office and how taking care of the military and the poor made the state better. He could finally relax a little. Or at least not have another uncomfortable discussion about his personal life. Now he just had to run to the cleaners and pick up his suit.

"Jackson," Teresa said, "this is really good and we're going to win this debate tonight."

"I'm glad you think so. We've put together the facts, what people need from their leaders, and how I plan to be accountable to them when they elect me."

"And I'm pretty sure we have the edge on anything Montgomery has planned. Like you said, he doesn't deal well in issues and facts. Noticed that throughout the campaign. Anyway, we can officially take a break."

"Good. I'm going to grab my suit and some food. Want me to bring you anything back?"

She shook her head. "Your idea of a vegan

meal is a salad. I need more than that." Pointing her finger at Jackson's chest, she said, "While you're out remember what you have to do to win."

He sighed, not wanting to say it out loud. But he knew he was supposed to stay away from Liza. "Yeah," he replied. "Be back in an hour." When he arrived at his car, Jackson checked his phone for the first time that day. He noticed that he hadn't gotten a call or text from Liza all day. He couldn't help but wonder if she was still going to make it to the debate. If she did show up, he wasn't going to ignore her. After all, he'd talked her into coming and he wouldn't mind hearing her thoughts on the debate once everything was over. Preferably in bed and naked.

Jackson couldn't deny that Liza knew her stuff, and under different circumstances, she'd be a part of his team. Maybe then he'd really get an understanding as to why people had to be on that social media network twenty-four hours a day. He had been glad that Teresa had gotten two college students to run the campaign's Facebook and Twitter accounts. That stuff gave him a headache, but in this digital society, it was a necessary evil.

Liza probably would've had us going viral,

he thought with a smile. Every time he thought about her he couldn't help but smile. He needed her in his life. He wanted more mornings where they'd wake up and have breakfast in her kitchen and more nights where she'd fall asleep in his arms. Would she want that if he ignored her until the election? It really wouldn't be fair to her for him to do that. But what would all these months of campaigning mean if he gave it all up for love?

Love? Was he in love with Liza Palmer?

He shook those thoughts out of his head as he pulled into the parking lot of the dry cleaner's. Jackson knew he had to keep his mind on the debate. If he wanted to win, then he had to be laser focused on the task at hand. Taking his claim ticket, he got his suit, then headed off to grab some lunch. Driving to Crisp on Seventh Street, he looked down at his phone to see if Liza had texted or called.

Still nothing. That's when he decided to text her. Hope you're having a good day. Will be looking for you tonight at the debate.

CHAPTER 23

The closing credits of *The Young and The Restless* rolled across the screen, but for the last hour Dayshea hadn't been paying attention to the show. The look on her face told Liza that she was mad as hell.

"So, he was engaged to you," Dayshea said as she nodded toward Chante then turned to Liza. "And was supposed to be your best friend. And he's a politician? Do you know how much that man paid me?"

"No," Chante said, then rolled her eyes. Liza tapped her friend on the knee. They had Dayshea on their side and they needed to keep her there.

"Seventy-five dollars. Talking about he needed a quick release and it wouldn't take long. I told him that I don't sell my body to married men or men who had pussy waiting at home. Then he wants to go all John Edwards on me. I'm not trying to be the

North Carolina version of Monica Lewinsky."

"And we're not trying to put you in that position, but you should tell the truth about the person that folks think will be the next senator," Liza said, struggling to keep her voice even. *Seventy-five dollars. Robert should be ashamed of himself.* "We want to let the voters know that they have an honest choice and a man who cheats on the woman he says that he loves."

"If a man does that to someone he loves, what do you think he's going to do to the people who would send him to Raleigh?" Chante asked. "It broke my heart to know that the man I was planning to marry had been unfaithful to me."

Liza handed Chante a tissue for effect. Chante wiped away her imaginary tears. "See," she continued, "that's why I can respect your policy of not having sex with men who are engaged or married. But when men aren't honest, they turn you into a liar. Don't you want to expose that? And clear your name? This will come out and you can be in front of the media blitz or you can get rolled over by it. Knowing Robert, he'll say you seduced him."

Oh, you're good, Liza thought as she watched her friend's act. Tears sprang into

Dayshea's eyes and she reached out to Chante. "I don't like a lying-ass man," Dayshea said. "I'll tell the truth about him because we have enough liars in power. Even Obama. You know he's a part of the illuminati."

Chante and Liza exchanged a quick glance but didn't say a word. Dayshea looked from Liza to Chante and smiled. "Oh, you didn't think I had that knowledge, huh?"

"Just make sure you two don't say anything about it when you're doing interviews with the local media," Liza said. "Everyone doesn't really understand or want to believe in that. And this has nothing to do with President Obama." Liza shuddered inwardly, thinking that if this girl got in front of a reporter and started talking crazy everything was going to blow up in their collective faces.

Dayshea nodded and pointed her finger at Liza. "You're right and I don't want to become a target of the Koch brothers either."

"Right," Chante said. She stood up and walked toward the door. "We're going to get going and start the process rolling."

"Wait a minute," Dayshea said. "I can't go on TV without getting my hair done. I need to go see my girl Mesha at . . ."

"Don't worry about any of that," Liza said. "I'm going to have a stylist come visit you. How long are you going to be home? She's going to call you and set up a time."

Chante and Liza wanted to run out of Dayshea's house, but instead they shook hands with her and calmly made their exit.

Once they were in the car, Chante shook her head and let out a string of profanities. Liza was shocked. She'd never heard her friend this angry.

"You need to calm down," Liza said.

"He was supposed to love me and he was out buying sex from a woman like her! I'm a fool. I'm beginning to understand why you don't put your heart out there anymore."

"Hold up," Liza said. "Both of us can't be vengeful and bitter. I think I have that down."

Chante closed her eyes and pounded the steering wheel. "Why did I believe that he was going to be the one? That this whole love at first sight thing was real?"

Liza thought about her connection to Jackson. It had been instant and intense. But was it real? Would she be crying on Chante's shoulder because reality wouldn't live up to the fairy tales she'd crafted in her mind?

"You know what I really was to him?" Chante continued. "I was a tool. A way to move the numbers in his direction so that he could win this senate seat. On paper, we were the perfect couple. Would've looked good at political events in Raleigh and in the papers. But he went out and paid that woman seventy-five dollars for sex. Who does that?"

Liza listened. Chante's words hit her like lasers. What was she to Jackson? Reaching into her purse, she pulled out her iPhone and smiled when she saw Jackson's message. Her day was getting better. And she couldn't wait to see him at the debate. She shot him a quick text telling him that she was looking forward to seeing him win the debate.

But the cynical side of her, bolstered by Chante's words, wondered if she was a tool for Jackson as well. The women headed back to Chante's office, where Liza grabbed her car and headed to her own office so that she could make Dayshea's appointment with the stylist. "You're going down, Robert!" she muttered as she drove through the streets of Uptown Charlotte.

Six o'clock can't get here fast enough ran through Jackson's mind like a mantra as he

311

and his camp put the final touches on the debate preparations. He hadn't had time to reply to Liza's text nor finish his lunch, and that had been hours ago.

He was excited, though. Ready to talk about the issues and win more voters. He hoped that Robert would keep his word about a clean campaign during the debate and focus only on the issues. Part of him worried that he would try to bring Liza into the debate; he didn't want things to get personal.

Liza was off limits. She was personal. She was his and he wasn't going to let anyone hurt her. Especially not Robert Montgomery. Jackson started to ponder if there was something more behind the falling-out between Robert and Liza. The last thing he wanted was to be blindsided again. *What if they had been more than friends? A lover's quarrel with political implications? Nah, I don't think she would let that happen. Who knows where Montgomery's head is. Then again, he was engaged to her friend,* Jackson thought as he crossed over to the window in the conference room. He hated that he was having doubts about her because he'd been stung so badly by Hillary. Granted, these women were like night and day. Still . . .

Teresa walked in, breaking into his

thoughts. "Calm before the storm," she said. "Are you ready?"

"As ready as I'll ever be."

"All you have to do is show the confidence that people have always seen from you. Think about how you saved that man from jumping off that roof. You're saving this whole district in the debate tonight."

Jackson nodded. "The last thing we need is a senator who uses personal attacks on people he no longer agrees with."

Teresa rolled her eyes. "What does Liza Palmer have to do with this election?"

"It's a pattern. Remember, you're the one who gave me his file from college and those allegations about rape and paying some girl off."

She smiled. "And all of this time, I thought you weren't paying attention."

"I'm still not bringing any of that up tonight."

Nodding, Teresa patted him on the shoulder. "Then let's get ready to rumble."

Jackson grinned, feeling relaxed and ready. "Let's do this," he exclaimed with a fist pump.

"That's my senator!" she said, mirroring Jackson's excitement. He looked down at his watch. Still a little more than two hours before the debate.

"Maybe we should go over to the venue," Jackson said.

"Reading my mind," she replied. "I want to make sure you hit your marks."

Jackson wanted to laugh. This wasn't the kind of theater that he was used to. Preparing for battle felt a lot easier than getting ready for this debate. Maybe it was better not to know your enemy so well.

About fifteen minutes later, Jackson pulled up to the Harvey B. Gantt Center in uptown, where the debate was to be held. As he got out of the car, he saw Robert and Nic walking into the building as well. Nic spotted him first.

"Mr. — er — Sergeant Franklin, it's nice to see you," he said. There wasn't a hint of sincerity in his voice. Robert stayed silent and sized up his opponent.

"Gentlemen," Jackson said with the same falseness. He certainly didn't think that either of them were gentlemen and he questioned if they were actually men. "Good luck tonight."

"I don't need luck," Robert said. "But I hope you brought your rabbit's foot."

Just as Jackson was about to react, Teresa walked up to him. "Nic. I'd say nice to see you but that would be nothing but a lie."

"Aww, Teresa, it's nice to see that a relic

like you is still trying to stay relevant."

"And a little prick like you is still making backroom deals to put scum in office." Teresa smiled as if she'd told him that his suit was amazingly tailored to his body. "Let's go."

"Bitch," Nic muttered to Teresa's retreating frame.

"There's some history there that's pretty brutal, huh?" Jackson asked Teresa when they entered the building.

"Yes. But we're not getting into that right now. We're going to work on beating the shit out of Robert Montgomery."

"At some point, you're going to have to tell me why this is so important to you."

Teresa paused. "I was Dominic's mentor on a campaign to elect Charlotte mayor Thomas Hankins. I thought Hankins was an honorable guy. He'd been on the city council for twenty years as an at-large member. That doesn't happen in this city." She closed her eyes and sighed.

"I had worked on five of his reelection campaigns and I pretty much thought I knew the guy. Fair. Clean. Honest. Well, his opponent was gay. It was kind of like the worst-kept secret in politics, but the man had never come out publicly. Nic, my little protégé, had spotted him in a compromis-

315

ing situation with another man. He brought this information to Hankins and I thought we were going to kick his little ass out of the office, but Hankins blackmailed that man and forced him to drop out. At that time, I'd never been so disappointed in a politician before. I quit; I cussed Nic for being a little shit and told him that one day his underhanded bull would come back on him. I'm still waiting for that day to happen."

As Jackson shook his head, it started to make sense to him why Robert would allow all of those things to be said about Liza. And since she wasn't a part of Jackson's campaign, officially, it still looked as if he'd kept the clean campaign promise.

"I'd love to expose Nic, but in this town image is everything and substance doesn't matter," Teresa said. "That's why you have to win and be above reproach. I can't have another one of Nic's cronies in an office he doesn't deserve."

Jackson nodded and then he and Teresa walked onto the stage. A few minutes passed before Robert and Nic walked in and took their place on the other side of the stage. Neither Jackson nor Teresa acknowledged their presence. But Jackson felt them looking at him. "Ignore them," Teresa whispered.

"They are showing that you're already winning."

Liza watched in stunned silence as the new and improved Dayshea walked to the front door. Gone were her cherry-red weave and spiderweb-looking eyelashes. Her hair was styled in a chic bob with some skin tone–appropriate auburn highlights. Her makeup was fresh and understated. And Liza wanted to jump up and down when she saw those garish acrylic nails were gone.

"Girl, I'm fancy now!" she said when she caught Liza's eye. "Shoot, I can hang out with you and your bougie gangster friend now."

"Chante isn't a gangster, unless you get her in the courtroom."

Dayshea stood on her tiptoes and looked over Liza's shoulder. "Where is she? Before the media gets here, I want to apologize to her. I hope I didn't cause the breakup of her engagement. Like I said, I don't fu—"

"And that's very honorable. What are you going to do now?" Liza asked. Dayshea shrugged.

"I was going to school, but money got tight and I got hooked up with the wrong damn man. Who knew he was mixing cocaine with my weed? Got me hooked on that shit and then he pimped me out. I started loving myself less and less every day. I'd see the women in uptown at night with men who loved them and the man who was supposed to love me wanted me to sell my body so we could get high."

Liza ached for her. Was she another user in this woman's life? "Dayshea," she said. The woman held up her hand.

"I didn't tell you that because I want you to feel sorry for me or give me some pity. I've messed up and I realize it's time for me to fix my life. I was slack when I took that money from Robert and didn't ask him if he had a woman at home. But I wanted my next hit so bad. When you walked in there, I was just embarrassed and ashamed."

"You're not the one who should feel that way. Robert lied to you and he's trying to pull the wool over the eyes of all of these people who will be depending on him for leadership."

"You sure you ain't just mad at him because of what he did to your girl?"

Liza shrugged. "I'm not going to lie and say I'm not upset. But don't you think it's time for us to stand up to men like him and your ex?"

"Oh, I shot him." Dayshea laughed. "He knows to leave Miss Dayshea alone."

Liza dropped her head and hid her grin. And just in the nick of time, Chante pulled up with a cameraman and reporter from Channel Fourteen.

"Where is everybody else?" Liza whispered to her friend when she walked up the steps.

"At the debate. This was the best I could do. But it will be on a twenty-four-hour loop."

Liza gritted her teeth as Dayshea led the reporter and cameraman inside. "A loop no one will see."

"Calm down. You, of all people, know how the Charlotte media works. No one is going to ignore this story."

Liza looked at her watch. "We need to get this rolling. I actually have to go to the debate."

Chante rolled her eyes, and even though she was through with Robert, she felt some kind of way about the turn in their relationship. Liza seemed to read those thoughts on her friend's face and wrapped her arm around her shoulder.

"It'll get easier."

Chante leaned her head on her friend's shoulder. "I feel like a fool. And part of me still wants his dream to come true."

"I always thought he'd be president," Liza replied. " 'Hail to the Chief' used to be his ringtone on my phone."

"So, how did we get fooled by the same man?"

Liza shrugged. "He knew how to play us and what we both wanted to hear. That means he's pretty much a psychopath, pathological liar, and so not the man for the job."

"But your boy Jackson Franklin is different?"

"This has nothing to do with Jackson. He won't even discuss politics with me. What we share . . ."

"What you share?" Chante wiggled her eyebrows. "This is something more than just a little stress sex?"

"I don't know." She expelled a sigh. "I hope it's more. I want it to be. I haven't felt this way in a long time."

Smiling, Chante tapped Liza on the arm. "Good luck, and if you're going to be at that debate on time, then you'd better get a move on."

"Are you okay with this?"

Chante nodded. "It's no longer just about him cheating. I was about to let Robert sink our friendship, our sisterhood. That's not cool, and I'm not going to sit by and let him think he got over."

"We've all made that mistake before. And

Robert knew you had thoughts about what went on with us in the past so he played on them. I have to admit, that is a skill that would have served him good in office. But if this interview gets traction, he won't be elected head of the PTA for the rest of his life."

Chante pointed at her friend. "I hope Jackson will teach you how not to always seek vengeance. You're like Batman with a Twitter account sometimes. I almost feel sorry for Robert."

"Really?"

"I said almost! Anyway, get going and let me know how everything turns out."

Liza waved good-bye to her friend and then dashed to her car. It was almost five-thirty and she knew traffic was going to be a little hectic. But she didn't want to miss the opening statements. Moreover, she wanted to see what Jackson was wearing. Smiling, Liza couldn't wait until the debate was over and she could celebrate with her man.

My man? Maybe I'm getting ahead of myself, she thought as she came to a red light. *This man has an election to win and there's no telling what his life is going to be like if he does win. How is he going to split time between here, Raleigh, and the voters? And where will*

I fit into all of this?

The angry blare of a horn alerted her to the fact that she'd missed the green and the yellow light at the intersection. She waved at the driver and forced herself to pay attention to the traffic signal and stop borrowing trouble.

It was about six-fifteen when Liza arrived at the center. She was actually surprised to see the number of people who were in attendance. The PR professional inside her wondered if the crowd was there because of the rumors floating in the media or if these were people who wanted to get information about the first state senator who would represent their district.

She took a seat in the back of the auditorium and listened to the evening's host tell the audience how the debate would be conducted: the time that each candidate had to answer questions and to make rebuttal responses. Liza stifled a laugh. There was no way that long-winded Robert would stay within the time frame of two minutes.

She looked up at Jackson. God, he looked good in that suit. His eyes were filled with determination. He deserved this seat. Not because it was something that he'd been preparing for over the years, but because he actually wanted to serve.

Glancing at Robert, she didn't see that desire and determination on his face. Simply a smugness that she'd managed to miss over the years. Maybe she should've listened to the rumblings about him when they were in college. There had always been rumors about shady things that Robert was involved in, and then there had been the alleged sexual assault. At the time, Liza had written it off as people hating on Robert, because there had been no way that he'd be involved in anything like that.

She'd even quit her column at the *Daily Tar Heel* because she hadn't agreed with the coverage that the student paper had given to the sexual assault, which allegedly involved Robert and his fraternity brothers. She'd also led a student protest against the paper, calling the editor and the majority of the staff racist.

Maybe if she'd paid more attention to facts back then, she never would've spent all of these years building Robert up to be this paragon of virtue. She turned her attention to the stage as Jackson stepped forward to give his opening statement.

"Ladies and gentlemen, North Carolina is facing a crisis. We're at a crossroads and if we are going to get on the right path, then we have to make the right choices. Protect those who have protected us and fought for this country. Make education a priority and pay teachers what they're worth. We're losing in the fight to educate our children, and without a foundation for a future, North Carolina will suffer. We have to cut the unemployment rate and bring industries to this area that will sustain growth. And if we're going to ask taxpayers to help us lure them here, then we need to make sure these businesses stick around.

"Our seniors need our protection. They need us to make sure that we don't cut Medicare, that we don't allow an agenda that protects the rich and powerful to hurt the seniors and the poor in this state. Sending me to Raleigh will ensure that the people in the state who need the assistance of the General Assembly the most will get it. It's time to stop sending the status quo back to Raleigh. It's time to have representatives in place who aren't out for power but have your best interests at heart. Tonight, I hope to earn your vote and go to the General Assembly to represent the best interests."

The thunderous applause almost made Jackson smile, but he remembered Teresa's coaching. Keep his face soft, but don't smile too much or show when he's upset. He needed to let people trust him.

Robert took to the middle of the stage, smiling at the crowd. "I'm Robert Montgomery, and when it comes to representing this district, we can't leave it in the hands of an idealist. I've worked with many of our General Assembly members and that's one of the reasons why I knew I had to throw my hat in the ring. I believe people want to do the right thing, but they just don't know how because there is so much noise about Republican versus Democrat. What we need to focus on is building coalitions and getting work done without the fighting and the arguments. That's not getting anything done. That's not helping the people of this district of the state of North Carolina.

"First, we have to heal rifts; then we can get people on the same page and make changes for North Carolina. We can provide better options for the people of this state and secure a future for North Carolina that will benefit all of the citizens of our great state." He took a bow and smiled at the crowd as the applause went up. Jackson fought to keep his composure. If he hadn't thought that Robert was an asshole before, he'd be sure of it now.

The moderator restated the rules of the debate and then started with the first question. Since Jackson gave his opening first, Robert answered the question — which was about coal ash being buried at Charlotte Douglas International Airport.

Robert walked from behind his podium as if he were channeling Mitt Romney. "Clean energy is important and we have to make sure we do everything that we can to save our drinking water supply. The airport in Asheville already has a program where they bury coal ash for Duke Energy, which is one of our largest employers in the state."

A rumble rippled through the crowd. Jackson chewed the inside of his jaw to keep from smiling. No one was happy with Duke Energy and Robert was losing any support he'd gained with his powerful opening statement. Jackson couldn't wait to answer the question.

"Mr. Franklin, your response?" the moderator asked.

Jackson stood behind his podium and turned toward the audience. "Charlotte Douglas is not a dumping ground, and the cities around this great state should not and will not be responsible for Duke Energy's waste. We're acting as if this is a department of the state and it is not. Duke Energy needs to be held responsible for cleaning up its own mess."

A thundering of applause erupted. The moderator called for quiet so that Jackson could continue. "A private company shouldn't have the power to buy legislation to increase its revenues. Let me ask this question: Does everyone in North Carolina work for Duke Energy? No, they don't. It's past time for the General Assembly to stop bowing to corporations and remember who put them in office."

"I wasn't suggesting anything like that," Robert interrupted. "But we have to remember that companies move to our state, and specifically this district, because it is easy to work with our government."

"That may be true," Jackson said. "But our government is first and foremost by the people and for the people. Of the companies that have moved here — to this district — in the last three years, two of them brought employees from the area that they moved from. Jobs were scarce to the unemployed residents of this area. So, if we're going to be easy to work with, then we need to make sure that everyone benefits."

More applause and a sneer from Robert let Jackson know that he was winning.

Thirty minutes passed and they answered questions about jobs, clean energy, and transportation issues. Jackson felt good about the direction of the debate and the fact that they stuck to the issues. And just when he thought the good feeling would last, during an exchange about experience, Robert went below the belt.

"And just what experience do you have?" he asked heatedly. "Leading soldiers in a war has nothing to do with working in politics. Your personal choices of whom you align yourself with show that. You have a former call girl working on your election campaign." Silence claimed the room. Jackson wanted to jump from behind the podium and choke the living hell out of Robert.

"Excuse me?"

"Liza Palmer."

"We're going to move on from this line of —" the moderator started to say.

"Liza Palmer is not working on my campaign, but she did work on yours. Why are you trying to say these things about her now?"

"Because once I found out about her character, I fired her."

"Gentlemen!" The moderator banged on the table. "We're moving on."

CHAPTER 24

Liza wanted to jump out of her seat, rush the stage, and beat Robert to within an inch of his sorry life. Did he seriously just call her a former call girl? That son of a . . . Gritting her teeth, she blinked back the tears in her eyes as she wondered why Jackson didn't defend her. *Now you're just being stupid. That man can't act like a jealous boyfriend. He's trying to win this debate.*

Still, it didn't stop her from wanting to see Jackson punch Robert in the face. Her professional side knew that could never happen, but sitting there listening to Jackson as he distanced himself from her hurt like hell. She decided that she needed to get out of Gantt Center before a reporter spotted her.

Ducking out the door, she was glad to see she had gotten away unnoticed.

Or so she thought.

"Liza," Nic said from behind her. "Aren't you going to stay for the finale?"

"Go to hell, bastard," she snapped as she kept walking.

"And you thought you were going to ruin his life because he cheated on your friend. Guess you should be a little more cautious about people you talk to," he said. Liza stopped in her tracks. She was mad as hell and someone had to feel her wrath. Nic would be the perfect verbal punching bag.

"You know what, you're an asshole. Nothing about you is good. Nothing. You and Robert deserve each other. But I'm not going to sit by and watch you two liars try to trick voters into thinking that Robert is going to Raleigh for anything other than the power and glory. He doesn't give a damn about this district or making anyone's life better. And you're just a puppet master, doing whatever it takes to get your boy elected no matter who you hurt."

"Do you really think you matter?" Nic laughed. "You play on the Internet and pretend you're making a difference. If this call girl thing doesn't gain traction, there are plenty of people who can tell the press just what kind of coattail rider you are."

"You pompous jackass."

"Your insults are juvenile. If I were you, I'd hop back on Twitter and stay away from politics. You can't run with the big dogs, little girl."

"Watch me," she said, then stomped away. "You have no idea who you're dealing with, old man." Pulling her cell phone from her pocket, Liza called Chante.

"How's the debate?" Chante asked when she answered the phone.

"That man. That piece of sh— Robert stood on that stage and called me a former call girl."

"He did what? Son of a bitch!"

"How did the interview go?"

Chante laughed. "Well, let's just say I'm glad I kept those pictures you sent me because the reporter didn't believe Dayshea at first. It's going to be the top story at eleven. So, Robert talking about call girls is really kind of ironic."

"Meet me at Amelie's," Liza said. "I need sugar."

"Wait, you aren't going to celebrate with Jackson?"

A chill ran through her body. There was no way she and Jackson could be together now, and she was still deep in her feelings about the way he responded to Robert's accusation about her. But what had she expected him to do — declare his love for her and lose the election?

"I don't think Jackson can afford to be

seen with me right now if he plans to win this election."

"I hate politics," Chante said. "See you in a little bit."

After hanging up, Liza dashed to her car, sat in the parking deck, and cried a little bit before heading to the bakery to meet her friend.

Jackson searched the crowd for Liza when the debate ended. He meandered through the crowd, shaking hands with audience members who'd stopped him, answering their questions while glancing around the room looking for Liza. He wanted to make sure she was all right after Robert called her out again. That bastard. He wished they could meet in a street fight. How dare he spread those lies so publicly.

"Mr. Franklin," a man said, "you earned my vote tonight. I can't stand how we kowtow to Duke Energy because they got their boy in the governor's mansion. Somebody needs to challenge that and it sure won't be Montgomery."

"Well, I appreciate your support," Jackson said as they shook hands. "It's time for government to hold companies responsible for their bad deeds."

"And that coal ash is going to kill us all.

My granddaughter lives near the Dan River. Twenty-three years old and she has breast cancer. That's not right." Tears welled up in the old man's eyes. Jackson's heart broke and he realized these were the voices that needed to be heard in Raleigh. It was people like this man who were suffering and disillusioned with the direction of local politics whom he would carry on his back if he won this election. Jackson handed him a business card from the center where he worked.

"Sir, if you ever need to talk, just call me."

The man took the card from Jackson's hand and smiled. "God bless you. And I hope you don't ever change or let that hooker bring you down."

Gritting his teeth, Jackson nodded and moved on. Did people actually believe what Robert said about Liza?

By the time the crowd thinned, Jackson realized Liza either was gone or didn't show up. Part of him hoped that she had missed the debate, didn't have to hear the person she thought was her friend tell a blatant lie on her. Then again, he was feeling some kind of way about her not being there when she said that she would be. Teresa crossed over to him and shook his hand.

"That was awesome. Now we do need to do a little damage control about Liza again, but you won hands down. If anyone here was on the fence, you pushed them over it."

"Did you see if Liza was here?" he asked.

Teresa frowned. "Really?"

"Yes."

"No, I didn't see her and I hope that she wasn't here. Robert and . . ." Teresa paused as her phone chimed. Jackson watched her as she began to laugh. "And this is on Channel Fourteen? Let me put you on speaker and repeat what you just said."

"Who is that?" Jackson asked.

"Just listen," Teresa mouthed as she pressed the speaker button on her phone.

"All right, T," a female voice said. "Channel Fourteen just aired an interview with Dayshea Brown, who has several arrests for prostitution, and she said that Robert Montgomery paid her for sex. Should I tweet the link?"

Jackson chuckled. "Maybe this is why he keeps bringing up call girls."

"And," the voice on the phone said, "there are pictures. Not some grainy, maybe-that's-his-forehead pictures either."

Jackson swore under his breath. Was this why Liza was missing?

"Thanks, Tabitha. And no, do not tweet the link to that story from the campaign's account," Teresa said, then ended the call.

"Looks like the tide is turning in our direction and we have clean hands."

Jackson was about to say he didn't know how clean their hands were since he knew the pictures came from Liza. "What?" Teresa asked.

"Nothing. I need to go," he said.

"Wait, I'm pretty sure the —"

"I'm not commenting on this," Jackson said. "If he has to buy sex, that has nothing to do with —"

"It speaks to his character. And it's illegal. We can't sit by silently and send a criminal to Raleigh. That should be our statement," she said excitedly.

"Sounds like a decent statement. Besides, we have enough criminals in Raleigh already," Jackson said.

"So why send another. That will be your one and only statement, but we have to say something."

"We can send it out in an e-mail, but I won't be talking about it on camera. Besides, with the election so close, why don't we show the people what I'm going to be focused on if they send me to the General Assembly."

Teresa nodded. "That sounds like a great idea." Her cell phone began vibrating and chiming with indications of text messages.

"The circus has begun."

Shaking his head, Jackson tried to hide his smile. Though he wasn't going to comment on Robert's troubles, he couldn't help but think it couldn't have happened to a better person. The lies he'd told on Liza had turned around and bit him on the ass. Still, Jackson wished Liza hadn't shared those pictures with the media. But he understood why she did it. Sometimes you had to fight fire with fire, and if Robert doubted that Liza could bring the heat, he knew better now.

Jackson pulled his phone from his pocket and sent a text to Liza.

Where are you?

Liza felt the vibration of her phone in her pocket as she and Chante sipped coffee at Amelie's. Figuring that it was another reporter — the reason she'd turned the phone off anyway — she decided to ignore it.

"You have to admit," Chante said, "Robert couldn't have picked a worse time to call you out when his skeletons are real and . . ."

"I really don't want to talk about this anymore," Liza said with a sigh.

336

Chante nodded. "But what did you expect Jackson to do? Defend your honor?"

"That's what the illogical side of me wanted. He could've said something other than 'Liza Palmer is not working on my campaign.' " She fingered the lid of her coffee cup and realized that she really should've been drinking tea tonight. Forget the tea, she needed something stronger.

"But didn't you do a press conference with him to say that exact thing? Oh, my. You're falling in love with him. Your feelings are hurt." Chante burst into laughter, and if she had been anyone else, Liza would've hurled her half-eaten éclair in her face.

"And yours wouldn't be? This is exactly why I don't date. These emotional roller coasters aren't who I am. I know what he was doing up there. And if he were a client of mine, I would've told him to do the exact same thing."

"It's just different when your heart is in it," Chante said. She picked off a piece of her torte. "That's why it was so easy for me to believe everything Robert said about those pictures. I thought I loved him."

"I never said I love Jackson!" Liza exclaimed.

"You don't have to say it; it's written all over your face. I'm actually happy to see

337

you like this. Well, not near tears because that man didn't risk what he's been working for all of these months to defend your honor. But happy that you've opened your heart to love again."

Happy would be the last word that Liza would've used to describe how she was feeling. Foolish, maybe. Like a schoolgirl with a big crush, definitely. But happy? Not unless she had his arms around her. Not unless . . .

"Liza." She looked up and saw Jackson standing in front of her. Did she just think him up out of thin air?

"What are you doing here?" she asked.

"I've been calling and texting you and didn't get a response. I figured I'd try my luck and check here." Jackson glanced over at Chante. "I'm sorry, am I interrupting?"

Chante smiled and picked up her empty coffee cup. "Not at all. I was just going to get a refill and check out some of the new pastries. Please sit down."

Liza closed her eyes. Chante was about as subtle as a brick through a window.

"Do you mind if I sit?" Jackson asked when he noticed the frown on Liza's face.

"Are you sure you want to be seen with me?" she snapped. She didn't mean for it to come out like that. But damn it, she was mad.

"You did catch the debate?"

Liza folded her arms as Jackson sat down beside her. "Yes, I did. Thought that denial of you and I working together was spot on."

Jackson touched her arm. "My natural instinct was to reach across that stage and choke the living shit out of Montgomery. But you and I both know that couldn't happen. And I've already told you that I want my personal life separated from politics."

Reluctantly, she nodded. "And," he continued. "I see you've been busy."

"I-I didn't do a thing that wouldn't have come out sooner or later. I just made sure Ms. Brown wouldn't be dragged through the mud like so many women who get caught up in political sex scandals."

"You're going tit for tat with Robert and . . ."

"It doesn't concern you, because *Liza Palmer is not working on your campaign.*"

"It does concern me, because if you get hurt in all of this I'm going to be the one picking up the pieces. What you're doing is personal with Montgomery."

"And what he's doing to me could ruin my business. Saying those things about me in a public forum like that and he's the one buying sex, I can't and won't allow him to get away with it. You want to play it clean

339

and run your campaign with no dirt, that's fine. But whether you become the first senator of district forty-five or not, I have to keep my business going."

Jackson stroked her cheek. "I almost believe that. But I know you. You like to destroy people who hurt you. And I know Robert has hurt you. How far are you willing to go with this?"

"As far as I have to. Again, Jackson, this isn't about you or this race. You talk about me taking it personal — there is no other way for me to take it. I'm not running for office." Closing her eyes, she sighed. "I can't and won't let him try to destroy everything I've built. I'm not going to be like my mother."

Jackson wrapped his arms around her and gave her a tight hug, then kissed her on the cheek. "Liza, I'm here for you but I don't want your vendetta to harden you to the point where . . ."

"Where it affects your campaign? You know what, Jackson, I see where this is going and I'm not going to go there with you. You want to win this election and I'm not going to stand in your way." Liza rose to her feet and started for the door. Jackson followed her, not wanting to make a scene in the bakery, but he damned sure wasn't going to let her walk out that door with so much between them unresolved.

"Liza," he said, touching her elbow and forcing her to turn around and look at him.

"What?" Anger flashed in her eyes, followed by a bolt of sadness. Then it hit him: Liza was trying to hide what she was feeling. And she wasn't doing a good job of it. Taking her face in his hands, he kissed her softly.

"I'm not letting you go," he said. "How can I when I'm falling in love with you more every day?"

"You're what?" she whispered.

"Falling for you."

She stroked his face. "Can we do this? I know you want this senate seat, and with everything that Robert is saying about me . . ."

"I don't give a damn about that. Do I want this seat? Yes, I've worked too hard for it and I'm not going to insult your intelligence and pretend that I'm going to give everything up and we're going to sail off into the sunset."

"I appreciate that."

"But," Jackson said, "I'm not going to be robbed of a personal life because I want to be a senator."

Liza lifted her chin to Jackson's lips. "But

what if your personal life costs you the chance to be the senator that this district needs?"

"That's for the voters to decide. I'm not going to borrow trouble. And I'm not doing anything illegal." He wrapped his arms around her waist and pulled her closer to his chest.

"I think we need to take this behind closed doors."

"As much as I want to," Jackson said, "I have an early morning meeting and . . ."

"That's too bad," she said, then nibbled on her bottom lip. Liza tried to hide her disappointment, because she understood that things were about to get really busy with Election Day creeping up on them. Still, you don't tell a woman you're falling for her and hit her with the "I have an early morning" line.

"Let's have dinner tomorrow," he said as if he read her mind. "And you bring the dessert."

She smiled. "Chocolate?"

"Of course," he replied, then kissed her again. When their lips parted, Jackson almost wanted to say forget the morning meeting and ask her to stay with him. But he had to focus. He had to make sure he would be the winner of the election. "See you tomorrow, babe."

"Bye," she said as he dashed to his car. Liza wrapped her arms around herself and shivered. How could she feel so good and so bad at the same time?

Returning to the table she and Chante shared, she saw her friend was waiting there with another cup of coffee and a salted caramel brownie.

"Are you trying to gain back all of the weight you lost to fit in your wedding dress in one night?"

"Ha," Chante said. "I just figured you needed some chocolate since Jackson left without you. You two have more sizzle than a steak on a grill."

"I wonder if that's all we have," Liza said quietly, then broke a piece of the brownie. She toyed with it for a moment, thinking that she was borrowing trouble because of the thoughts she was having about Jackson, then popped it in her mouth.

"You love looking for shadows when none are there," Chante said. "Don't make me take my brownie back. That man is trying to win an election that's about six days away. I bet he has a lot of work to do. And he needs to be focused."

"You would've been a great political wife," Liza said with a laugh.

CHAPTER 25

By the time Liza arrived home, she was feeling a lot better. Chante had given her a much needed reality check, and the infusion of chocolate had the right touch of mood-lightening chemistry.

For once, Liza intended to go home, not worry about media coverage or Google alerts, and head straight to sleep. She was about to get out of the car when she saw headlights behind her and a strange car pulling into her driveway. Panic gripped her. Who was that? Had she been followed? Was she about to become a victim of a random crime? *Oh, God,* she thought. *Maybe I should've watched the news a little more closely.* Glancing in her rearview mirror, she saw a tall figure emerge from the car. As he stalked over to her vehicle, Liza's panic turned into rage. What in the hell was Robert doing at her house?

She opened the door as he approached

her car just so she could slam it into him. "What the hell do you want?"

He bent over in discomfort and then stood up and looked at her. "You selfish bitch," he spat.

"The same could be said about you," Liza said as she got out of the car. She kept her finger on the panic button just in case she needed to get her neighbors' attention.

"Why did you find that woman and —"

"Stop! Just stop. You're going to show up at my house in the middle of the night after you called me a former call girl and you have the unmitigated gall to be upset because I found the woman you paid to bend over your desk? You want to be upset about something, be upset that you can't keep your pants zipped. Be upset that you didn't cover your tracks better. And definitely be upset that you found a prostitute with morals."

"You are a piece of work, Liza. All these years you made me believe you had my back. Told me that you believed in me and would always support me. When I needed you the most, you turned your back on me. Who does that?"

"Seriously? Who goes on television and calls his friend a hooker? Who cheats on a woman and can't take getting caught like a man? That would be you, Robert. Why would I continue to support a loser like you? You're that same non-responsibility-taking frat boy from college. Have you ever respected a woman? Or did you think your mouth would always get you out of everything? I was fooled for so many years. You raped that girl in college, didn't you?"

"Shut up! You're pathetic, and guess what, even if I lose, people will still wonder if you were or are a hooker. And let's see how many celebrities will be seeking your services — well, you know what I mean."

Liza slapped him. "You're nothing but a power-hungry piece of shit and I wish I'd known this years ago. Then I wouldn't have wasted so much time believing that you were someone special. I guess you're just the son of a crackhead seeking revenge on all women because your mother didn't want you."

He stepped toward her and Liza gasped. "And you wonder why no man, not even your father, wants anything to do with you. You're right about one thing, women — especially ones like you — aren't worthy of my time or effort. You'd better stay out of my way."

"Go to hell, Robert. And maybe you need to stay out of my way, because I have way more dirt than you paying for sex. Don't make me use it."

"This isn't a Twitter beef, Liza. I will destroy you, because lies travel just as far as the truth." He spat on the ground, then walked to his car. Liza slowly counted to ten, because she wanted to march over to his car and toss bricks at the windshield. Instead, she watched his car leave her driveway and then she headed inside. If Robert wanted to start a war, he'd messed with the wrong person. And he should've known that. Sleep was now the last thing on her mind as she walked into the house. She grabbed her laptop and sat on the sofa. After booting up the computer, she looked for links to stories about Robert and Dayshea. Liza wasn't the least bit disappointed that every news agency in the state had picked up on the story. However, an Op-Ed piece in the *News and Observer* gave her pause. She read where the author talked about her alleged connection to the South Park Madam and questioned if she'd been the one who'd set Robert up with the prostitute he'd been photographed with.

"Asshole," she muttered as she clicked on another link; this one was about Dayshea and her criminal past. "Of course we're going to blame the victim."

The next link was an exposé about Robert's disrespect of women, including the alleged rape of the college student. There were former secretaries from the law firm who said Robert had sexually harassed them, but they settled with the partners to keep it quiet.

"Thank God for the *Huffington Post*," she said as she retweeted the link and shared it on her Facebook page. She thought about writing a blog about it, but that would require more energy than she had at the moment. Yawning, she closed her laptop down and wrapped her afghan around her shoulders, then drifted off to sleep. When morning came, she had plans to drop the hammer on Robert and his chances to be a senator or even a damned sanitation director.

Jackson couldn't sleep. He tossed and turned until about three A.M., when he realized that the reason sleep wouldn't come was because he missed Liza. Her warmth next to him and the faint sound of her breathing, it amazed him how quickly he'd grown used to that. How comfortable she made him feel in the midst of this election cycle. And he was nervous. Wondering what the morning would hold with all the allegations about Montgomery, and the final get-out-the-vote rallies that he was expected to attend to sway more people to his side. Then there would be the media's questions about Liza and Montgomery. How many "no comments" would he have to deliver tomorrow?

Flipping on his back, Jackson stared at the ceiling. Was he built for this? Had this senate campaign been in vain? What was he going to do if he actually made it to the General Assembly? He may have won the debate, but Robert did touch on some insecurities that he didn't want to admit he had. Maybe he didn't have the experience that a senator needed. Maybe he wasn't ready to tackle all of the issues that politicians had to deal with while they were in session. He couldn't just push through sweeping changes for veterans and their families alone.

Closing his eyes, Jackson decided that all he could do was go to sleep and let tomorrow happen when it was time. Still, as he drifted off to sleep, he yearned for the touch of Liza's soft hands.

The ringing of his cell phone woke Jackson from a deep sleep and a delicious dream of making love to Liza. It was a little after six and he was sure that it was Teresa.

"Yeah?" he said when he answered, not bothering to look at the caller ID.

"Did I wake you? I'm sorry," he heard Liza say. "I figured after last night's debate you'd be up and doing the morning shows."

"Not yet. I actually overslept. I had a lot on my mind."

"Really? Anything you want to talk about?"

"Mmm, I'd rather show you all of the things that I've been thinking about. They all involve you."

"Interesting, because you were the first thing on my mind this morning when I woke up. But I still waited an hour or so before calling you."

"We should've just woke up together. I'm sorry I didn't take you up on your offer last night."

"A mistake I'm sure you won't make again." She laughed and Jackson's morning wood twitched with desire.

"What are you doing right now?" he asked.

"Waiting for my coffee to brew."

"How long would it take you to get here, with some of your delicious coffee?"

Liza laughed. "All you want is my coffee?"

"Not at all. I want every part of you. Especially the most intimate parts."

"I'll see you in ten minutes," she said, and

350

then the line went dead. Jackson hopped out of bed and into the shower.

Liza brushed her teeth and then tossed cold water on her face. She was glad that she'd taken her shower as soon as she woke up. It was a cold shower to cool her hormones after dreaming of Jackson all night. She missed waking up in his arms this morning and she tried to ignore what she was feeling. She knew this man had a busy day; she'd been on his campaign website and seen that his first event was at ten, and that's why she decided to call him so early. She wanted him. Wanted to taste his lips and feel him deep inside her. Liza skipped putting on a bra or panties as she pulled her bandeau dress over her head. She pushed her hair back, then grabbed her purse and headed for her car. Part of her expected to find slashed tires or a broken windshield after her encounter with Robert, but her car was intact, so he hadn't lost his mind. Driving to Jackson's, she tried to forget what had happened with her and Robert. She wasn't going to tell Jackson about it at all. All she wanted to tell him was how deep she needed him to go.

It took her about fifteen minutes to arrive at Jackson's house, and when he opened the door, she threw herself into his arms. They kissed long and deep. Jackson's hands pushed up the bottom of her dress and stroked her naked bottom. Liza moaned as his fingers danced across her cheeks.

Her body tingled at his touch, hummed when his index finger found her throbbing bud of desire. She bit down on his bottom lip as he drew circles on her clitoris. Her moans turned into screams of passion as he thrust his finger in and out of her hot and awaiting valley. Liza's knees went weak as they broke their kiss and he thrust deeper into her with two fingers. Then Jackson dropped to his knees and brought his lips to the center of her desire. He sucked and licked her as she gripped his neck. Liza howled as she met a quick climax. Jackson continued to lick and suck the sweetness of her climax.

"Oh, Jackson," she moaned as he lashed her with his tongue. Liza stroked the back of his neck as if she was encouraging him to keep his mouth right where it was. It didn't take much encouragement for Jackson to get his fill of Liza's sweetness. The more he licked and sucked, the more he wanted her. And when her explosion dampened his face with her passion, he wanted nothing more than to bury his hardness deep inside her walls.

After pulling his mouth away from her, Jackson rose to his feet and scooped Liza into his arms. He took her into his bedroom and laid her on the bed, where he'd dreamed of doing this all night. The gleam in her eyes as they looked at each other made his erection grow harder. He reached into his nightstand drawer and pulled out a condom. After sliding the sheath in place, he spread Liza's thighs apart and entered her. She pierced the air with a guttural moan. Jackson thrust in and out of her while gripping her hips.

Liza pressed forward, matching his intensity. Jackson buried his lips in her neck, licking and kissing her as she ground against him. "Yes, yes, yes," she repeated like a mantra. Her moans encouraged him to dive deeper, finding all of her hot spots, every spot that made her moan, made her wetter, and brought her closer to climax.

Liza tilted her head back and screamed his name. Her release poured down her thighs and Jackson reveled in the hot wetness falling on him; it felt like a summer rain. "That's it, baby, come for me," he whispered in her ear.

Liza's walls gripped his heated erection as

she had another orgasm. And this time, Jackson came with her. Sated and sweaty, they collapsed in each other's arms. Silence enveloped them as Liza snuggled against Jackson's chest, inhaling his clean scent. Though she could've stayed wrapped in his arms all day, they had work to do.

"Liza," Jackson said.

"Mmm?"

"What happened to my coffee?"

She snatched the pillow from underneath his head and playfully hit him across the chest.

"Ouch, woman," he quipped, then rolled her over on her back. Pinning her arms down, he captured her lips in an ardent kiss that lit her body on fire. She wrapped her legs around his waist as their tongues tangoed. She parted her thighs and Jackson swam in her hot wetness. Liza had never felt such intense pleasure, felt so desired and wanted.

"Kiss me," Jackson ordered. Liza complied, adding a few nibbles to his bottom lip. Jackson growled as he exploded. Holding Liza tightly, he released a satisfied sigh. "Whew, I think if I had that coffee now, I'd have a heart attack."

She smiled and kissed him on the cheek. "Besides, this is a better way to wake up."

"You won't get an argument from me," he said, then glanced over at the clock on his nightstand. "Damn."

"I guess we have to get out of bed now," she said, taking note of the time.

"Unfortunately, but tonight, I won't make the mistake of sleeping alone. Will you stay with me tonight?"

"Yes, because I really missed you last night."

"Not nearly as much as I missed you. I know things are getting hectic right now and when I pick up that cell phone real life is going to creep in and steal more time out of my day."

"But this is what you have to do so that you can be that voice in the Senate for the wounded warriors, for the poor families in this state living paycheck to paycheck, and the seniors who depend on Medicare."

"Somebody has been on my website," he said with a grin.

"You'd better live up to those campaign promises or I might have to tweet about you."

"And that really does scare me. What is it about people and Twitter? Just because they read it in a tweet it's true? And then you with that blog. People love it. I'm kind of hoping that I never make you want to post about me on it."

"You mean I can't sing the praises of my war hero?" she joked. When Liza saw the frown on his face, she was a bit confused. "I was just joking."

"It's not that," he said with a sigh. "I hate being called a hero. I'd rather be on the battlefield than running for political office. When I was over there, I did what I was trained to do. I tell you what, when I went through those skin grafts and surgeries to remove the shrapnel from my leg, I didn't feel anything but pain. But when the doctor said I'd never see combat again, I felt like my life was over. I loved being a soldier. When I couldn't do it anymore, I felt useless."

"Jackson, I'm sorry."

He shook his head, then kissed her on the cheek. "It's not your fault. We all have our demons and mine is being called a hero. It just makes me remember that I can't do what I feel like I should be doing."

"And here I am pulling the scab off a wound. I'm sorry."

Jackson sat up and then eased out of the bed. "Come on, let's take a shower."

"I thought you had someplace to be, because you know if we get in that shower together, there won't be much cleaning going on."

Winking, he said, "I'm willing to take that chance. Besides, we have time."

CHAPTER 26

It was about eight-thirty when Jackson and Liza emerged from his house. She gave him a quick kiss, then turned on the ringer on her cell phone as she headed to the car. She wasn't surprised at the number of missed calls and text messages she had on her phone. Some from reporters, three from Chante, and, surprisingly, a text from Robert.

"Oh, he has a damned nerve," she muttered as she read his threat.

You'd better not try to use what happened last night against me. That was my last-ditch effort to save your ass. The gloves are off, Liza. If you cost me this election, I will make you suffer.

Common sense told her to ignore his text. But Liza was pissed. First, he'd followed her home, and now he was sending threats

— and in the form of a text! Either he was never as smart as she thought he was or he was desperate.

It didn't matter as she dialed his number. She just planned to give him a huge piece of her mind.

"Montgomery for Senate, this is Robert speaking."

"Robert, I had no idea you were an idiot."

"Liza Palmer? Why are you calling me?"

She could smell the setup. Either she was on speaker or he was recording the conversation to try to discredit her. Did he forget that she knew how he played his games? Hell, she'd given him the playbook.

"I was simply responding to your text message, Robert. It's illegal to text and drive so I thought I'd call you."

"I asked you not to contact me anymore."

"Then why did you text me? Should I do a screen shot and put it on Twitter so that the voters can catch you in yet another lie?"

The line went dead. *Check and mate,* she thought as she headed back to her house to change into something more appropriate for the office and possible media appearances. When she got home, she dressed in a pair of tailored black slacks and a ruffled pink tunic, then called Chante.

"Where have you been all morning?"

Chante asked. "I've said 'no comment' so many times that my throat is dry."

"I'm sorry, I really meant to get a statement together for you this morning, but I got sidetracked. And you know that fool Robert had the nerve to show up at my place last night."

"What? Why?"

"Other than the fact that he's a lunatic, I guess he figured out who found Dayshea."

"I haven't heard from him at all," Chante huffed. "And I don't even understand why I'm pissed about it."

"Neither do I," Liza replied. "What do you expect him to do? Apologize?"

"I guess I want to know if he used me or if he ever cared. Stupid, I know."

"It's not stupid. It just shows you have a heart. But I don't think you're ever going to get those answers."

"I kind of figured that out. How did I miss what was really going on? This had nothing to do with love. It was all about politics. We looked good on paper. But when we were alone, the passion fizzled."

Liza felt guilty because she'd introduced them. Felt as if she had some responsibility for Chante's heartache. Then again, she did try to warn her friend and it took her a month to listen. *Now is not the time for "I told you so,"* Liza thought. "I thought you two were . . ."

"I know, we're lawyers and being a successful lawyer means you're a skilled and crafty liar. Enough about that. I need you to get over here and help me respond to these reporters before I file an injunction."

"I'm on my way," Liza said, then made an illegal U-turn.

When she arrived at Chante's office, she walked in on a shouting match between Chante and Taiwon, the asshole partner Liza wanted to choke the other day.

"Don't you think a little warning about your fiancé's affection for whores would've been nice? Now this firm is —"

"I told you not to have that fund-raiser for him. But, like you always do, you ignored what I had to say. So, don't sit up here and tell me that I'm responsible for your fucking poor judgment!"

Liza wanted to applaud her friend, but she was in such a state of shock that she simply stood there with her mouth open.

"Well, you can kiss your partnership chances good-bye. The last thing we need here is to be associated with such filth!" Taiwon glanced at Liza. "See, this is just what I'm talking about."

"Get the hell out of my office!" Chante

361

snapped. Liza could feel the anger and heat radiating from her friend. She crossed over to her as Taiwon left the office.

"I never knew you had that in you," Liza said. "I'd be proud, but with what he just said about your partnership . . ."

"A self-destruct button. That's what I have." Chante shook her head. "I can't believe I just stood here and cursed out one of my senior partners." She leaned back on the desk. "I've lost my mind."

"Or maybe you found it. There's only so much a person can take before he or she snaps. I'm pretty sure you've taken a lot from that jerkface over the years. Add to that the fact that men always want to blame a woman for a man's inability to keep his pants zipped."

"He can't say he wasn't warned. I wonder if they still gave him the donation."

"He just has fucking poor judgment," Liza parroted her friend. The women broke into laughter.

"You know if our big sisters heard us now, they'd probably want to take their pink and green back."

Liza fanned her hand. "As hard as we worked for those colors, they'd have a fight on their hands. Now, let's get out of here and return these phone calls and e-mails with a well-written and brilliant statement."

Chante sighed. "How could he do this to me, though? I'm more embarrassed than hurt right now. But when he was buying sex from Dayshea, I was planning a wedding. Thought I had a future with this wonderful man who fell head over heels in love with me and didn't mind that I was just as ambitious as any man in this field. He thought it was amazing that I was so driven. Do you know how many men are just intimidated by that?"

Liza nodded. "Preaching to the choir."

"That's why I thought Robert was perfect and wanted to believe that he was telling me the truth about you."

For a moment she bristled, but she could understand where Chante was coming from. It didn't mean she had to like it.

"I'm sorry," Chante continued. "Sorry that I became one of those dizzy broads who put a man before someone who has had her back for years."

"We've all done it," Liza said, though she couldn't remember a time when she made such an error.

"You're trying to make me feel better and you really don't want to tell me what a bitch I was."

Liza shrugged. "Well, you said it, I didn't."

"I knew you were thinking it. It's all right, because it will never happen again."

"How can you be sure?" Liza quipped.

Chante snorted. "Because I'm done with men and through with love. But that doesn't mean that I don't want to be the one to lead the sweetheart song at your reception."

"Now, you're getting ahead of yourself, don't you think?"

"Nope. I think you have finally found the real thing in Mr. Jackson Franklin. Don't mess it up and don't let this election come between you two. And please don't elope. That would be so Liza, eloping and tweeting a wedding picture."

Liza wondered, *Are we really a two? Is there more between us than hot sex and desire?*

"Come on, girl, let's go before we start crying," Chante said. She grabbed her laptop and stuffed it in her purse. "Just in case Taiwon does lock me out of my office."

Liza shook her head. "I'm sure he won't do that."

"You don't know how big of an asshole he is."

They headed to their favorite place, Amelie's, and hunkered down in a corner, where Liza hammered out a statement for Chante to e-mail the reporters who'd contacted her.

■ ■ ■ ■

"Jackson, Jackson, Jackson!" the crowd yelled. He stood on the stage at the voter's rally and smiled at the crowd. Teresa had estimated that only a few hundred people were supposed to show up. But over three thousand people showed up. Maybe they'd come out to see if there was going to be some drama after the debate or if Jackson was going to bad-mouth Montgomery, but what they got was the full view of Jackson's platform, some real-life answers to questions that they had about Medicare, the Affordable Health Care Act, and coal ash.

By the time he finished talking to them, Robert was nearly forgotten. "They love you," Teresa said as he walked off the stage. "I feel like we won their hearts and votes today."

"We will see for sure in the next few days, when it counts. You think voter turnout is going to be as low as the experts are predicting?" he asked, trying to sidestep what he knew was coming when he saw a horde of reporters heading their way. Teresa glanced over her shoulder and shook her head.

"Jackson, I've held the press off as long as I can about Montgomery," she said. "We have to issue a statement or the questions are going to keep coming."

"I'm not going to comment further on what he's done. Let the media keep milling for drama somewhere else."

Teresa shook her head. "Is that what Liza told you to do?"

Jackson narrowed his eyes at her. "What do you have against her?"

"Nothing. I'm sure she is an amazing woman. But she's too much of a distraction. There is just too much history between her and Montgomery for me to believe that they're just not friends anymore."

"It's not for you to believe or disbelieve," Jackson said firmly.

"I know one thing, I'm sick and tired of arguing with you about Liza Palmer. If you can't see that she's trouble —"

"How is she trouble? Because of these rumors and lies being spread about her? Just how is she responsible for that?"

"It's not about the truth. All it takes is a couple of misplaced howls and you could find yourself going from front-runner to joke. Just ask Howard Dean."

"I think it's more than that. We're at a point now where this is our election to win. You keep trying to find problems where there aren't any."

"Don't count your victory before votes are cast. What is it about her that has you willing to risk everything we've fought for?"

"Maybe I'm smart enough to know that love means more than anything else."

Teresa raised her right eyebrow. "You're in love with her?"

Jackson wasn't ready to admit that yet, but he knew that's where things were going. He loved everything about her. Her drive, her passion, and her desire. He wanted and needed Liza in his life because she'd already planted herself in his heart. Maybe he *was* ready to admit that he was in love with her.

"Yes, I am."

"Does she know that? I get the feeling that she isn't the kind of woman who's ready to settle down and live the straight and narrow life of a politician's spouse or girlfriend. How are you going to get anything done if you're always putting out social media fires involving her?"

"You have a really low opinion of Liza. Why?"

Before Teresa could answer, a crush of reporters swarmed on them. Most of the questions focused on what he'd said to the voters and how he planned to get the governor to change his mind on Medicare and taking federal money. Then there were questions about the military and wounded warriors. Just when he thought he'd gotten off scot-free and wouldn't have to answer a question about last night's debate, Liza, or Robert and the hooker, he heard, "Mr. Franklin, are you and Liza Palmer working together to discredit Robert Montgomery? Was that what your meeting was about a few weeks ago?"

Teresa looked to see who'd asked the question but couldn't find the reporter or campaign spy.

"I've done nothing to try to discredit Mr. Montgomery."

"What are your thoughts on the allegations Dayshea Brown made against him in an interview last night?"

"I don't think his personal life has anything to do with this election, and if he has broken laws, then it's up to the police and district attorney to handle. Other than that, I have no further comment."

"Don't you think that this speaks to his character? Why not condemn his behavior?"

"Because," Jackson began, "we don't know if this is his behavior or a rumor, much like a lot of things that have come out in the media during this election season. And that's all." He and Teresa headed for the parking lot, ignoring the other questions about Robert. Though Jackson wanted to finish his conversation with Teresa about her feelings toward Liza, he knew that he had less than ten minutes to make it across town to the Stevenson Senior Center. This was the third stop of the morning and Jackson was fired up to meet the people who may put him in office. The more he spoke to people, the more his excitement grew. But it was the questions that threw him off. It seemed as if the media didn't listen to anything he said and only focused on the rumors and the controversy during the debate. It seemed as if the statement his campaign had released didn't mean anything. He'd hoped that the sound bite from earlier would've been enough. But after the senior center event, the questions were the same: What did he think about Robert and the allegations?

By the time he stopped at the VA hospital on Harris Boulevard around one that afternoon, he'd reached his limit.

"Listen, when are we going to focus on the issues?" he snapped. "I'm sure the seniors trying to keep their Medicare don't give a rat's . . . don't care what I think about my opponent's personal life or if he had to pay for sex. If he broke the law, I'm sure the appropriate action will be taken. What more can I say?"

Teresa dropped her head, then ushered him out the door. "You can't afford to lose it now," she said. "Do you know how many times you're going to have to answer tough questions if you make it to Raleigh?"

"Tough questions are one thing; this is just stupid. Why don't they just go ask Robert?"

Teresa held up her cell phone. "They have."

He read the headline from the *Charlotte Observer*'s political blog: LIES AND FABRICATED DRAMA.

"They are keeping the machine going," Jackson said. "How is this . . ."

"He mentions that your girl and his former fiancée teamed up to bring him down. I'm just glad they didn't say anything about us. But it's not going to be long before your link to Liza Palmer comes up again." Teresa sighed. "She's a beautiful and smart woman. If she and Robert hadn't been joined at the hip, then you and Liza would be awesome together."

"I can't allow rumors and innuendos to change how I live my life."

"These rumors and innuendos you want to brush off can mean the difference between you winning and helping all of these people you claim you're running to help and losing. I didn't devote all of this time to you and this campaign to watch you throw it away behind a woman!" Teresa rolled her eyes, then took a deep breath. "Make a decision."

"What?"

"If you want my help for you to win this thing, then you have to decide what's more important — a relationship with Liza or winning this election! I will quit and watch from afar as you piss away your chance to make a difference right now."

"Fine."

Teresa gasped. "Well, if that's how you want it."

"It's not, but I'm not going to be dictated to by you or anyone else. If I want to be with Liza, then I'm going to do it."

"I hope she's worth it," Teresa said, then stormed away from him.

Jackson dropped his head. What in the hell had he just done? How was he going to win this election without Teresa? Was Liza worth it?

It didn't take long for Jackson's inner circle to find out about his row with Teresa. The first call he received was from Daniel. "Jackson, have you lost your mind?" his boss asked. "Why did you let Teresa walk?"

"Word travels fast," he said as he slipped into his car.

"It just so happens that I called her to congratulate you guys on the endorsement from the *Charlotte Observer* and she said she's no longer affiliated with your campaign. When I asked her why, she told me that you know why and she's not going to talk about it. She was your ace in the hole."

"I'm not letting anyone tell me how to live my life and who I should associate with."

"Oh no? You don't think the voters aren't going to hold you accountable for the people you associate with? Just ask your boy Robert Montgomery. What you need to do is go talk to Teresa."

Jackson sighed and realized that Daniel was right, but nothing had changed. He wasn't going to choose between the election and Liza. He wanted both. And he was going to have both. He headed to his campaign headquarters and hoped to find Teresa there.

CHAPTER 27

Liza and Chante sat in the studio of WCNC waiting for Ramona Holloway of *Charlotte Today*. They both loved Ramona, and when she'd asked for a comment on the situation with Robert, Liza talked her friend into going on the popular local show for a live interview.

Of course, Chante had to be coaxed into doing it. "I really don't want to go on TV and talk about this, Liza," she'd said as Liza ran a brush through her friend's hair.

"This will be the last interview you'll have to give. It's not as if you have anything else to do," Liza had replied, referring to the suspension Chante had received from the law firm just hours earlier.

"I can't believe those bastards suspended me because of Robert. Calling me a distraction!" Chante had been livid and pushed Liza's hands away. "Let's do it."

That had been about forty-five minutes

ago, and now, Chante was even more nervous than she'd been while Liza had done her makeup.

"Are you sure it's not too late for me to run out of here?" Chante whispered. "How many people are going to be watching this show? And the video is going to be on their website, isn't it? Please don't tweet the links."

"You aren't leaving until the interview is over," Liza replied.

"And you're positive that the questions are going to be the ones that we went over and nothing more?"

"Yes," Liza said. "The producer gave us her word that they won't go off script."

The producer walked onto the set and smiled at Liza and Chante. "Ramona is on her way, so, Liza, we're going to have to move you off set. You can watch with me in the control room," she said with a smile.

"Is that all right with you, Chante?" Liza asked.

She shrugged. "I guess I need to be a big girl." Liza smiled at Chante, then followed the producer to the control room, where they'd watch the interview. Liza made a mental note to get a picture with Ramona before she left. Of the media stars in Charlotte, Ramona had to be her absolute favorite. Maybe it was the way that she ruled the TV and radio airwaves. There was no compromise in Ms. Holloway and Liza wanted to believe that she followed in her footsteps. Now, she hoped that Ramona would stick to the questions they agreed on so that she would still be a fan after the interview.

Liza watched in rapt attention as Ramona and Chante bantered back and forth like old friends. Then the questioning started.

"So, you and Robert Montgomery are engaged?" Ramona asked.

"Were engaged," Chante said, then waved her left hand, which was ring free. Liza had dusted some bronzer around the tan line so that it looked as if she'd taken the ring off a long time ago.

"Did you know he'd been unfaithful and was entertaining call girls?"

"A good friend tried to warn me after the incident she'd witnessed with Dayshea Brown, but I didn't want to believe it. I'd been the stereotypical woman, accusing my single friend of being jealous of my relationship. But then I noticed a change in Robert and things that he'd been saying didn't make sense. I'm a lawyer, I deal in logic. So, I had to evaluate my relationship."

Good answer, Liza thought.

"Then why didn't you let your friend make her case when she first came to you?"

Liza looked at the producer. "That's not on the list."

"Shh. It's a logical follow-up question."

"The hell you say," Liza snapped and rose to her feet. But what good would it do for her to go and interrupt the interview?

"Well, I-I," Chante began. "I wasn't expecting that question. But if I'm totally honest, I didn't want to believe her. I thought I was in love and I thought I was loved in return. She walked in my house when I was planning my wedding telling me that my then fiancé was cheating on me. What would you have done, Ramona?"

Liza applauded her friend. "Great comeback."

"And we'll be back after these messages," Ramona said.

Following the interview, Chante stormed out of the studio — no selfies with Ramona at all. Liza had to run to keep up with her friend. "Chante."

She whirled around. "What was that all about? Did you two sneak that question in, because it damned sure wasn't on the list?! You said that I wouldn't look like a fool."

"I didn't know she was going to ask that. And you didn't look like a fool. The producer said . . ."

Chante folded her arms across her chest. "Oh no? Funny, everyone else was mentioned by name — but you."

"Just what are you accusing me of?" Liza snapped.

"I know you, Liza. You put your reputation above everything else, no matter who you throw under the bus. No wonder you and Robert were so close. You two are just alike."

"Oh, I threw you under the bus?"

"No, but you gave me a great push off the curb. I'm out of here." Chante dashed to the car and Liza swore under her breath. How in the hell was she going to get back downtown when she rode to the studio with Chante?

"Damn!"

Jackson was heading into his headquarters just as Teresa was walking out carrying a huge box. "Teresa," he said, causing her to stop.

"What?"

"Can we talk about this?" he asked. "I need you and . . ."

"You need me?" She laughed. "Most of the people I've worked with who've needed me actually listened to what I had to say.

377

You've made your choice and now you have to live with it."

Jackson stood in front of her and took the box from her hands. "You know what," he said, "I probably don't deserve you. I should have listened to you more, and if I was smarter, I never would've gotten involved with Liza Palmer. But I can't deny what I feel for her and pretend that I don't know her or I don't want to be with her. Still, I know that I didn't spend all of these months trying to win this election with you by my side to throw it away now."

"I guess those emerald eyes and strong arms work on most of the women you meet, but, Jackson, when I'm done, I'm done. You're going to tell me what I want to hear right now and then ten minutes later you're going to be in Liza's arms, risking the press seeing you together. Or more stories coming out about her that will reflect badly on what we're trying to accomplish. Did you catch the interview that Chante Britt gave on *Charlotte Today* about Robert? When asked why she didn't believe her friend, Chante stammered. I'm guessing when Liza set up that interview, she didn't tell her bestie that she'd be asked that question. How can you put so much faith in a woman who doesn't value friendships that are decades old? Are you sure that's the kind of woman you want to be with?"

"I didn't see the interview," Jackson said. "But that's not why I'm here. I said I need you, Teresa, and that's no lie."

"What do you need more? Me, leading you to victory, or whatever it is that you think you and Liza share?"

"I have to see this thing through. I started this campaign because I wanted to help the military families and wounded warriors, whom the government has seemed to turn its back on. I don't want to stop now. I don't want to see the status quo continue."

"What about Liza?"

Jackson sighed. "What about her? She's not running for office and she's not . . ."

"To be trusted. Even if she accidentally does something, she could ruin everything we've worked for. Why don't you see that?"

"What is it that you want me to see? That the woman I love is out to take me down?"

"That the media gives and takes. And why in the hell do you think you're in love with her?" Teresa slapped her hand against her forehead. "If I'm wrong about Liza, please show me. Because after what I saw on *Charlotte Today,* if that's how she treats her friends, I'd hate to see what happens if her man ever disappoints her."

Jackson furrowed his brows. He knew what had happened to Liza's ex, but did that mean she hadn't matured? "What happened?" he asked, not genuinely wanting to know the answer.

Teresa cleared her throat, then gave him the play-by-play of the interview with Ramona Holloway and Chante Britt. "So, when she asked about the *friend,* Liza wasn't mentioned. She comes off smelling like a rose, while Chante looks like a total idiot."

"But that's her friend. I can't imagine that she set her up on purpose."

"And when you talk like that, I can't take anything that you say seriously. Why do you think you would fare any better? I'm done."

"Teresa," Jackson said. "You and I haven't worked this hard for it to end like this."

"I stand by what I said. It's the campaign or Liza Palmer."

Jackson was about to make his choice when he saw Liza walking up the steps. "If I'm standing in the way of you winning this seat," she began, "then, by all means, continue what you've been working for."

Teresa turned and looked at Liza, then shook her head. "The choice is yours, Jackson," she said.

Jackson looked from Liza to Teresa. He

thought about what he wanted to accomplish as the senator from district forty-five. Then he thought about the way he felt about Liza. The way she made him feel and how much he cared for her. This was unfair. This was a choice he couldn't make. Not right now. Not while looking into Liza's bewitching eyes. Looking at her, he knew that she hadn't purposely done anything to make Chante look foolish or to hurt her. He'd known that she wanted nothing more than to help her friend. But did Liza's help come with a price? Did he really want her more than he wanted to win this election?

Jackson reached out and stroked her cheek. "In another time . . ."

She shook her face free of his hand. "I understand. This is important to you and I don't want to stand in your way. I guess I'm just bad news for everybody." The heartbreaking look in her eyes made him want to pull her into his arms and kiss her until she knew that she was all he wanted. Instead, he let her walk down the steps and get into her car.

Teresa placed her hand on his shoulder. "Let's go inside and get some work done," she said. Jackson gave Liza a fleeting look and then followed Teresa inside.

Jackson couldn't sleep and it was after midnight. He knew the polls opened at six A.M. He also knew he was expected to be at his precinct to vote; Teresa had given the media his voting location and he was supposed to cast the first vote. He hoped that he'd wake up in time. More than anything, he hoped the turnout would be what he and Teresa expected. The experts were calling for a 10 percent turnout and Teresa said they were just undercounting.

"People are going to vote because they have too much to lose by staying home," she'd said the night before.

Jackson and the other volunteers had agreed 100 percent.

Now, he was wide awake, trying not to think about Liza. Trying not to think about the last time he saw her and how sad she looked when he chose his campaign over her.

Was it worth it? Would winning the election and losing Liza be worth it? He picked up the phone and dialed her number. He just wanted to hear her voice. Then maybe he could go to sleep.

Liza wasn't about to admit that she needed reading glasses. Maybe she needed to turn the lights on or just go to sleep. Why was she still following this damned election? She tried to tell herself that the outcome didn't matter. Neither candidate was in her life anymore.

Chante still wasn't speaking to her because of something that she had no control over. The only thing she had going for her right now was the fact that business had picked up. She'd been so busy that until tonight she hadn't looked at the political columns in the local papers.

But she wasn't busy enough to notice that Jackson had disappeared from her life. She hadn't heard from him and it hurt like hell. She'd done it again — hitched her wagon to the wrong man. She closed the cover on her iPad and sighed. She wanted Jackson to win and hoped that he'd live up to his campaign promises. More than that, she wanted to kiss him and make love to him again.

I guess he wanted the power more, she thought as she reached for her blanket.

When her cell phone rang, it nearly sent her into cardiac arrest. No one called her after midnight unless it was a serious emergency. Since she'd dumped her young professional athlete clients, she hadn't been getting those calls. Fumbling for the phone, she was shocked when she saw Jackson's number emblazoned on the screen.

"Hello?"

"Did I wake you?" he asked.

"Who is this?" Liza asked sarcastically.

Jackson chuckled. "I deserved that. How are you, Liza?"

"How am I? Feeling a little tossed aside, but other than that I'm awesome. Don't you have an election to win? After all, I thought that's why we couldn't see each other."

"Liza, this election is important to me, and in a few hours, the voters are going to make their decision. But I have a decision that I have to make right now."

"What's that?"

"I want and need you in my life."

"I'm a hot-button issue. Your people think you should stay far away from me."

"You want to know what I think?"

"I already know. You want to win this election and I'm a distraction or something like that."

"I'm glad I'm the mind reader and not you," he quipped. "What I was thinking was I want you and I need you by my side today, win or lose."

"Is that smart?"

"Who cares? Liza, these past few days without you have been hell."

She groaned and started to tell him that didn't even describe how lonely she'd felt without him. But she wasn't going to blink. What had she done to deserve this blackout from him? Yes, the public relations professional inside her knew what he did made the most sense. The rumors, the ties to Robert, her feud with Chante — it was a distraction. But the woman who was falling for Jackson Franklin wanted to be in his arms. Wanted him beside her when she had a tough day and wanted to hear him telling her that everything would be all right.

"Jackson," she began, "wouldn't it be better for your career if you just continued ignoring me? It was fun while it lasted but I don't want you to ever look back and say, 'I could have if it weren't for her.' "

"I'd never think of you like that. If I win or lose, it has nothing to do with you. Unless you don't vote for me."

"Well, you know damned well I'm not voting for your competition."

"How have you been holding up through all of this? I mean, you lost a lot during this election cycle."

"My two best friends, my reputation, and my heart," she said, then immediately regretted that last part.

"Your heart, huh?"

"That came out wrong," she said. "I-I . . ."

"You can lie to yourself, Liza, but don't lie to me. I know what I feel for you isn't one-sided. And I did lose my heart."

"Then why am I the only one feeling as if mine is broken?" Her voice was low and she felt tears welling up in her eyes.

"That's the last thing I want you to feel. I need you, Liza, and I'm willing to tell anyone who has a problem with that where they can go."

"Maybe I don't want this," she said, though the lies burned her lips. "When you win this election, you're going to be spending more time in Raleigh than you will be in Charlotte. You're going to face more scrutiny, and then when you start trying to get controversial bills passed the lobbyists are going to come after you. I don't want to be caught up in the crossfire — and then there are the groupies."

"Whoa. You've just laid out my political life as if you have a crystal ball attached to your MacBook."

"I'm just saying I expect big things from you and big things don't happen without a little controversy and a lot of sacrifice."

"Then I'm going to need you on my side to help me steer clear of that type of thing and by my side to make me feel better when my bills get voted down."

"Like Olivia Pope? I don't think so."

"No. Like Liza Palmer-Franklin."

"What?"

"I don't think I could be any clearer," he replied. His laugh vibrated in her ear and made her body tingle.

"That sounded like you want to fake a marriage."

"Baby girl, I don't do fake. But if I'm going to ask you to be a part of this intrusive new life I'm about to have, I can't just ask my girlfriend to do it."

"Girlfriend? I didn't even think we'd gotten that far. No, wait, we did, because you did dump me."

"I didn't dump you. I just needed to focus. . . . You know what, I let you down and I will never let that happen again."

"That's what you say now. But . . ."

"I'm giving you my word, and in this world, that's all I have."

Liza sighed and toyed with the frayed edge of her blanket. "Don't you have to get up early in the morning?"

"Yeah, but I'm not hanging up this phone until I know that we're okay and you're going to join me after you vote so that we can monitor the returns together."

"All right," she said. "I'll be happy to

watch the returns with you. And I guess I need to get those flowers and cupcakes."

"And don't forget the kisses."

"As I recall, that was only if you won, right?"

Jackson chuckled again. "And you think I won't?"

"I know you will. I'll call you after I cast the winning vote for you," she said. "Good night, Jackson."

"Sweet dreams, Liza."

After hanging up, sleep didn't come easy for Liza. Was Jackson serious with all that talk of . . . Nah! She was going to chalk it up to his nerves. Why would he spend all of this time away from her and just jump to marriage? That didn't make sense. Love stories like that didn't happen to her. Granted, she knew he wasn't trying to use her to gain voters. Hell, most people would probably turn away from him if they knew about their relationship. Relationship. Is that what this thing was?

Groaning, she rolled over on her stomach. This was even more confusing than ever.

CHAPTER 28

Jackson hopped out of bed at five A.M. After hanging up with Liza, he didn't sleep more than three hours. Had he lost his mind when he quasi-proposed to her? Did he mean it? Yes. He wanted to spend his life with her and he would tell the world that, but was he ready to trust Liza with his heart? He only questioned himself because the last time he felt this way about a woman, he was the one who ended up heartbroken and on the verge of suicide. Things were different this time. He wasn't returning home from war. He actually knew more about Liza than he'd known about Hillary. He knew Liza was kind, sweet, daring, and loyal. Loyalty meant a lot to him. Maybe that was why he'd fallen for her as quickly as he had. He didn't care what Teresa or anyone else thought about him being with Liza.

And he didn't plan on explaining himself

to anyone. But would his love for her make what he'd worked for all these months in vain? Jackson had to tell himself that it wasn't a forgone conclusion that he was going to win today. Maybe voters would still choose Montgomery over him. He was the typical Charlotte politician and people voted for what they knew. Maybe his last few weeks of campaigning had connected with voters. He'd actually stuck to the issues, stopped with the rumors about Liza, and talked about his life growing up in foster care. He'd even made a pledge to fix the broken system.

That probably gained inroads with voters. But Jackson knew Robert was a snake and he felt as if his promises were hollow and full of lies. *Robert wants to win and he'll do anything to do so,* Jackson thought as he got out of the shower.

It was now five-thirty and he had to meet with the volunteers who were going to be handing out literature about him at the polling precincts. He grabbed a banana and put a K-Cup in his Keurig coffeemaker. He smiled as he drank the single cup of coffee and silently thanked Teresa for buying the system for him. After eating the banana, he headed upstairs and dressed. It took him about ten minutes to drive to his voting place, and when he arrived, Teresa was there with the press.

"Good morning," she said when he crossed over to her. "Senator elect."

"Getting a little ahead of yourself?" he quipped.

"Got to believe it and put it in the universe. Are you holding up all right?"

Jackson shrugged, then smiled as he saw the news crew coming their way. "Let the show begin." He walked into the precinct and smiled at the women at the table who recognized him and explained the voting process to him. He could tell they were being a little extra for the camera, but it was all right.

It felt funny to vote for himself and to see his name on the ballot. But this was what he'd worked for. This was why he'd sacrificed and worked the long hours. Now, all he could do was wait for the payoff. He hoped that he'd done enough to win the support of the voters of the district.

Liza cursed as the heel on her shoe snapped the second she walked out the door. She had been hoping to avoid the long lines at her voting place. Actually, she wanted to see Jackson sooner, rather than later. And she'd watched him on the news casting his vote and then heading out with his band of supporters. Jackson was probably going to hit all of the voting places in the city. And as much as she didn't want to think about it, she figured Robert would as well. She wanted to avoid that asshole at all costs.

Who knew that today she would actually be rooting for someone else when this had been something she and Robert had dreamed of for years and planned out as undergrads like most girls planned their dreamed wedding.

Kicking her shoe off, she groaned. Liza wished that she could've made peace with Robert and Chante. More Chante than Robert. She headed back inside and changed her shoes, then decided to call her sorority sister.

This feud and anger had gone on long enough. Dialing Chante, Liza silently prayed her friend would listen to her.

"Hello?"

"Chante?"

"Who else is going to answer my phone?"

"How are you?" Liza asked, feeling at a loss for words.

"Well, lucky for you, I was about to go for a run; otherwise you would've been waking me up. What do you want, Liza?"

"I miss you and . . ."

"Liza, I've been thinking about everything that's happened over these last few months and I've been a hard person to get along with."

Not wanting to voice her agreement, Liza simply listened as Chante continued. "If I were you," Chante said, "I'm not sure if I'd keep reaching out."

"We've been friends too long to let misunderstandings —"

"And Robert."

Liza laughed. "And Robert to come between us. That interview with Ramona . . ."

"I know. It wasn't something that you did. I know how reporters work, and I guess it's just that the question hurt me because I should've listened to you. I know who you are and that you had my best interest at heart. If I look foolish, it's my fault."

"You're not the first woman to be taken in by a lying man."

"That doesn't make it any better. He's out here trying to further his career, I'm still suspended from the firm, and there's nothing I can do but lick my wounds until all of this passes."

"Have you voted today?"

"Hell no, and I might not. Then again," she said with a click of her teeth, "I'm going to vote for your boy Jackson and pray that I'm the one vote that makes Robert lose."

"Glad to see that you're going to do your civic duty," Liza said with a laugh. "I wish we had a reset button on all of this. I would've stopped with the matchmaking, stayed out of politics, and probably wouldn't be thought of as a call girl in some circles."

"That is tough. If you want to sue, I'll take the case."

"Are you all right moneywise?"

"Yeah. I've got everything under control on that aspect, but I'm bored. So, if you know of anyone who needs a lawyer or if you need to sue the hell out of somebody call me."

"I think you need a vacation," Liza said.

"Maybe you're right. I've been meaning to go see my grandmother in Charleston. She's doing some renovations on her house, and I could go down there and make sure the contractors aren't taking advantage of her and the work is getting done in a timely manner."

"Or you could just go relax."

Chante laughed. "Hello? I think my phone is broken — Elizabeth Palmer just told me to relax? When is the last time you took your own advice? Still sleeping with your Mac-

Book? Oh, wait, you have Jackson now — right?"

"Well," Liza began, "it's been a little complicated lately."

"I hate politics," Chante said. "All right, I'm going for my run. Want to meet for breakfast?"

"Sounds good. I'll call you after I vote."

Once she and Chante said good-bye, Liza headed out. Arriving at her polling place, she saw Jackson and a group of volunteers handing out literature and shaking hands with voters. When she locked eyes with Jackson, he winked at her while talking to an elderly man. She felt a blush rise to her cheeks. He looked so handsome in his dark blue suit and red tie. He looked like a senator. He looked delicious. Glancing to her right, she saw Robert's car pulling into the parking lot.

"Damn," she muttered as she watched him get out of the car. Nic pulled up behind him in a van with his own team of volunteers. Liza rolled her eyes and started for the entrance.

"Liza," Nic called out. "I hope we can count on your vote." His sarcasm wasn't missed, and as much as she wanted to flip him off, she was well aware of the news crews in the area and simply walked inside to vote for Jackson. This was one time that she wished she could vote twice.

Teresa rolled her eyes as she watched Robert and Nic set up shop. Jackson touched her shoulder. "Remember, *you* said we'd probably run into them today and this is one of the largest polling places in the district."

"I don't always follow my own advice."

Nic walked over to Teresa and smiled. "Good luck," he said, then extended his hand to her. Teresa rolled her eyes and walked away. "Still bitter?"

"Mr. Hall," Jackson said. "Don't you have your own candidate to assist right now?"

Nic smiled. "I'm just trying to be gentlemanly and wish you good luck, Mr. Franklin. You're probably going to need it."

As Nic walked away, Jackson took a deep breath and braced himself for the reporters heading his way. It was time to shine and win over the last-minute voters. Robert was doing the same thing as well.

In the middle of his interview, Jackson noticed Liza walk out of the building and saw two reporters walk up to her. As much as he hoped she'd be left alone, he knew Liza was still considered a newsmaker.

"What has the turnout been like out

here?" a reporter asked him, forcing him to focus on his own interview.

"It's been steady and it gives me hope that people are taking their civic duty very seriously. As we all know, in the next year or so, voting is going to be harder in North Carolina."

"And if you win today, will that be something that you plan to fight against?"

"Absolutely," Jackson said. "Now, if you will excuse me." He headed over to a group of voters near Liza. Of course, he wanted to shake hands with them, and he planned to swoop in and save his woman if he needed to.

"Miss Palmer, you've been an interesting piece to this election," the reporter said, and Liza fought to keep from rolling her eyes.

"I'm just a voter," she replied with a smile.

"But you've been linked to both camps. Who won your support today?"

Liza folded her arms across her chest and didn't fight her frown. "We vote by secret ballot in this country for a reason. But, since you asked, I voted for the man who has been focused on the issues from the start of this election season. The man who is a hero but doesn't want credit for anything he does. I voted for the man who will go to Raleigh and won't be blinded by power, lobbyists, or the trappings that have brought down many men and women who were supposed to represent us. I voted for Jackson Franklin."

"But weren't you saying the same things about Robert Montgomery a few months ago?" another reporter asked.

"I'm not perfect. I was wrong. Excuse me," she said as she pushed through the reporters. Jackson reached out and touched Liza's arm.

"Hey, are you okay?"

"Sure you want to be seen with me right now?" she asked.

"What did I say to you this morning? I haven't changed my mind," Jackson said, then pulled her into his arms and gave her a tight hug. Cameras pointed in their direction and Liza closed her eyes.

"I hope this doesn't cost you the election." She opened her eyes and saw the smirk on Nic's and Robert's faces.

Jackson stepped back from her. "Let's clear some things up with the media," he said as he watched a group of reporters come their way.

"Mr. Franklin, are you and Miss Palmer

now working together?" a reporter called out.

"No, we're not."

Liza kept her face neutral, wondering what he was about to say. After all, he started the PDA and he was the one who had to answer for it.

"Then, what was the embrace about?" another reporter asked.

"While Liza and I are not working together professionally," he said, then smiled at her, "we are very good friends. She's an important part of my life. I'd appreciate some privacy as Liza and I move forward."

She could've been bowled over with a feather after hearing what Jackson said. Did he really just . . . "Liza? Any comment?" a reporter asked.

"No, nothing other than polls close at seven-thirty. Don't forget to get out and vote." She and Jackson headed over to his volunteers, and it wasn't lost on her that the reporters had crossed over to Robert and his camp.

Teresa grabbed Jackson's arm. "Have you lost your damned mind?" she gritted.

"Teresa, I'm not going to —"

"Jackson," Liza interjected. "Let me talk to Teresa, alone and away from the cameras."

Teresa rolled her eyes and then nodded. "Sounds like a good idea."

The two women walked over to Liza's car and hopped inside. Liza glanced at Teresa as she started the vehicle. "Is Starbucks okay with you?"

"Fine," she replied curtly.

"You don't like me very much."

"I don't trust you and I've been doing this long enough to know that leopards don't change their spots overnight. Your history of supporting Montgomery goes a long way back. Hell, for all I know this was a huge setup to turn him into an underdog, and your PDA with my candidate . . ."

Liza burst out laughing. "I'm sorry, I'm sorry. But what part of this political circus makes sense for me? Why would I, someone who puts out PR fires, allow myself to be called a call girl, linked to the South Park Madam, and risk losing my best friend? What would be my end game?"

"A posh job in Raleigh, money, anything," Teresa replied.

"I have money. I've never been political; hell, I failed my pol. sci. class at UNC." She glanced at Teresa. "But you already know that."

"Yes, I do. All right, Liza, let's cut the

400

bullshit. How do you go from being a man's biggest supporter — I mean, you stood by him through more than a cheating scandal before — to supporting his political rival?"

"Because some people take years to realize that they've made a huge mistake. I just happen to be one of those people. I thought Robert was someone he wasn't. Honestly, he reminded me of a man who hurt me more than anyone in the world. . . ."

"Your father?"

"Damn, how thick is that file you have on me?"

"I do my research," Teresa said. "Maybe I'm wrong about you, and for your sake, I hope that I am. Working with Jackson, I've come to believe in him. I'll be the first to tell you that I've been wrong about a politician before."

"Yeah, you were really deep in John Edwards's corner for years," Liza said as she pulled into the parking lot of Starbucks.

"I see you've done your share of research as well."

"Well, I was trying to figure out who the competition was, but after I got to know Nic, I wasn't sharing anything. That man is an asshole with a capital *A*."

"Don't I know it. He has people fooled."

"But not you."

"Nope. Not me. I sniffed that snake out when he came up with the inane plan for John. But that's neither here nor there. I hate corruption and dirty tricks." She focused a cold stare on Liza. "Don't be a dirty trick."

Liza held back her laughter and told herself that Teresa was the kind of woman you definitely wanted as your friend.

Jackson counted to ten when he saw Robert walking his way. He still wanted to punch this man for all of the lies he told on Liza. "Jackson, I guess congratulations are in order," Robert said, sarcasm dripping from his words like honey.

The cameras were gone now, but some midmorning voters were making it to the polling place. "I don't want to talk to you right now," Jackson gritted.

"But you're cuddled up with my former best friend. I just hope she makes you happy."

Jackson laughed sardonically. "I'm sure you do, Montgomery. Maybe you need to go shake some more hands and see if you can gain some more votes."

"Aww, but your little public display with Liza probably gave me all the ammunition I need to trounce you."

"Get. Out. Of. My. Face."

Robert folded his arms across his chest. "What are you going to do, deck me because you fell for a whore?"

Jackson's jaw tensed. "Funny, you're the one who pays whores. Or are we supposed to forget about Miss Brown because your mama left you at a fire station?"

Robert glared at Jackson. "You sorry —"

"No, that's you." Jackson smiled. "You're the one who played dirty and started those rumors about Liza hoping to turn the tide in your direction. All because she caught you being the sorry piece of shit you are. Liza was right about you — if the woman you love can't trust you, why should the people in the state think they can?"

"We'll see what happens when the polls close and when you're nothing. Then Liza will turn her back on you and you'll return to being a damned brick."

Oh, if only he had a brick to slam against his thick skull. "Good luck, Robert. You're going to need it." Jackson walked away and rounded up half of his volunteers so that they could move on to their next voting place.

CHAPTER 29

It was more like lunchtime when Chante and Liza finally met up. Liza had dropped Teresa off at the polling place where Jackson had moved his party. Liza had an idea as to why he left and she couldn't blame him at all.

Knowing Robert, after all of the cameras had been turned off he probably started some low-key mess. Joining Chante at 300 East, she was happy to see her friend with a smile on her face.

"Sorry about the delay."

Chante waved her hand. "I saw the news. Bold move by your man."

Liza tried to hide her smile, but she couldn't. Just thinking of Jackson as her man made her tingle with happiness.

"So," Chante said, pointing to her "I voted" sticker, "where's the victory party going to be?"

"I'm not sure," Liza said, realizing that

her talk with Teresa had kept her from having a conversation with Jackson about his plans for the evening.

"Well, I have a great dress that I'd like to wear, if I'm invited."

"Of course you are. Girl, we have a lot to celebrate and it's going to start with you not marrying a jerkoff."

Chante rolled her eyes. "While I was waiting for you, I got a call from the office. Taiwon said my suspension will be lifted in a month."

"That's good, right?"

"Maybe it's time for me to take control of my destiny. This is the very excuse they need not to make me partner. I'm tired of busting my ass for men who don't value what I do or what I bring to that firm. One million dollars in billable hours last year."

"That's a lot of damned money."

She nodded. "Yet, I have to beg them to make me a partner? Then I have to put up with Taiwon. What an ass. I'm betting he was bullied as a child or dropped on his head."

Liza laughed, agreeing with her friend. "I don't see how you've put up with it as long as you have."

She shrugged. "I guess it was what I was supposed to do. Or rather, what I was expected to do. You go to law school, graduate at the top of your class, and get a job with one of the most prestigious firms in the state."

Liza reached out across the table and placed her hand on top of Chante's. "You know what this means, right?"

"What?"

"It's time for you to stop doing what's expected and do what you want, finally."

"You're right. Now, if I could figure out what that is."

Liza was about to reply when her cell phone rang. It was Jackson and she excused herself from the table to take the call.

"Hi, how's it going out there?" she asked.

"I'm tired and hungry, but it's well worth it."

"Where's the victory party tonight? Chante and I want to be there to help you celebrate."

"You and Chante made up, that's reason enough to party even if I don't win." She could hear the smile in his voice.

"Why do you think you aren't going to win? I've seen a few exit polls and they have you up two to one."

"It's still early. Where are you?"

"Three hundred East."

"Umm, an Asian tuna burger would be

delicious right now," he said. "Wait for me. I think it's time for a break."

"I'll be here," she said. Returning to her table, she smiled at Chante. "That was Jackson."

"The smile on your face gave it away." She wiped her mouth with her napkin and then set it on the side of her plate. "And while you were outside talking to your Mr. Wonderful, I got a call of my own. Robert Montgomery is truly the definition of insanity."

"What the hell did he want?"

Chante laughed. "Me to come to his *victory* party tonight. Said we could make up when he wins and show the public that love can overcome anything. I was like, fool, I am not Tammy Bakker."

"Yeah, that is insane. What did he say in response?"

She looked over her shoulder. "He didn't have a chance because I told him to hug and kiss my black ass. And that couple over there heard me because I got a little loud. That's why they keep staring at me."

"Forget them. That was a good one, though. I'm going to use that."

"Yeah, in the throes of passion with Jackson," she quipped, then waved for the waiter. "I need a really big glass of wine."

Liza looked at her watch. "Umm, it's not even one-thirty."

Chante rolled her eyes as the waiter approached the table. "It's five o'clock somewhere." She turned to the young man and ordered a four-ounce glass of merlot.

"And you, ma'am?" he asked, turning to Liza.

"I'm good," she replied. "Just a refill on my tea. And I need an Asian tuna burger."

When the waiter returned with the wine, Jackson was also walking over to the ladies. "Hello," he said to Chante and Liza. Then he looked at Chante's choice of drink. "Hard day?"

"You have no idea," she said, then took a big gulp of her wine.

"You two need to be alone?"

Chante shook her head, then put her glass down. "No," she said. "You two need to be alone. I'm going to take this wine to the bar and give my grandmother a call. I think a trip to Charleston is in order. And, Jackson, I voted for you today; I hope you win." She rose to her feet and headed for the bar. Jackson sat down and smiled at Liza.

"What was that all about?"

"Robert. But you know what, we're not talking about him. I ordered your food, and

408

for the next hour or so, you are going to relax."

"Relax? Are you seriously telling someone to relax? I'm impressed."

Liza rolled her eyes. "I'm tired of hearing that."

"Need I remind you that you're the woman who said she didn't have an off switch?"

"And you simply showed me that a pause button is worth using sometimes," she said, then took a sip of tea.

After lunch, Jackson headed back out on the campaign trail, while Liza and Chante headed to their respective homes to get ready for what they both hoped would be Jackson's victory party at The Ritz-Carlton in uptown.

Jackson sat in the silence of his headquarters and prayed. He prayed for the Lord's will to be done. If this was his election to win, then he would leave it in God's hands. Saying amen, Jackson stood up and grabbed a room-temperature bottle of water. He drank it down quickly. There were two hours before the polls closed and he'd already written his concession speech. In it he thanked the voters and the volunteers. Then he congratulated Robert on his win and asked that he remember the trust that the people put in him as he made decisions in Raleigh. He reminded Robert that the children of North Carolina and the elderly were depending on him. Told him it wasn't the huge corporations that made the state great, but it was the people and the military that made North Carolina an amazing place to live and it was his job to protect those people and make sure he always spoke truth over power.

He'd memorized the four pages that he'd written. Especially the last few lines:

Liza Palmer. You're an amazing blessing and I want to publicly say, I love you. Thank you for being in my corner even when I told you to stay away. Let's make this official. Marry me.

No matter what speech he gave tonight, the ending would be the same. His life was going to start with Liza — win or lose.

The lights flickered on and Teresa walked in. "I figured you were in here. Have you finished your victory speech?" she asked with a smile.

"Nope. But the concession speech is ready."

She rolled her eyes. "You're not going to need that. I have a confession to make."

"You fixed the election?" he joked.

"Don't even go there. Liza and I had a talk today and I have to say I was wrong about that young lady."

"Let me write this down. Teresa Flores admits that she was wrong about something."

She smacked him on the shoulder playfully. "You're something else, you know that? She's special, Jackson. You'd better hold on to this one."

He smiled. Oh, he planned to hold on to her very tightly. "What changed your mind?"

"A few things. But mainly, the way she lights up when she talks about you. And Liza's sharp. You deserve a woman like that and she actually deserves you. So, while I was blinded by my dislike for Nic and the fact that she had been Robert's champion for all of those years, I see she's the kind of woman who cleans up her mistakes."

"Kind of like looking in a mirror, huh?"

"Now, you're just going too far. There is only one Teresa Flores, all right? Maybe in a few years she'll be half the force that I am. That is, if you don't saddle her down with six or seven babies by then." Laughing, Teresa flounced out of the office and Jackson found the inspiration to write a victory speech.

Liza and Chante felt as if they were back in college getting ready for a sorority social. They had emptied their closets and talked themselves out of and into several different outfits. Chante had decided against the dress she'd planned to wear when she and Robert were together. She decided that it gave her a Stepford Wife look and Liza agreed wholeheartedly.

Neither of them was going to be caught dead in red! Even if Liza thought the red sleeveless band dress that Chante had brought over was absolutely adorable. "We should just go shopping," Chante said as she looked at the stack of outfits on Liza's bed.

"No. We have enough clothes right here to start a boutique. Oh, my! I'm such an idiot."

"What's up?" Chante asked as Liza dashed into her closet. When her friend pulled out a pink bag, Chante shook her head. "I guess you went shopping without me. I've been dying to try this place."

"You know I run their social media accounts."

Chante grinned. "Of course you do. So, what's in the bag?" Liza unzipped the bag and pulled out two brilliant dresses, one a strapless pink satin gown and the other a bright yellow razorback dress with a beaded bodice. Of course, Chante reached for the pink one.

"It's way too short for your long legs and you're probably going to be filmed more than me anyway. Besides, you have better arms."

"Hello, this dress is strapless."

"I know, but I thought I'd throw that in to confuse you."

"Ugh," Liza said with a laugh. "Take the pink one. I wanted to wear this yellow one anyway."

"That's right, be that man's ray of sunshine."

Liza smiled, knowing that Jackson was definitely the brightness in her life. She couldn't believe that she'd fallen so hard and fast for him. And he for her. It felt good to care for someone and know they felt the same way in return. She didn't have to worry about late-night phone calls from other women or catching him chatting it up with his lover. He was a man she could be totally devoted to and not feel like a fool about it.

"Liza," Chante said, snapping her out of her thoughts. "What do you think?" She spun around in the dress and looked like a total knockout.

"Yes, that is you. I want you to keep it."

"I can't do that. It's brand-new."

"And? Maybe the next time you wear it, you'll be going out with your brand-new boo. Ooh, I have the perfect shoes for this dress. And those, I will be taking back." Liza walked into her closet and grabbed a pair of nude heels, then handed the shoes to Chante.

"I don't know, girl. These shoes are fierce and I don't recall you ever wearing them, so you should give them to me."

"Just because you haven't seen me in them doesn't mean I don't have big plans for them." She headed back into the closet and grabbed a pair of silver stilettos to pair with her dress.

About two hours later, they were both dressed and ready to go to The Ritz-Carlton. The polls had been closed for five minutes, but Liza had been too nervous to take a peek at the early results. If she saw that Robert was in the lead, she'd probably cry and she'd worked too hard to get her makeup to pop tonight. And if she saw that Jackson was in the lead, then she would be a ball of nerves. So, she wasn't going to look. She was just going to be there to celebrate with her man. Liza prayed she wasn't going to have to do any consoling.

People aren't going to vote for Robert. They can't be that stupid.

Jackson had gotten to the point where he was beginning to hate ties. He couldn't remember when he had to choose between so many different ties, and for what? He glanced at himself in the mirror of his hotel suite. "You are about to be the first senator of the forty-fifth district," he said. "You ran a clean race, you connected with the voters, and you're going to be the voice that the people deserve."

Bolstered by his short pep talk, he chose a Carolina blue and white polka dot tie to accompany his heather gray suit and white oxford shirt. He pinned his 82nd Airborne decal pin on his lapel, then brushed his hand across his face. It was time to learn his fate. Jackson headed down to the ballroom, where the party was in full swing. Waiters floated around the room with trays of wine and champagne. The first people to approach him were Carlton and Barbara.

"Hey, Sarge!" Carlton said, his eyes bright. Jackson was so happy to see him in good spirits, and the smile on Barbara's face told him that the therapy was working.

415

"Carlton, I'm glad you guys could make it." He gave the couple a hug.

"You know we had to come celebrate with you," Barbara said. "I drove about thirty people to the polls today."

"Thank you so much," he replied, giving her a kiss on the cheek.

"It was my pleasure."

Carlton nudged him in the ribs. "So, what's really going on with you and the lady you were hugging on the news?"

Just as he was about to say her name, Jackson spotted Liza from across the room. God, she looked amazing in that yellow dress hugging her like a second skin. The silver hoops that hung from her ears made her look like a 1970s sex symbol. If she'd had a wide Afro and she would've been Cleopatra Jones reincarnated. Carlton and Barbara followed his stare.

"You're a lucky man," Carlton said.

"Almost as lucky as I am." Barbara punched her husband on the arm.

"Good save, soldier," she said. "Jackson, I hope she keeps that smile on your face."

"She will," Jackson replied. "Excuse me."

He quickly crossed the room and stood in front of Liza as she chatted away with Chante. Jackson touched her shoulder. "It should be a crime to look this good."

"Jackson," she said as she wrapped her arms around him and hugged him. "You look great as well. Very senatorial."

"Hi, Chante," he said. "You look great too."

"Thank you," she said with a small bow. "Excuse me for a moment." Chante took off in search of a glass of wine, leaving Jackson and Liza in each other's arms.

"Are you ready to get up on that stage and be introduced as the first senator from district forty-five?" Liza asked as she stroked his lapel.

"You know something that I don't?" he quipped. "The results aren't official yet."

"I know in my heart that you won. You are the best man for every job." She leaned in and kissed him on the cheek.

"You sure know how to stroke a brother's ego," he said with a wink. "Win or lose, I still got the victory tonight."

"Is that so?" she asked.

"I got you and that's all I need."

Liza beamed. "But you want that seat, I can see it in your eyes."

"I'm not going to lie and say no. This has been a long, hard battle."

"And you kept your integrity intact. You should be proud of that."

He nodded. He was proud of how he and

Teresa ran his campaign. He was proud of the way they stayed above the fray and kept it clean. Stroking her smooth arms, Jackson smiled, then brushed his lips against hers. "Thank you," he said.

"For what?"

"Coming into my life and being special."

"I should be thanking you. You had no reason to trust me or believe that I wasn't some kind of spy. And then when all of that . . ."

He placed his finger to her lips. "That doesn't matter and I never believed any of the rumors about you for a second."

She looked out at the crowd and smiled. "I hope the voters felt the same way."

"Here it is, here it is," Natalie called out as she turned up the volume on the big-screen TV.

WSOC's anchorman Blair Miller's image filled the screen. "With 100 percent of the precincts reporting, North Carolina's new district forty-five has its first senator. Former Army Sergeant Jackson Franklin is predicted to be the winner, with 60 percent of the vote."

A roar erupted from the crowd as cameras snapped and balloons fell from the ceiling. Jackson kissed Liza as the crowd shouted his name. "I love you," he said, then ran to the stage in the middle of the ballroom. The applause was deafening and Jackson felt tears burning in his eyes.

"Thank you! Thank you!" Jackson said. "This is only the beginning. I'm going to Raleigh to represent every last one of you. Everything I said as I asked for your vote, I want you to hold me accountable for it. I'm your senator, not big business and not the people who want to take away your rights. Being on this stage is surreal to me."

"We love you!" a chorus of voices yelled out. "You're our hero!"

Jackson smiled. "I hope I can live up to that," he quipped. "I'm not a hero. I'm just a man who wants to make a difference. I've seen too many people hurt by indifference. Watched good men die because of red tape and bureaucracy. It's time for that to stop. It's time for the government to be for the people, not just for the rich, not just the business owners and corporations who want to do business with our state at your expense. There has to be a balance. There has to be growth that doesn't choke the life out of the rest of us. That's what I'm going to fight for."

More applause erupted.

"I'd be remiss if I didn't thank the people who helped me run this campaign. Teresa

Flores," he said, then pointed her out in the crowd. "Thank you for having my back and wanting the best for me. Daniel Keter, your support and encouragement means as much today as it did when I said I was going to take this crazy ride. He could've told me that I didn't have a chance in hell. What did I know about politics or running for office? But he said I was just what this district needed and helped me put a team in place that taught me more than I thought I could learn in this time span. Hoorah!"

Daniel lifted his glass to Jackson.

"To all of you who stood by me, led rallies, and took your friends and family to vote — either early or today — thank you seems too hollow to say. But you made this happen." Jackson locked eyes with Liza. Her smile radiated warmth and happiness. Made him feel like he was the luckiest man in the world because she was smiling at him.

"There's one more person I'd like to say something to," he said, then motioned for Liza to join him at the platform. "Liza Palmer."

Whispers whirled through the crowd as she headed toward the stage to join him. If she was feeling any kind of way about what was being said or if she paid it any attention, it didn't show in her cool demeanor as she walked up and stood beside him. Jackson took her hand in his. "The way we met wasn't the stuff that dreams are made of," he said, then smiled. Liza shook her head. "The closer I got to you, the more it seemed to hurt you. The lies and rumors that circulated about you to hurt me were unfair. But you stood tall through it all and there's one thing that I have to ask of you."

Liza kept smiling at Jackson even though her heart was pounding like a drum corp. After all of the attention she'd received during the election cycle, she should've been calm, cool, and collected. But she felt as if she was going to faint at any minute as Jackson and the thousands of people in the room looked at her.

"I love you, Miss Palmer."

Awws and ooohs filled the air.

"I love you too," Liza replied with a shaky voice.

"Will you do me the honor of being my wife?" he asked.

"Say yes, before I do," an older lady called out as Liza stood there with her mouth wide open.

"Shut up, Gladys," another woman said, causing the crowd to break into laughter.

Liza looked into his emerald eyes as tears filled hers. "Jackson, I-I . . . I don't know what to say. I'm speechless."

"I haven't heard the one word that I'm waiting for," he said with a smile. He reached out and wiped a single tear from her cheek. Liza smiled at his tender touch. Was she crazy to be standing up there in silence? Pretty much.

"Yes. Yes. Yes! I will be more than happy to be your wife." Jackson pulled her into his arms, dropping the microphone and kissing her to thunderous applause.

As the party began to wrap up, Liza hung in the background, smiling at her fiancé as he shook hands with his supporters. But she was ready for these people to go home. Teresa crossed over to her and smiled.

"I have to give it to you, Miss Palmer," she began. "You're a class act."

"Really?"

"Since the campaigning is over, I can be real. If Robert and Nic had tried to smear my name the way they did yours, the story would be about how their bodies were found floating in Lake Norman."

"Oh, I had those thoughts but orange has never been my color."

"He's a great guy. And I can imagine the moves you two are going to make in the state."

"I kind of like not mixing business with

pleasure."

"And just how long is that going to last? Jackson is lucky to have you on his team — professionally and personally. Don't let him forget that."

"I feel like this is a dangerous combination right here," Jackson said as he approached Liza and Teresa.

"Not at all," Teresa said. "I was just telling Liza how much I look forward to watching you two grow as a power couple."

Jackson glanced from Teresa to Liza. "If you say so."

"Well," Teresa said, hugging Jackson and then Liza, "I'm going to take off and give you two some quiet time. Then the real work begins!"

Once they were alone, Liza looked into Jackson's eyes and smiled. "Mr. Senator."

"I like the sound of that. But you know what sounds even better?"

"What?"

"The future Mrs. Jackson Franklin."

She smiled, feeling her cheeks heat up. "I'm still in shock. You know, I've never made love to a senator before." Liza licked her bottom lip and smiled saucily at him.

"Then I say let's head to my room upstairs and change that." He took her hand in his and they headed for the elevator. Although

Liza wanted to kiss her man in the elevator, she was well aware of videos from security cameras being leaked to the press. So when Jackson drew her into his arms and kissed her with a steaming passion, she was shocked, but after about five seconds, she succumbed to the sweetness of his kiss.

A soft moan escaped her throat as he sucked her bottom lip. "We probably shouldn't be . . ."

Jackson pulled back and brought his finger to her lips. "I know. But I couldn't resist. You know what I thought when I saw you walk in?"

"Tell me," she said as he cupped her bottom.

"I thought that is the most beautiful woman I've ever seen, and yellow is her color. Then I wondered, is she wearing panties and how amazing that dress is going to look — off that amazing body."

"And here I was thinking that you hadn't even noticed me."

He ran his hands down her sides. "A blind man would've regained his sight to notice you in that dress." The bell dinged and the doors of the elevator opened. Jackson pulled his key card out of his pocket as they headed down the hall to his room. He couldn't get the door open fast enough. As soon as they were inside, he pressed Liza against the door and slipped his hands underneath her dress. There were panties, lace and barely there panties.

"Disappointed?" she quipped as his fingers slipped inside the waistband of the lace boy shorts.

Jackson grinned. "Not at all." He pulled the underwear down and Liza stepped out of them. "Now, let's lose the dress."

"Nope. You strip first," she said, then slipped her hands inside his jacket and pushed it off his broad shoulders.

"Yes, ma'am," he replied as he untied his tie. Liza unbuttoned his shirt once he tossed the tie away. She rubbed her hand across his chest and smiled.

"Looking good, Senator."

Jackson took her hand and placed it on his belt. "You haven't seen anything yet."

Unhooking his belt, she shivered with anticipation as she felt his erection growing. Jackson took hold of her hands and made quick work of unzipping and stepping out of his slacks. He stepped back from her and did some flexing. "You see something you like?"

"Oh, yeah," she replied with a smile. She stepped closer to him, then pulled his boxers down his hips and eased down to her knees. Taking his thick erection in her hands, she stroked him slowly, back and forth. He threw his head back in ecstasy as her lips took the place of her warm hands. Licking. Sucking. Kissing. She made his knees quiver as she took him deeper and deeper inside her hot mouth.

"Liza, Liza, Liza," he moaned as he ran his fingers through her hair. When she flicked her tongue across the tip of his penis, Jackson had to fight the urge to climax. Pulling back from her, he gripped her shoulders. "Now, it's time for you to shimmy out of this dress," he groaned. Liza rose to her feet and unzipped the back of her gown. With two quick shakes, the dress pooled at her stiletto-clad feet. Jackson released an appreciative whistle. "Simply beautiful," he said, then drew her into his arms. Liza wrapped her leg around his waist and brought her lips to his.

"Make love to me," she moaned, then ground against him. Jackson plunged into her wet valley. She was so hot and felt so good as he thrust in and out. She kissed and licked his neck as they matched each other thrust for thrust. Liza moaned, gritted out his name, and reached her climax as he gripped her round cheeks.

"That's it, baby," he cried. "Come for me."

Liza shivered as her orgasm took hold. "Oh, Jackson. Oh, Jackson," she cried. Her body shook and she felt as if she was about to collapse. He walked them back to the bed and they fell into each other's arms. Sweat poured from their bodies and their hearts began to beat in sync.

"I'm so proud of you," she whispered as she followed a bead of sweat down his chest with her finger.

"Mmm, I'm just glad you stood by me during all of this."

"It wasn't easy," she admitted. "I thought you'd chosen this seat over us. And I couldn't blame you."

"I wanted both, you and this senate seat. But if I had to choose, Liza, you would've won. I can't see my future without you."

"Jackson," she intoned.

He stroked her cheek. "I love you. I love everything about you. From the way you smile at me to the fierce way you protect those you care about. One thing I know for sure, I'm never going to let you go."

Tears of joy filled her eyes as she rested her head against his chest. This man had opened her heart and showed her that real love could come into her life and this was something she'd cherish forever.

"Thank you," she said.

"For what?"

"For loving me, for accepting me flaws and all. Jackson, you've made me happier than I thought I deserved to be."

"Baby, this is just the beginning. You haven't seen anything yet."

Smiling, she hugged him tightly, knowing that the best was yet to come and she'd spend the rest of her life wrapped in the warmth of Jackson's love.